ANGELOPOLIS

ANGELOPOLIS

DANIELLE TRUSSONI

VIKING

VIKING
Published by the Penguin Group
Penguin Group (USA) Inc., 375 Hudson Street,
New York, New York 10014, USA

USA | Canada | UK | Ireland | Australia | New Zealand | India | South Africa | China

Penguin Books Ltd, Registered Offices: 80 Strand, London WC2R 0RL, England
For more information about the Penguin Group visit penguin.com

ISBN 978-0-670-02554-1
ISBN 978-0-670-78590-2 (export edition)

Printed in the United States of America
1 3 5 7 9 10 8 6 4 2

Book design by Francesca Belanger
Set in Centaur MT Std

For Angela

One of the original branches of theology, angelology is achieved in the person of the angelologist, whose expertise includes both the theoretical study of angelic systems and their prophetic execution through human history.

*And she began to speak to me—so gently
and softly—with angelic voice.*

—Dante, *Inferno*

ANGELOPOLIS

33 Champ de Mars, seventh arrondissement, Paris, 1983

The scientist examined the girl, his fingers pressing into her skin. She felt his touch against her shoulder blades, the knobs of her spine, the flat of her back. The movements were deliberate, clinical, as if he expected to find something wrong with her—a thirteenth rib or a second spine growing like an iron track alongside the original. The girl's mother had told her to do as the scientist asked, and so she endured the prodding in silence: When he twisted a tourniquet around her arm she did not resist; when he traced the sinuous path of her vein with the tip of a needle she held still; when the needle slid under skin, and a rush of blood filled the barrel of the syringe, she pressed her lips together until she could no longer feel them. She watched the sunlight fall through the windows, blessing the sterile room with color and warmth, and felt a presence watching over her, as if a spirit had descended to guard her.

As the scientist filled three vials with blood, she closed her eyes and thought of her mother's voice. Her mother liked to tell her stories of enchanted kingdoms and sleeping beauties and brave knights ready to fight for good; she spoke of gods who transformed into swans and beautiful boys who blossomed into flowers and women who grew into trees; she whispered that angels existed on earth as well as in heaven, and that there were some people who, like the angels, could fly. The girl always listened to these stories, never quite knowing if they were true. But there was one thing she did believe: In every fairy tale, the princess woke and the swan transformed back into Zeus and the knight overcame evil. In a moment, with a wave of a wand or the casting of a spell, the nightmare ended and a new era began.

The First Circle

LIMBO

V. A. Verlaine pushed through the barrier of gendarmes, making his way toward the body. It was nearly midnight, the neighborhood deserted, and yet the entire perimeter of the Champ de Mars—from the quai Branly to the avenue Gustave Eiffel—had been blocked by police cars, the red and blue lights pulsing through the darkness. A floodlight had been set up in a corner of the scene, the harsh illumination revealing a mutilated body resting in a pool of electric blue blood. The features of the victim were unreadable, the body broken and bloodied, her arms and legs angling at unnatural positions like branches cracked from a tree. The phrase "ripped to shreds" passed through Verlaine's mind.

He had studied the creature as it died, watching the wings unfold over its body. He'd watched it shiver with pain, listening to its sharp, animal grunts as they dulled to a weak whine. The wounds were severe—a deep cut to the head and another to the chest—and yet it seemed that the creature would never stop struggling, that its determination to survive was endless, that it would fight on and on, even as blood seeped over the ground in a thick dark syrup. Finally, a milky film had fallen over the creature's eyes, giving it the vacant stare of a lizard, and Verlaine knew the angel had died at last.

As he looked over his shoulder, his jaw grew tense. Beyond the ring of police stood every variety of creature—a living encyclopedia of beings who would kill him if they knew he could see them for what they were. He paused, assuming the cold, appraising position of a scholar as he cataloged the creatures in his mind: There were congregations of Mara angels, the beautiful and doomed prostitutes whose gifts were such a temptation to humans; Gusian angels, who could divine the past and the future; the Rahab angels, broken beings who were considered the untouchables of the angelic world. He could detect the distinguishing features of Anakim angels—the sharp fingernails, the wide forehead, the slightly irregular skeletal structure. He saw it all with a relentless clarity that lingered in his mind even as he turned back to the frenzy surrounding the murder. The victim's blood had begun to seep past the contours of the floodlight, oozing into the shadows. He tried to focus upon the ironwork of the Eiffel Tower, to steady himself, but the creatures consumed his attention. He could not take his eyes off their wings fluttering against the inky darkness of the night.

Verlaine had discovered his ability to see the creatures ten years before. The skill was a gift—very few people could actually see angel wings without extensive training. As it turned out, Verlaine's flawed vision—he had worn glasses since the fifth grade and could hardly see a foot in front of himself without them—allowed light into the eye in exactly the right proportion for him to see the full spectrum of angel wings. He'd been born to be an angel hunter.

Now Verlaine could not block out the colored light rising around the angelic creatures, the fields of energy that separated these beings from the flat, colorless spaces occupied by humans. He found himself tracking them as they moved around the Champ de Mars, noting their movements even while wishing to shut out their hallucinatory pull. Sometimes he was sure that he was going crazy, that the creatures were his personal demons, that he lived in a custom-made circle of hell in which an endless variety of devils were paraded before him, as if amassed for the purpose of taunting and torturing him.

But these were the kinds of thoughts that could land him in a sanitarium. He had to be careful to keep his balance, to remember that he saw things at a higher frequency than normal people, that his gift was something he must cultivate and protect even as it hurt him.

Bruno, his friend and mentor, the man who had brought him from New York and trained him as an angel hunter, had given him pills to calm his nerves, and although Verlaine tried to take as few as possible, he found himself reaching for an enamel box in his jacket pocket and tapping out two white pills.

He felt a hand on his shoulder and turned. Bruno stood behind him, his expression severe. "The cuts are indicative of an Emim attack," he said under his breath.

"The charred skin confirms that," Verlaine said. He unbuttoned his jacket—a vintage yellow 1970s polyester sport coat of questionable taste—and stepped close to the body. "Does it have any kind of identification?"

His mentor removed a wallet, its pale suede stained with blood, and began to sort through it. Suddenly Bruno's expression changed. He held up a plastic card.

Verlaine took the card. It was a New York driver's license with a photo of a woman with black hair and green eyes. His heart beat hard in his chest as he realized that it belonged to Evangeline Cacciatore. He took a deep breath before turning back to Bruno.

"Do you think this could really be her?" Verlaine said, watching his boss's expression carefully. He knew that everything—his relationship with Bruno, his connection to the Angelological Society, the course of his life from that point forward—would depend upon how he handled himself in the next ten minutes.

"Evangeline is a human woman; this is a blue-blooded Nephil female," Bruno replied, nodding toward the bloody corpse between them. "But be my guest."

Verlaine slid his fingers between the buttons of the victim's trench coat, his hands trembling so hard he had to steady himself to make out the shape of her shoulders. The features of the woman were utterly unrecognizable.

He remembered the first time he had seen Evangeline. She had been both beautiful and somber at once, looking at him with her large green eyes as if he were a thief come to steal their sacred texts. She had been suspicious of his motives and fierce in her determination to keep him out. Then he made her laugh and her tough exterior had crumbled. That moment between them had been burned into him, and no matter how he tried, he had never been able to forget Evangeline. It had been over a decade since they had stood together in the library at St. Rose Convent, books open before them, both of them unaware of the true nature of the world. *"There were Giants on the Earth in those days, and after."* These words, and the woman who showed them to him, had changed his life.

He hadn't told anyone the truth about Evangeline. Indeed, no one knew that she was one of the creatures. For Verlaine, keeping Evangeline's secret had been an unspoken vow: He knew the truth, but he would never tell a soul. It was, he realized now, the only way to remain faithful to the woman he loved.

Verlaine tucked the driver's license into his pocket and walked away.

Paris was full of angelologists and, as such, one of the most dangerous places in the universe for an Emim angel like Eno, who had a tendency toward recklessness. Like the rest of her kind, she was tall and willowy, with high cheekbones, full lips, and gray skin. She wore heavy black eye makeup, red lipstick, and black leather, and often wore her black wings openly, unafraid, daring angelologists to see them. The gesture was considered an act of provocation, but Eno didn't have any intention of hiding. This would be their world soon. The Grigoris had promised her this.

Even so, there were angelologists lurking everywhere in Paris—scholars who looked like they hadn't left the Academy of Angelology's archive in fifty years, overzealous initiates taking photographs of whatever creature they could find, angelological biologists looking for samples of angelic blood, and, worst of all as far as Eno was concerned, the teams of angel hunters out to arrest all angelic creatures. These idiots often mistook Golobiums for Emim and Emim for the more pure creatures like the Grigoris. Hunters seemed to be on every corner lately, watching, waiting, ready to take their prey into custody. For those who could detect the hunters, life in Paris was merely inconvenient. For those who could not, each movement through the city was a deadly game.

Of course Eno had strict rules of engagement, and her first and most important rule was to leave the risk of being captured to others. After she had killed Evangeline, she'd removed herself from the scene quickly and walked on the Champs-Élysées, where nobody would think to look for her. She understood that sometimes it was best to hide in plain sight.

Eno folded her hands around the Styrofoam cup, taking in the ceaseless motion of the Champs-Élysées. She would be going back to her masters as soon as possible now that her work in Paris was finished. She'd been assigned to find and kill a young female Nephil. She'd tracked the creature for weeks, watching her, learning her patterns of behavior. She'd become curious about her target. Evangeline was unlike any other Nephil she had seen before. According to her masters, Evangeline was a child of the Grigori, but she had none of the distinguishing characteristics of an angel of her lineage. She had been raised among regular people, had been abandoned by the Nephilim, and—from everything that Eno had observed—was dangerously sympathetic to the ways of humanity. The Grigoris wanted Evangeline dead. Eno never let her masters down.

And they, she was certain, would not let her down either. The Grigoris would take her home to Russia, where she would blend into the masses of Emim angels. In Paris, she was too conspicuous. Now that her work was done, she wanted to leave this dangerous and loathsome city.

She'd learned the dangers of Parisian angelologists the hard way. Many years ago, when she was young and naïve to the ways of humans, she had nearly been killed by an angelologist. It had been the summer of 1889, during the Paris World's Fair, and people had flooded into the city to see the newly erected Eiffel Tower. She strolled through the fair and then ventured into the throngs in the fields nearby. Unlike many Emim, she adored walking among the lowly beings that populated Paris, loved to have coffee in their cafés and walk in their gardens. She liked to be drawn into the rush of human society, the exuberant energy of their futile existence.

In the course of her stroll, she noticed a handsome Englishman staring at her from across the Champ de Mars. They'd spoken for some minutes about the fair, then he took her by the arm and led her past the crowds of foot soldiers, the prostitutes and scavengers, past the carriages and horses. From his soft voice and gentlemanly manner, she assumed him to be more elevated than most human beings. He held her hand gently, as if she were too delicate to touch, all the while examining her with the care of a jeweler appraising a diamond. Human desire was something she found fascinating—its intensity, the way love controlled and shaped their lives. This man desired her. Eno found this amusing. She could still recall his hair, his dark eyes, the dashing figure he cut in his suit and hat.

She tried to gauge whether the man recognized her for what she was. He led her away from the crowds, and when they were alone behind a hedge, he looked into her eyes. A change came over him— he'd been gentle and amorous, and now a wash of violence infused his manner. She marveled at his transformation, the changeable nature of human desire, the way he could love and hate her at once. Suddenly the man withdrew his dagger and lunged at her. "Beast," he hissed, as he thrust the blade at Eno, his voice filled with hatred. Eno reacted quickly, jumping aside, and the knife missed its mark: Instead of her heart, the soldier sliced a gash across her shoulder, cutting through her dress and into her body, leaving the flesh to fold away from her bone like a piece of lace. Eno had turned on him with force, crushing the bones of his throat between her fingers until his eyes hardened to pale stones. She pulled him behind the trees and destroyed all traces of what she had found beautiful in him: His lovely eyes, his skin, the delicate fleshy curl of his ear, the fingers that had—only minutes before—given her pleasure. She took the man's peacoat and draped it over her shoulders to hide her injury. What she couldn't hide was her humiliation.

The cut had healed, but she was left with a scar the shape of a crescent moon. Every so often she would stand before a mirror examining the faint line, to remind herself of the treachery that humans were capable of performing. She realized, after reading an account in the newspaper, that the man was an angelologist, one of the many English agents in France in the nineteenth century. She had been led into a trap. Eno had been tricked.

This man was long dead, but she could still hear his voice in her ear, the heat of his breath as he called her a beast. The word *beast* was embedded in her mind, a seed that grew in her, freeing her from every restraint. From that moment on her work as a mercenary began to please her more and more with each new victim. She studied the angelologists' behavior, their habits, their techniques of hunting and killing angelic beings until she knew her work in and out. She could smell a hunter, feel him, sense his desire to capture and slaughter her. Sometimes she even let them bring her into custody. Sometimes she even let them act out their fantasies with her. She let them take her to their beds, tie her up, play with her, hurt her. When the fun was over, she killed them. It was a dangerous game, but one she controlled.

Eno slid on a pair of oversize sunglasses, the lenses black and bulbous. She rarely went outside without them. They disguised her large yellow eyes and her unnaturally high cheekbones—the most distinct Emim traits—so that she looked like a human female. Leaning back in her chair, she stretched her long legs and closed her eyes, remembering the terror in Evangeline's face, the resistance of the flesh as she slid her nails under the rib cage and ripped it open, the frisson of surprise Eno had felt upon seeing the first rush of blue blood spill onto the pavement. She had never killed a superior creature before, and the experience went against everything she had been trained to do. She had expected a fight worthy of a Nephil. But Evangeline had died with the pathetic ease of a human woman.

Her phone vibrated in her pocket, and as she reached for it, she checked the crowds walking by, her gaze flicking from humans to angels. There was only one person who used that number, and Eno needed to be certain that she could speak privately. Emim were bound by their heritage to serve Nephilim, and for years, she had simply done her duty, working for the Grigoris out of gratitude and fear. She was of a warrior caste and she accepted this fate. She wanted to do little else but to experience the slow diminishing of a life, the final gasping for breath of her victims.

Fingers trembling, she took the call. She heard her master's raspy, whispery voice, a seductive voice she associated with power, with pain, with death. He said only a few words, but she knew at once—from the way he spoke, his voice laced with poison—that something had gone wrong.

Before he'd found Evangeline dead beneath the Eiffel Tower, Verlaine had had a presentiment of her death. She had appeared to him in a dream, an eerie creature woven of light. She spoke, her voice resounding through the corridors of his mind, her words inaudible at first but then, as he strained to hear them, becoming clearer and clearer. *Come to me,* she said as she hovered over him, a beautiful and horrible creature, her skin glowing with luminosity, her wings gathered about her shoulders like a gauzy ethereal shawl. He understood that he was dreaming, that she was a figment of his imagination, something he'd conjured up from his subconscious, a kind of demon meant to haunt him. And yet he was terrified when she leaned close and touched him. Placing her cold fingers upon his chest, she seemed to be feeling his heartbeat. Heat passed from her hands and into his body, the current moving from her fingers into his chest, burning through him. He knew with terrifying clarity that Evangeline was going to kill him.

It was always at this moment in the dream that he would wake, unable to breathe, overcome by fear, love, desire, hopelessness, and humiliation at once. He would emerge into consciousness knowing that an angel of darkness had been with him. If not for Bruno's intervention, Verlaine might still be caught in an endless loop of terror and desire.

Still reeling, Verlaine headed toward the street, trying to reconcile the woman in his dream with the dismembered corpse. His Ducati 250 was parked on the rue de Monttessuy. The very sight of it—the chrome fenders polished, the leather seat buffed—helped bring him back to the present moment. He'd bought the Ducati his first month in Paris and restored it, sanding away the rust and re-painting it red. It remained one of his favorite possessions, giving him the feeling of freedom whenever he rode it. As he pulled it off its kickstand, he noticed a jagged scratch gouged into the paint. He swore under his breath and rubbed it to see how deep it went, though, in truth, the scratch was just one of the many abuses the Ducati had endured in recent years. Ironically he associated each dent and scratch with his own experiences over the past decade. He had been injured more times than he could count and—unlike the restored Ducati—he was beginning to show his age. Catching his reflection in a passing storefront window, he noted that the motor-cycle was better preserved than he was.

As he reached the quai, something else caught his attention. Later, when Verlaine examined the moment he saw Evangeline, he would tell himself that he'd felt her presence before seeing her, that a change in the atmospheric pressure had taken place, the kind of imbalance created when a gust of cold air sweeps through a warm room. But at the time, he didn't think. He simply turned and there she was, stand-ing near the Seine. Verlaine recognized the sharpness of her shoul-ders and the glossy blackness of her hair. He recognized her high cheekbones, the same green eyes that had just stared back at him from the driver's license. He simply wanted to stare at her, to make certain that it was really her, a flesh and blood being and not a fig-ment of his mind. Verlaine held her eye for a second, and in that moment, he felt a slow turning in his perception, as if some rusty lock had clicked open. He caught his breath. A cold sensation grasped his spine and moved through his body. The mutilated woman below the Eiffel Tower was a stranger. He propped the Ducati on its kickstand and made his way to his Evangeline.

She crossed the street as he grew near and, without giving it a sec-ond thought, he fell into step behind her, following her as he would any other target. He wondered if she could sense him behind, feel his eyes upon her. She must have known he was there and purposely led him onward, because she never moved too far ahead, but never allowed him to get too close either. Soon he was close enough to see her reflection appear and disappear in the glass of a parked van, her image silvery, wavering, fluid as a mirage. As the image stabilized he saw that her hair had been cropped in a messy pageboy and she seemed to be wearing dark makeup. She could be any one of the thousands of young women walking through Paris, but her disguise didn't fool Verlaine. He knew the real Evangeline.

As she increased her pace, he struggled to keep up. The streets were packed with people; Evangeline could disappear easily, in an instant, washing away in the swirl of the crowd. In all the hunts in which he'd participated, he had done his job impeccably. He followed, captured, and then imprisoned the creatures without question. But everything about this chase was different. He wanted to catch her, but he couldn't follow the usual protocol if he did. Most troubling of all, he only wanted to talk to her, to understand what had happened in New York. He wanted an explanation. He felt he deserved that much.

Verlaine felt the soles of his favorite shoes—a pair of brown leather wing tips he'd worn for years—slipping with each step. A shiver of fear moved through him, gathering into a solid ball in his stomach at the thought of losing her again. He knew that, if she chose, she could easily outrun him. Indeed, she could open her wings and fly away. He had watched her do it before. The last time he had seen her she'd lifted herself away from him, moving high into the vault of the sky, her wings bright under the moon, a beautiful monster among the stars.

He hadn't told anyone about this—not the angelologists who had been part of the New York mission and not the men and women who certified him as he passed through his courses at the academy. Evangeline's true identity had remained his secret, and his silence had made him complicit in her deception. His silence was the only gift he could give her, but that gift had left him feeling like a traitor. He'd lied to everyone. Earlier, as he stood at the crime scene, he couldn't look Bruno in the eyes.

Verlaine hated the feeling. He'd spent too many years hunting the creatures, worked too long and too hard to capture them, to be so shaken. No matter what had happened between them, years had passed. He was a different man. If he caught Evangeline, he would have to capture her. He had to remember what she was and what she was capable of doing to him. If he caught her, he would take her into custody. If she attacked him, he would fight. He needed to move fast, to put his feelings aside. He needed to convince himself that she was just another angel and this was just another routine hunt.

In the distance the lights of the Eiffel Tower glimmered against the night sky, bright as a constellation fallen to earth. Verlaine ran, his hand trembling as he reached for his gun. Drawing it from his belt, he switched it on. With its two hundred volts of electricity, the gun was powerful without being lethal. If placed over the furcula of an angel, and the shot directed into the solar plexus, the creature would be stunned for hours. He didn't want to use force, but he wasn't going to let Evangeline slip away again.

Axicore Grigori peered through the smoky glass of the limousine window. It was a clear spring night, with the streets filled with people, which made it very unlikely that he would leave the dark enclosure of the car. He detested *Homo sapiens*, and the thought of getting out into the soup of humanity made his skin crawl. When he had to venture out among people, he kept his distance. He didn't walk among them, he didn't eat in their restaurants, he traveled in a private jet. He never so much as touched the hand of a human being without feeling deeply, essentially violated. The very idea that his ancestors had been attracted to such vile beings filled him with wonder. *What on earth*, he wondered, looking at the people walking by, *had the Watchers been thinking?* How his twin brother, Armigus, had managed to remain in Russia while Axicore found himself on a filthy Paris bridge like some common Gibborim was beyond him.

His great-aunt Sneja Grigori believed that one of these repulsive creatures, a young woman named Evangeline, was the granddaughter of her deceased son, Percival. It all seemed so far-fetched to Axicore—even more so after his most trusted mercenary angel had observed the subject in question for weeks. Eno had reported everything back to Axicore. He learned that Evangeline was short, thin, dark haired, and utterly human in appearance. She lived simply, did not exhibit her wings, had no Nephilistic contacts, and spent the majority of her time moving among normal human beings. She bore none of the typical characteristics of the Nephilim, nor any of the various identifying markings that ran through purebreds, much less the Grigori family traits.

The contrast between them could be drawn by a simple comparison with his own bearing, a perfect exemplar of the Grigori. He was a head taller than human beings, his skin fine and pale, and his eyes white blue. He dressed impeccably, as did Armigus—they often wore matching attire and never the same suit twice. That morning's shipment had come from their grandfather Arthur's favorite Savile Row tailor, the brushed velvet smooth and black as the coat of a jaguar. With their elegant clothing and thick blond hair that fell over their shoulders in a chaos of curls, the twins were stunning, classically handsome, startling enough to make the most beautiful women stop and stare, especially on the exceedingly rare occasions that the twins went out into the human world together. In this they resembled all the Grigori men, and the late Percival Grigori in particular. The twins were princes among peasants their mother used to say, regal creatures forced to walk the earth, drawn into the material plane when they should be among the ethereal beings in the heavenly spheres.

Of course, with the dilution of their race over the past millennia, such physical traits were only superficial. The true markings of the Nephilim were more subtle and complicated than that of complexion, eye color, and body type. If Evangeline was, in fact, Sneja's flesh and blood, Axicore concluded, she was the ugliest Grigori ever born.

Tapping a long, white finger on the window glass, Axicore tried to put aside his repulsion and concentrate upon the task at hand. He had retrieved Eno from an establishment on the Champs-Élysées, and although she sat next to him in the limousine, she was so silent, so ghostly, that he barely registered her presence. He admired her enormously, thought her one of the most fierce Emim he had ever seen, and—although he would never openly admit this—found her much more attractive than most lower angelic creatures. Indeed, Eno was a beautiful killing machine, one he admired and secretly feared, but not the most clever angel in the heavenly spheres. Her outbursts of rage could be violent. He had to handle her with care. And so it was with some delicacy that Axicore resumed the explanation he had begun on the phone. Eno had made a grave error. Evangeline was alive.

"You're certain?" Eno said, the yellow fire of her eyes piercing the lenses of her dark sunglasses. "Because I never make mistakes."

She was angry, and Axicore wanted to use her ferocity to his advantage. "Absolutely certain," he said. "And I'm not the only one—an angelologist is hunting her at this very moment. An angel hunter."

Eno took off her sunglasses, the light from her eyes breaking through the darkness. "Have you identified him?"

"One of the typical crew," Axicore said, feeling uneasy at the thought of what she would do to this angel hunter if she caught him. Axicore had seen Eno's victims. Such gruesome violence almost evoked his sympathy.

"We'll take care of this now," Eno said, sliding her sunglasses back over her eyes. "And then we will go home. I want to get out of this horrid city."

Axicore sat back in his seat, remembering his childhood in Russia. They would leave their city apartments and spend months in the Crimea, where their family estate stood at the edge of the water. The Grigori clan would gather for tea, and he and his brother would unfurl their wings—great golden wings that shimmered like sheets of pounded foil—and lift themselves into the air, performing tricks for their adoring relations. They would do twists and turns and acrobatics that elicited the approval of the older generation, four-hundred-year-old Nephilim who had given up on such athletic maneuverings long before. Their parents were there, dressed entirely in white, gazing up with pride. They were the golden children of an ancient family. They were young, beautiful, with all of creation at their feet. There seemed to be nothing at all that could bring them down to earth.

Passage de la Vierge, seventh arrondissement, Paris

Verlaine felt a cold presence deep in the shadows of the passage and knew that Evangeline was there, standing in the darkness, so close he could feel the icy chill of her breath against his neck.

He took a step back, trying to see her more clearly, but she seemed little more than an extension of the shadows. There were so many things he wanted to say to her, so many questions he'd rehearsed, but he couldn't begin to formulate them. The contradictions he felt about Evangeline—the affection he'd felt for her, the anger—left him enraged and confused. His training hadn't prepared him for this. He wanted to take her by the arm and force her to speak to him. He needed to know that he wasn't imagining everything that happened between them.

Finally, he reached into his pocket and removed the driver's license. Holding it out to her, he said, "I think you lost something."

She met his eye and slowly took the card in her hand. "You believed it was me back there."

"All evidence pointed in that direction," Verlaine said, feeling his stomach turn at the thought of the bloody mess at the Eiffel Tower.

"There was no other way." Her voice was no more than a whisper. "They were going to kill me."

"Who was going to kill you?"

"But they made a mistake," she said, her eyes wide. "I led them in the wrong direction. I let them kill someone else."

Verlaine felt a strange, double-edged sensation of wanting to protect Evangeline from whoever had tried to kill her and wanting to take her into custody himself. His first instinct was to call Bruno and bring her to their prison in La Forestière. "You're going to have to give me more than this."

Evangeline slipped her hand into the pocket of her jacket and removed something large and round, and dropped it into Verlaine's hand. It was some kind of egg. He examined the hard brilliance of the enamel, the jewels that encrusted the surface like chunks of rock salt. He removed his glasses, cleaned them on his shirt, and slid them on again: The intricacy of the egg clicked into focus. He turned it in his fingers, letting the jewels glint in the weak light.

"Why would they want to hurt you?" he asked, meeting Evangeline's eyes. Even the green of her irises struck him as hazardous and hypnotic. With this thought came a sharp pang of longing for the person he had once been—trusting, optimistic, young, his future wide open before him. "You're one of them."

Evangeline drew close to him, bringing her lips to his ear as she whispered, "You must believe me when I say that I was never one of them. I've wandered from place to place trying to understand what I had become. It's been ten years and still I don't understand. But I know one thing for certain: I am not like the Grigori."

Verlaine pulled away, feeling as if he were being broken apart inside. He wanted to believe her, and yet he knew what the Nephilim were capable of doing. She could be lying to him.

"So tell me," Verlaine said. "What brings you back now?" Verlaine tossed the jeweled egg in the air and caught it in his hand. "The Easter Bunny?"

"Xenia Ivanova."

"Vladimir's daughter?" Verlaine asked, turning serious. The death of Vladimir Ivanov had been just one of many fatalities of their failed mission in New York. It had been Verlaine's first brush with the murderous treachery of their enemies.

"Vladimir was one of the only people I had known outside the convent," Evangeline said. "He'd been close to my father. His daughter, Xenia, took over the café after he died, and she was kind enough to let me work and live in a small apartment in the back of the shop, deducting the rent from my salary. Years went by this way. I became close to Xenia, although I was never certain if she fully understood the kind of work her father had done, or my family's connection to him."

"I'm sure you didn't go to great lengths to fill her in, either," Verlaine said.

Evangeline looked at him for a moment, decided to ignore his comment, and continued. "And so I was surprised when, one day last month, Xenia told me that she had something to discuss with me. She took me upstairs to her father's apartment, a room still cluttered with his possessions, as if he'd only just left. She showed me the egg you have in your hands. She told me she was surprised to have found it among Vladimir's effects after his death."

"It's not really Vladimir's style," he said. Vladimir was remembered for his ascetic ruthlessness. His café in Little Italy was a cover for a life of extreme austerity.

"I think he was merely holding this egg for someone else," Evangeline said. "It was the only object of this kind among his possessions. Xenia found it wrapped in a cloth at the back of one of his suitcases. She believed he'd brought it to New York from Paris in the eighties. Xenia didn't know what to do with it, so she simply held on to it. But then, a few months ago, she took it to an auction house to have it appraised and, not long after this, strange things started happening. Nephilim began to follow her. They searched her apartment and the café. By the time she told me about the egg, she was terrified. One night two Gibborim broke into her apartment and tried to steal the egg. I killed one and the other escaped. After this I knew that I needed to tell her the truth. I explained everything to her—our fathers' work, the Nephilim, even my own situation—and, to my surprise, she knew more about Vladimir's work than I had initially believed. Eventually Xenia agreed to close the shop and disappear. I took the egg. It's why I came here. I had to find someone who could help me explain what it means."

"And Xenia?"

"If I hadn't intervened, Xenia would be dead."

"Was that her body at the Eiffel Tower?"

"No." Evangeline shook her head, her expression serious. "That was just some random Nephil who looked a bit like me. I planted my ID on her and led the Emim to believe she was me."

Verlaine considered this, realizing how far Evangeline had gone in her efforts to survive. "So they think you're dead," he said at last.

Evangeline sighed, a look of relief on her face. "I hope so," she said. "It will give me enough time to hide."

As Verlaine considered Evangeline, his eyes drifted to her neck, where a chain of bright gold glittered against her skin. She still wore her pendant, the very one she had worn the day they'd met. Legend had it that the infamous angelologist Dr. Raphael Valko had fashioned three amulets from a rare and precious metal called Valkine. One pendant he had worn himself, one he had given to his daughter, Angela, and the third was worn by his wife, Gabriella. Evangeline inherited Angela's pendant upon her mother's death; Verlaine wore Gabriella's pendant, which he had taken when Gabriella died. Verlaine brought his fingers to his neck and pulled out the pendant, showing it to Evangeline.

Evangeline paused, looked for a moment at the pendant. "I was right, then," she said, reaching for the egg in his hand. The brush of her finger against his palm gave him such a shock that he nearly dropped it. "You're meant to have this. Gabriella would have wanted it that way. Keep it safe." She closed her hand around his, as if locking his fingers around the egg.

"They want this thing," Verlaine said, glancing down at the egg. "But what in the hell is it?"

"I don't know," Evangeline said, meeting his eye. "That is why I need you."

"Me?" Verlaine said, unable to imagine how he could be of any use.

"You're an angelologist now, aren't you?" Evangeline asked, her voice challenging him. "If anyone can help me understand this, it's you."

"Why not go to the others?" Verlaine asked.

Evangeline stepped away and the air around her seemed to fold, as if heat emanated from her clothes. The smooth surface of the air buckled with electricity. Her human appearance dissolved in a fluctuation of warped space, flesh wavering and twisting as if she were made of nothing but colored smoke. A wash of light exploded around her as her wings unfolded.

Verlaine blinked, holding—for a strange and disorienting moment—Evangeline's dual selves in his vision, the surface illusion of a woman and the underlying reality of the winged creature. The images of human and angel were like holograms that, with a turn of the light, bled into each other. She opened her wings, extending first one and then the other, rotating them until they stretched to the walls of the passage. They were immense and luminous, the layered feathers deep purple shot through with veins of silver—and yet they were transparent, ephemeral, so light he could see the texture of the brick wall behind them. He watched them vibrate with energy. They pulsed with the slow rhythm of her breathing, brushing her shoulders and sending shivers through her hair.

He leaned against a wall, steadying himself. For years Verlaine had tried to imagine Evangeline's wings, to reconstruct them. When he had first seen them a decade before, it had been from a distance, and with the untrained eyes of a man who couldn't tell the difference between the varieties of angels. Now he could decipher all the small distinctions that marked her, subtle as inclusions in quartz. He could see the iridescence of her skin in the shadows, the strange colored glow that appeared around her hair. He walked around her, studying her as if she were a winged statue in the Louvre, and he wondered what it felt like to live outside of time. Evangeline wouldn't age like human beings, and she wouldn't die for many hundreds of years. When Verlaine was an old man, Evangeline would be exactly the way he saw her now—as young and lovely as a figure cut from marble. He would die and she would remember his existence as something brief and insignificant. He realized now that she was more special than he could have ever guessed. He could hardly breathe. Evangeline was a thing of wonder, a miracle playing itself out before his eyes.

"Now do you understand why I cannot go to them?" Evangeline whispered.

"Come here," Verlaine said, and to his surprise, Evangeline stepped toward him. He could feel the movement of the air swirling around her wings, smell the sweet fragrance of her skin. Her wrist, when he took it to feel her pulse, was cold as ice and slicked with the plasma characteristic of the Nephilim. He wanted, suddenly, to bring his lips to her skin. Instead, he pressed his finger to her vein. Her pulse was low and shallow, almost nonexistent.

"Your blood?"

"Blue."

"Eyesight?"

"Better than perfect."

"Temperature?"

"Thirty-three degrees Fahrenheit, sometimes lower."

"It's strange," he said. "You have both human and Nephil characteristics. Your heartbeat is extraordinarily slow—less than two beats per minute, much slower than the average Nephil rate." He squeezed her arm. "And you're practically frozen. But your skin is flushed. You look every bit as human as I do."

Evangeline took a breath, as if bracing herself. "Have you killed many creatures like me?"

"I have never in my life encountered a creature like you, Evangeline."

"The way you say that," she said, holding his gaze, "makes it seem like you understand what I've become."

"Everything I've done, all the hunting, has been so that I could understand you."

"Then tell me," Evangeline asked, her voice trembling. "What am I?"

Verlaine looked at her, aware that his measured caution was giving way to the strength of his feelings. At last he said, "It is clear from your wings—their color and size and strength—that you are one of the elite angels. You are a Grigori, a descendant of the great Semyaza, granddaughter of Percival, great-granddaughter of Sneja. But you are human, too. You are incredible, a kind of miracle."

He stepped away and looked at Evangeline's wings once more, touching the gooseflesh under the feathers. "There's something I've always wanted to know," he said. "What does it feel like to fly?"

"I wish I could explain it," she said. "The sensation of weightlessness, the lightness, the buoyancy, the feeling that I might evaporate in a current of air. When I was human, I could not have imagined what it was like to step into a void, to fall fast and then sweep up, suddenly, into the wind. At times it feels like I belong less on the earth than to the sky, that I must recalibrate all of my movements just to remain earthbound. I used to fly out over the Atlantic, where I wouldn't be seen, and I would go for miles and miles without tiring. Sometimes the sun would rise and I would see my reflection in the water and think that I should keep going. I would have to force myself to go back."

"It's in your nature to fly," Verlaine said. "But what about the other characteristics of the Nephilim? Did you experience those as well?"

Her expression changed, and Verlaine could see at once that she was afraid of her capabilities. "My senses are slightly altered—everything is stronger and sharper; I don't need food or water in the way I used to—but I have none of the desires attributed to the Nephilim. I am physically different, but my inner life is unaltered. My spirit has not changed. I may have inherited the body of a demon," Evangeline said softly, "but I would never willingly become one."

Verlaine touched the pendant resting against her skin. It was so cold that a sheet of frost covered the metal. His finger melted a watery print on its surface. "You're freezing."

"Did you expect my skin to be like yours?" Evangeline asked.

"I've been in crowds of Nephilim; I've spoken to them in close proximity. You can feel the ice running in their veins—they are cold, but it is a different kind of coldness, like the dead walking among us. They have no soul and so they feed on the souls of human beings. Even a mediocre angelologist can identify them easily. But you're not like that. If I hadn't known the truth, I would have believed you to be human. You could pass for one of us."

"Do I frighten you?"

Verlaine shook his head. "I have to trust my instincts."

"Meaning?"

"That you may look like them, but you're not one of them. That you're different. That you're better."

Evangeline's skin shimmered in the half light of the moon. He wanted, suddenly, to pull her close, to warm her in his arms. Perhaps he could help her. He felt as if nothing mattered but this moment with Evangeline. He brushed her cheek with his finger and slipped his arm around her, feeling the dusty surface of feathers brush over his hand as he drew her to him. He wanted, for just a moment, to feel as if the world beyond them was all a distant dream, an unreality. Angelologists and Nephilim, the hunters and the hunted—all of this didn't matter. In all of existence, there was only the two of them. Verlaine wanted the illusion to last forever.

But holding her was like trying to embrace a shadow. She slipped away, her attention drawn to something behind him. Verlaine caught a sweep of movement in the corner of his eye. Suddenly a car pulled into the passage, its headlights breaking through the darkness. The door opened and an Emim angel leaped from the car. Before he could move, Evangeline ran through the passage and, with a speed and grace that he recognized as belonging to the most adept creatures, she lifted into the air, landing on the rooftop above. The Emim angel opened her wings—large black wings, immense and powerful—and flew after her.

1973 Alfa Romeo, rue Bosquet, seventh arrondissement, Paris

Bruno roved the streets, unsure of where to look for Verlaine. He'd discovered his Ducati abandoned near the Seine, and Bruno knew instantly that his strange evening was only going to get stranger. Something was going on with Verlaine, that much was obvious. He loved his Ducati and was rarely without it. Leaving it thrown on the sidewalk—especially at this time of night, when the restaurants and cafés were closed and the seventh arrondissement was little more than a calcified forest of shuttered windows—was wholly out of character.

Bruno reached into his pocket, took out a flask filled with Glenfiddich Solera Reserve, and took a long drink. The whole damn neighborhood was full of Nephilim. After his time in New York, he thought he'd seen the worst of it. But the area between the Bon Marché and the Eiffel Tower had proved to be the most concentrated collection of old-world Nephil families in the world.

Over the course of Bruno's time as an angel hunter—thirty years of service in Jerusalem, Paris, and New York—he had watched the Nephilim grow more and more reckless. It used to be that the creatures feared exposure, creating elaborate methods to shroud their existence in secrecy. For many hundreds of years, the creatures' survival depended upon blending into the surrounding population of humans. Now there seemed to be a total disregard for such machinations. Among the new generations of angels there was a tendency toward exhibitionism. Reports, confessions, photographs, and videos were everywhere. Once such testimonies would have been relegated to sensational magazines, their claims printed next to UFO and yeti sightings. Bruno had watched it all with interest and, in recent years, growing alarm. Such exhibitionism was pure arrogance: The creatures believed that they were strong enough to come out in the open. And yet, strange as it might have seemed, Bruno had found that the more the angels exposed of their secret lives, the less shocking they were to the human population. There was no general awareness of them, no fear, no real inquiry into the nature of the Nephilim. Human beings were so saturated with the supernatural that they'd become desensitized. Bruno had to admit that there was a certain brilliance in it all: The creatures had chosen the perfect moment in history to step out of their shadow existence. After thousands of years of living in seclusion, they'd embraced the present era of exhibitionism.

Of all his agents, he believed Verlaine best equipped to handle the change in the creatures' behavior. Bruno had studied Verlaine at the crime scene as attentively as he'd studied the corpse and, as always, he'd liked what he saw: a young man with the potential to become a great leader. Sure, Verlaine was still struggling to find his place in their organization, but he was talented. He was also unusual, without the typical family history, without the normal education, and with a scary talent for locating and capturing angels. Acting on gut feeling alone, Bruno had plucked Verlaine out of his ordinary life as an academic in New York, brought him to Paris, and trained him with a rigor he saved for only the strongest and brightest recruits. He'd seen something unique in him, a rare balance of intelligence and intuition. And, sure enough, once he had entered training, Verlaine exemplified all the elements of an angel hunter—a sixth sense for the creatures mixed with the physical stamina to capture them. And, on top of everything, Verlaine had the remarkable ability to see the angels plainly, without assistance.

Within the various departments of the society, angel hunters were the most covert, well funded, and selective. As director of their Paris bureau, Bruno handpicked his team, training each member personally. It was a painstaking process, as delicate and refined as the education of a samurai warrior. Verlaine had bypassed the academic track—a difficult and lengthy course of study rooted in the traditional practices of textual and archival study—and began his apprenticeship as a hunter straightaway.

Now he was one of Bruno's best. The young American scholar who'd once been in limbo about his future could now decipher the presence of angels with extraordinary precision. He understood the physiology of the Nephilim and demonstrated a clear ability to differentiate between human and angelic anatomy. He could detect the small distinguishing physical markings of the Nephilim—the sharp, opalescent fingernails, the wide forehead, the slightly irregular skeletal structure, the large eyes. He understood that the Nephil body was designed for flight, with thin, hollow bones that rendered their skeletons as light and agile as birds'. He noticed the scintillating quality of the skin, the way it shimmered as if dusted with tiny crystals. The structure of the wings themselves—the efficient retraction, the airy composition of the feathers, the struts and trusses that fortified the muscles—had fascinated Verlaine from the start. He had mastered every method of identifying angels, capturing them, binding them, and interrogating them, skills known by only the elite of the society. Bruno believed Verlaine could already be considered a great hunter, but he suspected that his protégé could become more: a mythic angel hunter, the kind of hunter to emerge once in a generation.

And still there was something holding Verlaine back, a weakness that Bruno could feel lingering below the surface but could not readily identify. He'd made it his personal responsibility to help Verlaine overcome this Achilles' heel and succeed.

Something in the distance caught his eye. It seemed to him that there was a commotion at the far end of the street. Bruno pulled over, cut the engine, and got out of the car, trying to see more clearly. There was an Emim angel, its black wings stretched, the light of the moon casting a gray brilliance over the feathers, giving them a smoky fluidity. Although Bruno couldn't see beyond the creature, he was sure—from the belligerent stance and the extended wings—that it was preparing to attack. He was certain that an Emim attack had just occurred at the Eiffel Tower. Given the proximity of the passage, there was a good chance that he'd found the killer.

He pulled out his smartphone, snapped a series of photographs of the angel, and, after logging onto the society's encrypted network, sent the images for identification. A series of Emim profiles popped onto the screen, but there was only one that interested him.

Name: Eno

Species: Emim

Height: 200 cm

Hair color: Black

Eye color: Black

Domain: Unknown. Three unconfirmed sightings in St. Petersburg, Russia (see call reports).

Distinguishing features: Classic Emim angel features; black wings measuring twelve feet wide by four feet high; normally works exclusively with members of Nephilim species.

Surveillance history: First documented angelological encounter occurred in 1889, during the Paris World's Fair, and resulted in the death of an agent. Subsequent encounters have included extended surveillance during the Second World War (see agent notes in dossier), DNA sample retrieved from strands of hair, and a series of photographs taken by agents at various Paris locations (see photographs below). Eno is characterized by outbursts of extreme violence, especially sexual violence enacted upon human males she has seduced (see autopsy reports).

Although the surveillance report on Eno suggested she was in St. Petersburg, Bruno was certain that she was the angel at the end of the street, and that she was responsible for the murder at the Eiffel Tower. Bruno recognized Eno's signature in the brutality of the slaughter, the great skill and strength of the killer, the peculiar way the body had been mutilated. He took a deep breath and tucked his phone into his pocket. Nothing had changed. Eno was as sadistic as ever.

In his twenties, he had come under Eno's spell during a hunt. She was unbelievably deft at evading their best agents, a vicious Emim who had been wanted for over a hundred years, and Bruno was determined to capture her. He'd known she was deadly. One of the murdered agents cited in Eno's profile had suffered third-degree burns over his chest, indicative of electro-induction shock, and his body had been found with rope burns to the neck, wrists, and ankles, signifying that he'd been tied up and tortured. Lacerations to the face, torso, buttocks, and back confirmed this. He had been castrated and dumped in the Seine.

Bruno understood the kind of creature he was dealing with, but when he was near Eno, it was as if he had stepped into a field of electricity, one that made all rational thought impossible. Of course, the original attraction between the Watchers and humans was purely physical, a dark and persistent sexual allure, a phenomenon of sheer lust, something that didn't disappear over time. So it shouldn't have come as a surprise that he'd fallen into a dangerous, obsessive pattern of hunting her. That he could lose his place in the society, that he could be disgraced or even killed—all of this had faded in the pursuit of Eno. She was beautiful, but that wasn't what interested Bruno. There was something hypnotic about her very existence, something dangerous and exciting about the knowledge of what she would try to do to him if he succeeded in capturing her. She made him feel alive even as she planned to kill him.

Verlaine climbed onto the ledge of a window, grasped the iron bars of the balcony, and, swinging his legs to gain momentum, pulled himself up toward the rooftop, the soles of his wing tips slipping as he climbed. He took a breath and continued. There were four more balconies above him, each one just out of reach, each one a step closer to Evangeline. He could see her there, above, perched on the roof tiles like a gargoyle.

By the time he'd hoisted himself over the balustrade of the final balcony, his muscles burned. The resistance felt good. His body was lean, his muscles tight and long, his endurance high. He would be forty-three years old in less than a week and he was in the best condition of his life, able to run for miles without breaking a sweat. Verlaine threw one leg over the ironwork balustrade and pushed himself onto the slate-roof tiles.

The Emim angel swooped past him, the wings brushing against his back as she flew into the sky. He felt the shiver of air against his skin, felt the strength of the creature's body as it slid past. If he were to grab her wings, she would take him with her into the air. He watched her twist upward, the lights and rooftops of Paris stretching beyond. As the Emim angel lowered herself to the rooftop, Evangeline rose. Soon the two creatures stood at the center of the rooftop, one facing the other, their wings moving in time.

There was no doubt in Verlaine's mind that the Emim was an exceptionally powerful angel. There was a rarefied, ghostly transparency to her skin and a certain distinction to her carriage that marked her as the higher order of warriors. As he examined the creature's bone structure and facial features he saw that everything—her large, alien eyes and her sinuous body—coalesced to form a strange and inhuman beauty. One rarely came across such a striking Emim. He took a deep breath and wondered what kind of god would fashion such a seductive and evil being.

Verlaine heard something behind him and turned to see Bruno emerge from a balcony just below. He knew that he should have called for assistance right away, that following Evangeline without backup went against all that he'd been trained to do, but Verlaine hadn't even thought to alert Bruno.

"I see you have a death wish," Bruno said.

"I thought that was one of the criteria for this job."

"Going solo against a creature like Eno is suicide," Bruno said, gasping for breath as he pulled himself over the ledge. "Believe me, I've been there."

Verlaine noted the hesitation in Bruno's movements and the self-conscious way he spoke, and strained to imagine what sort of connection to Eno could provoke this reaction in his boss. Veraline turned to the two angels facing off at the center of the rooftop. "I think there's something else happening here."

Verlaine stared at Evangeline and Eno for a moment, as if considering their actions with the eye of an anthropologist. The Emim angel traced a circle around Evangeline, marking her territory, and slowly opened her enormous black wings. They were magnificent, falling in sweeping tiers, the small feathers graduating into large opaque bursts of plumage. While the powdery feathers appeared heavy and substantial, he knew that if he were to touch them, his hand would pass through, as if skimming through a projection of light. Most Emim were repulsive, but this one was alluring, with all of the defects of the breed altered to create a disturbing and dark beauty. Verlaine was captivated. He wanted to remember each minute detail of what he was seeing, to store it in his mind so that he could examine the creature again in the future.

As if to demonstrate the power and agility of her wings, Eno curled them around her body and, with a pulse of strength, puffed them outward, so that they flared like the hood of a cobra. Although the subject of years of intensive investigation, Verlaine was never quite prepared for the mystery, the sheer inexplicable magic, of angels' wings. Strength, breeding, and classification in the heavenly sphere—all of this became instantly evident with a flash of a wing.

When Evangeline looked down at her opponent preparing to attack, she opened her wings in response, so that a layer of purple light wrapped around her body in a shimmering cloud. Silver streaks shot through the feathers, quick and electric, as if charged with a current. She swiveled and turned, moonlight sliding over her. The display was meant to terrify and impress.

"Pay close attention," Bruno whispered, his manner agitated. "You might never see an identification ritual like this again." He leaned closer to Verlaine, lowering his voice further. "First, they will display their wings to establish hierarchy. When there is a great disparity in strength, the weaker angel will submit straightaway. But clearly this match isn't going to be like that. There are two females creatures, both with extraordinary wings, one with a pedigree that should put her among the elite angels, the other with the strength of a mercenary. The dominant creature isn't obvious. If they can't establish a pecking order, they'll fight a duel."

Verlaine watched, fear growing in his stomach. The duel was an ancient angelic ritual, one that was considered outdated by modernized Nephilim. For centuries the custom had remained embedded in Russia, however, where the presence of the most powerful Nephilim, those descending from ancient angelic families, reside. Human beings once copied the practice, challenging one another in the name of honor, marking off paces and shooting at close range. In time, human beings had left the practice behind. Now only the most traditional Nephilim fought duels.

In the abstract, Verlaine found the ritual to be beautiful, a kind of call-and-response between creatures of strong but quite distinct species. Verlaine had watched archival footage of duels between Nephilim many times, but Eno's aggressive posturing, and Evangeline's defensive reaction, was unlike anything he had seen in the case studies he'd encountered. A duel between angels was theoretically a confrontation to the death. Only one of the angels would make it out alive. And although Evangeline was of a higher species of angel, he couldn't help but sense that Eno would win.

Evangeline fixed the angel in her gaze. Verlaine could see that she was struggling with her thoughts, that the confrontation was unexpected, that she didn't want to fight. He remembered what she had said about choosing not to become like the Nephilim, about being born with the characteristics of the beasts but refusing to accept her fate. Every impulse told her to kill Eno, and yet he knew she would not allow herself to do it.

Suddenly, Eno leaped into the air, her wings pushing her high above the rooftop once more. Evangeline stretched her wings and swooped into the sky. Eno hovered, waiting for Evangeline, watching her, preparing to attack. In a swirl of motion, the fight began. From a distance they looked like dragonflies twisting and circling in the moonlight.

As Verlaine studied their movements, he saw that Evangeline was far more adept than he had initially thought. Eno dove and struck, harrying Evangeline, darting at her, circling her, teasing her. Evangeline responded, slamming into Eno full force. Eno fell back, tumbling through the air. Recovering herself, she held her knees to her body, pushed herself forward, and turning in a somersault, spun once, twice, three times, gaining momentum with each rotation until she was a ball of fire. She launched herself at Evangeline, striking her with a force that threw her to the roof in a clatter of slate tiles. She lay still, stunned from the force of her fall.

With an elegant flick of her wings, Eno descended and walked to

Evangeline. She was trembling from the effort, her long black hair falling over her shoulders, her breathing heavy. She stood over Evangeline and drew her wings back, preparing to deliver a final blow, when Evangeline pushed Eno with an inhuman strength, landing a hit to the solar plexus.

"Very nice," Bruno said under his breath, and Verlaine had to agree: The solar plexus was the weakest point of all angelic creatures. A solid strike there could end the duel in a second.

"The Emim angel isn't wearing a shield," Verlaine noted, surprised. Mercenary angels often protected thier chest.

"She likes the challenge," Bruno said. "And if she gets hit, she likes the pain."

Eno buckled, raising her hands to defend herself. Evangeline kicked again, striking her with enormous force, her movements precise, perfectly delivered, vicious. In a matter of seconds she gained dominance over her opponent, pinning her to the floor, pressing her boot into the curve of her elegant neck, as if to crush her throat. Evangeline was the stronger angel. She had the power and the skill to kill Eno if she chose, kill her without effort, kill her as easily as if she were pressing the body of an insect under her boot. Despite himself, Verlaine was proud of her. He watched, waiting for her to deliver the death blow.

Instead, Evangeline bent on one knee and folded her wings over her shoulders in submission. Verlaine stared, shocked, as Eno recovered her bearing and, losing no time, began to bind Evangeline's hands behind her back. Evangeline met his eye, and he knew, with one look, that this act of surrender was a message for him. Evangeline had the powers of the Nephilim, but she chose not to be one of them. It was clear now that all his dreams, and every angel he had tracked, had led him back to Evangeline. Now he was about to lose her again.

Bruno must have been thinking the same thing, because he was ready to go after Evangeline. He stepped forward, his gun in his hand. Verlaine knew the standard procedure: Shoot the creature with an electric stunning device, sending a stream of electricity at the angel until the wings were immobilized. The stunned creature would lose control and fall to the ground, where the angel hunter would bind it. Verlaine felt a rush of panic at the thought of harming Evangeline. Although the method was meant to simply stun the furcula, the force of the electricity could cause enormous pain.

"Don't shoot," Verlaine whispered, panic making him feel unsteady as he moved across the slate tiles toward Bruno.

"It's not Evangeline I'm after," Bruno said under his breath.

Eno yanked Evangeline to her feet, wrapped an arm around her waist, and, with a push of her wings, flew into the night. Bruno and Verlaine stood in silence, watching Eno ascend. It seemed to Verlaine that a part of himself was in Eno's hands, that as she moved farther and farther into the sky, he, too, was beginning to fade away. When Bruno put his hand on Verlaine's shoulder, Verlaine wanted to believe that his mentor understood his burning anger, his rage, his need for revenge. "We're going after them," Verlaine said.

"It's useless to try to track Eno in Paris," Bruno said, as he walked to the edge of the roof and began to climb down to the balcony. "If we want to capture her, we'll have to hunt her on her own territory."

The Second Circle

LUST

Winter Palace, State Hermitage Museum, St. Petersburg

I f Vera Varvara were permitted to do as she wished, she would leave her office, with its chipping white plaster and disorderly papers, and walk through the vast Baroque hallways of the Winter Palace. She would make her way through the ancient corridors, with their gilded mirrors and cut crystal chandeliers, free as a child in a palace built of rock candy. She would cross the immense Palace Square, walk under the arches of the southern façade, and wander to the museum, where a flash of her ID card would open every door. Among paintings and tapestries and porcelains and statues—all the beautiful things amassed by the Romanovs during their three-hundred-year rule of Russia—she would feel as unfettered as a princess.

Instead she twisted her long blond hair into a chignon, went to the window, and pushed the pane open. There were angelic creatures below; she could feel them lingering, their presence like a high frequency vibrating her ear. She ignored them and let the chill night wind sweep over her. A lifetime in the swampy climate of St. Petersburg had given her a strong constitution, one that resisted every kind of illness and allowed her to get through harsh winters without much discomfort. Vera was neither tall nor short, thin nor fat, beautiful nor plain. In fact, she considered herself to be a perfect example of physical mediocrity, and this knowledge empowered her to live entirely in her mind, to push herself intellectually, to forget the frivolous lives led by so many women she knew—lives filled with shopping and husbands and children—and to excel in her work. In this regard, she had a difficult time coming down to the level of the people she met on the street; she simply didn't want to hear about their everyday successes and failures. An old boyfriend had once complained that her mind was like a metal trap—it hung open, inviting one to engage, and then clamped down hard on whoever dared come inside. She had never had a relationship with a man for more than a month or two, and even that duration of time she found to be cloying.

Leaning forward, Vera craned her neck outside, taking in the green-and-white marble of the Winter Palace, the onion dome rising in the distance. The river Neva, floes of ice floating and sinking, rushed by. All that she found ugly about St. Petersburg—the Communist apartment blocs, the gaudy trappings of the nouveaux riches abutting the glaring poverty, the lack of political freedom of Putin's government—seemed far away when she was ensconced in her tiny corner of the Winter Palace. Vera's position as a junior researcher revolved around the study of Russian Nephilim, their infiltration into the royal family and the aristocracy, their artifacts, their genealogies, and their fates during the revolution of 1917. She'd grown up in post-Soviet Petersburg, surrounded by the lush Italianate buildings of the Romanovs, and this—along with her training in angelology—had influenced her taste profoundly. She did not yearn, like so many young Russians, to experience the opulence of the past, to feel the luxuries and excesses of another era, and yet she didn't perceive such decadence as a kind of sickness either, as the Communists had. She was able to accept the layers of historical accretion as one accepts the layers of an archaeological dig: The effects of the Nephilim on the earth could be found underneath the social, economic, and political structures humans experienced each day. She knew that the creatures had infected the essence of her country once and, with the angelic population rising, would do so again.

With only two years of work outside of her training period, Vera was at the lowest position on the totem pole and, as such, was charged with sorting and cataloging artifacts. Just a fraction of the

Hermitage collections were on permanent display. The rest of the three million treasures were kept in massive storage rooms below the palace, hidden from public view. Among these she'd found uncountable remnants of Romanov treasures: ancient books that had been ripped apart; Rembrandts with red numbers painted on the canvases to mark their place in the Soviet inventory; furniture destroyed by water and fire. Many of the objects had been part of Catherine the Great's private collection but had been significantly augmented by Tsarina Alexandra Feodorovna before her fall from power in 1917. Picking up the pieces strewn about by history, and putting them back together—rebinding books, matching chipped enamels, removing the mar of red paint—was work she loved. Such opportunities were rare, and ones that allowed access to a collection like that of the Hermitage were almost nonexistent. Past curators had left the artifacts locked away for nearly a hundred years, uncertain of what to do with such strange treasures. Whenever she entered the storage rooms she felt as though she had walked into a time capsule, one as eerie as an Egyptian tomb, filled with secrets too strange to be shared with the world. She found segments of the collection to be a highly unnerving, almost frightening, accumulation of bizarre curiosities. For example, there was an entire storage room filled with canvases depicting angels and swans and young women, presumably virgins. It made her wonder at the motives for collecting such objects. Had the Romanovs actively singled them out or had the pieces been procured for them at random? For some reason, the taste of the collector mattered to her.

One day earlier that year, while Vera was searching through this bizarre collection of swans and virgins, she come across a sheaf of etchings. She'd found many odd things, but these were magnetic, perhaps because they were so unusual. Each print contained a portrait of an angel unlike any she had seen before. The creatures seemed utterly unique, with details that set them apart, and it was clear that they were very pure beings, perhaps archangels. Checking the signature, she realized that the prints were the work of Albrecht Dürer, a fifteenth-century artist, mathematician, and angelologist whom Vera deeply admired. His Apocalypse series was taught extensively in angelological courses as a vision of what would happen if the Watchers were ever released from their subterranean prison.

But these etchings seemed like a departure for Dürer. Oddly, they reminded her of the photographs taken by Seraphina Valko during the Second Angelic Expedition, in 1943. The renowned Dr. Valko and her team had located a dead angel's body, measured it, photographed it, and positively identified it as belonging to one of the Watchers who had been banished from Heaven for falling in love with human women.

Vera had seen the photos firsthand, during a conference in Paris the year before. Although they were black-and-white, taken in conditions that were far from ideal, the body of the dead angel was clearly visible. The long limbs, the hairless chest, the ringlets of hair falling over its shoulders, the full lips—the creature seemed vital and healthy, as if it had only closed its eyes for a moment. Only a broken wing fanning from the torso, its feathers folded at an unnatural angle, revealed the truth: The angel had been dead for thousands of years. The creature was male, with all the recognizable organs of human anatomy, a truth the pictures demonstrated with graphic accuracy. Seraphina Valko's photographs proved that the Watchers were physical beings, more like humanity than traditionally believed. Angels were not sexless beings but physical creatures whose bodies were but a more perfect expression of the human body. And most important of all, the photos had proven that angels were capable of fathering children. All of Vera's ideas about the Watchers, and all the work she had done to support her theories, depended upon this conclusion.

Vera drew away from the window and leaned against her desk, a Brezhnev-era affair with rusting metal legs. She slid open a drawer and removed the envelope she'd hidden under a stack of magazines. The portfolio was too bulky to keep on her desk, where anyone stopping by to chat could see it. With such limited access hours to the Hermitage, and the strict ban on bringing objects up from the storage rooms, she had had little choice but to smuggle the prints out of their tomb. It was her only hope for making progress on her own research. If there was one thing she knew about her field, it was this: Nobody was going to help her to advance but herself.

Gently unwinding the string of the clasp, she spread the sketches over the desk, marveling at the intricacy of the figures, the leaden hue of the line, the sheer genius of Dürer's composition. Originally, it was her fascination with Dürer's artistry that drew her to covet the etchings. But now, in the privacy of her office, the drawings seemed to become animated with movement and energy. Only an artist as masterful as Dürer could make a viewer viscerally understand how a Watcher could, like Zeus, seduce a virgin. Gazing at the prints, Vera imagined the encounter: In a swirl of wind, an angel appears before a young woman. He opens his wings, blinding her with his brilliance. She blinks, tries to understand who or what has come to her, but is too afraid to speak. The angel tries to comfort her, wrapping the terrified woman in his wings. There is a moment of terror and empathy and attraction. Vera wanted to feel it: the tangle of feathers and flesh, the heat of the embrace, the conflating of pain and pleasure and fear and desire.

The lights in the cabin had been switched off. Most of the passengers were twisted in their seats, trying to sleep. Bruno pulled down the plastic table and set out his dinner, bought at Roissy before boarding: a baguette sandwich with ham and a bottle of red wine from Burgundy. If there was one thing he understood about the present situation, it was that he couldn't think on an empty stomach.

Bruno found two plastic cups and poured the wine. Verlaine accepted one, took a pillbox from his pocket, and swallowed two pills, washing them down with the wine. He was obviously too jittery to eat anything. Verlaine tried to hide his state of mind, but Bruno could see it clearly: Finding Evangeline had opened a door to another lifetime, one Verlaine had nearly forgotten. Bruno knew, at that moment, that his suspicions about Verlaine were correct: His Achilles' heel, that secret weakness he'd detected, was now clear.

No one knew it, he hoped, but Bruno was also wrestling with his own demons: He couldn't forget Eno—the way she moved, her strength, her beauty. Calling up the profile he'd downloaded onto his phone, he scrolled through the supplementary documents, glancing at the DNA report before stopping to examine—admire, if he were honest with himself—the photographs of her exquisitely cold features. It was no use pretending to himself that her penetrating black eyes hadn't burned into his heart.

"What are you looking at?" Verlaine asked, squinting through his glasses.

Bruno passed the phone to Verlaine. "Eno," he said, opting to tell him the truth. "This creature inspires pure obsession among our agents," he said. "There is something about her, something that makes the challenge of capturing her almost irresistible. Our official stance has been to discourage our agents from becoming too tied up in hunting a particular creature. Often they don't heed this advice."

As Verlaine looked at Eno's profile on the phone, a look of horror spread over his face: *"The victim suffered burns to the neck, wrists, and ankles; lacerations to the face, torso, buttocks, and back. The body was marred by what appears to be—from autopsies documenting previous victims—ritualistic castration. Organs are never left at the scene and assumed to be kept as a trophy."*

"She's not someone you want to take home for a quiet romantic evening," Bruno continued. "No matter how much one likes to think himself the hunter, Eno is the one doing the hunting. She's young, by the standards of the Emim angels, and hungry."

"But what does she want with Evangeline?" Verlaine asked.

It was an interesting question for Bruno. The last time he had seen Evangeline, she'd been at the center of an operation that ended in unqualified disaster: They had lost their outpost in Milton, New York, not to mention a number of agents, and an artifact of untold value to their cause. Evangeline's own grandmother Gabriella, a close friend of Bruno's, had been found dead on a subway platform. Evangeline had disappeared completely. For the past ten years Bruno had considered her AWOL at best; at worst she was a traitor, guilty of crimes against their society.

Not that he was perfectly in line with society regulations himself. Bruno took a long sip of his wine, trying to think through the consequences of his decision to go after Eno and Evangeline. Flying to Russia on the spur of the moment was totally unsanctioned. Of course, Bruno had leeway to go after dangerous creatures, and he didn't ask for permission for every hunt, but this was not the usual situation. He'd bought the tickets himself, to keep the flight off the record, and he knew that he would have to work without the usual backup. It was an act of insubordination worthy of Evangeline, but even more so of Evangeline's mother, Angela Valko, one of the most daring angelologists in recent memory.

When Bruno arrived at the academy in Paris, Angela Valko was already legendary. Even then she was considered to be their most brilliant scientist. Her reputation was varnished by her husband, an infamous angel hunter named Luca Cacciatore. Angela's pedigree was the envy of every student in the school. As the daughter of Gabriella and Dr. Raphael Valko, she was personally tutored by her parents and was thus their heir in spirit as well as in name. As it turned out, she was the rare case of a well-connected child exceeding the glories of the past: Angela's work was so advanced that it didn't matter who her parents were or what they had done to help her. Her work changed the direction of the battle against angels—angelologists began to focus on the possibility of destroying the Nephilim en masse.

As with the chatter about any celebrity couple, much of what Bruno heard was gossip, but there must have been at least a little truth in the stories. Whenever an antiquated tradition or the red tape of the society held her back, Angela had simply changed the rules. If she couldn't change the system, she created a new one, beginning with her marriage to Luca, whom she met when he was a guest from the academy in Rome. When the council members—old and conservative angelologists who liked to keep the school staffed with their own kind—rejected Luca's application for a position in Paris, Angela helped him to create the angel hunter unit. Together they recruited the first fleet of angel hunters and the rest was history.

In the end their work had gone terribly wrong. Angela was murdered, Luca died alone and forgotten in America, their daughter was raised by nuns at St. Rose Convent—strangers, really—who hadn't been able to protect her in the end. The reality of Evangeline as a fully formed angelic creature was the final blow to the once inviolable Valko legacy. For Bruno, the truth about Evangeline was a total shock to the system. Seeing her perched on the rooftop, her wings tucked behind her, had produced a chemical reaction, pure and simple. He'd repressed an instinctual desire to destroy her.

"To discover what Eno wants with Evangeline might take some digging," Bruno said, finally answering Verlaine's question. "Eno's motives are never clear. She confounds the best of us."

"I'm more interested in finding Evangeline than in theorizing about her abductor," Verlaine said.

Suddenly Bruno wondered if his obsession with Eno tinted everything he did and said. "She works exclusively for the Grigoris. If she wants Evangeline, there's something important going on."

"This might have something to do with it," Verlaine said, reaching into his backpack.

Bruno watched him unwrap a gaudy, gem-encrusted egg. It was clearly valuable but, in Bruno's mind, a piece of kitsch that he wouldn't have looked at twice under normal circumstances. "How'd you make it through security with that thing?"

Verlaine held the egg before Bruno's eyes and said, "Watch this." He pressed a tiny button and the egg split in two, springing open on an invisible hinge and revealing, tucked inside its center, another egg. This egg, in turn, split apart, revealing two small miniatures: an intricately constructed gold chariot and a cherub, its body enameled and jeweled and gleaming, as if rendered in oil paint and varnish. What was once compact as a stone had expanded, as if by some magic mechanism, into an intriguing diorama.

"Evangeline slipped it to me," Verlaine said. "I was hoping you might know why."

Bruno looked it over, unsure of what to make of it, and closed the contraption, feeling the cold metal click into place as each mechanism retracted. "I can't tell you. But if there's a connection, we're going to the right place to find out."

Bruno felt his stomach lift as the plane descended. Pushing up the window shade, he looked out through the warped lens of thick acrylic plastic. In the distance, beyond a haze of darkness, the lights of St. Petersburg sparkled. He strained to see the twist of the Neva and the dome of St. Isaac's Cathedral, but could make out only a faint gradation of gray hovering at the edges of the lights, like smudges on an abstract painting. As the wheels hit the tarmac, and the plane bounced with the weight of the impact, Bruno could almost feel the density of the angelic population, as if their presence created another layer in the atmosphere. Eno was there, among these creatures. Turning to Verlaine he saw that his best hunter understood what they were up against. He would risk his life—he would risk everything— to find Evangeline.

Against his better judgment, Armigus left the human creature to scream. He knew it would be much less trouble to end its life quickly and be done with it. He had a dagger—a piece of sharpened bone that had been passed down for generations by the Grigori men—ready, he had the human's hands tied and the plastic sheets ready to catch the blood, but the doorbell was ringing on the first floor, the sound echoing through the vast plaster and marble interior. As Armigus left the room the human looked at him, pleading, desperate. He wanted to die quickly, Armigus could see it, but there was no choice but to put a pause to this little amusement. It could be his brother back from Paris, after all. And if Axicore had to wait, he would be furious.

Armigus walked the long stretch of hallway from one side of the house to the other, passing an array of modern glass-and-steel furniture, a shelf filled with Tibetan copper bowls, and a collection of Shivas cast in bronze. The apartment had been occupied by a lesser branch of the imperial family before the revolution, a period the twins disliked, and so, in defiance of the stuffy nineteenth-century moldings and the elaborate marble floors, Axicore and Armigus filled the space with modern furniture, tatami mats, Japanese manga, folding silk screens—anything to dispel the musty air of the past.

They had the same tastes in everything. In conversation one twin would finish the other's sentences. As children they would switch identities, so as to confuse their teachers and friends. When they were older they would take each other's women to bed, sharing lovers without disclosing the truth to their partners. Indeed, Axicore and Armigus Grigori were identical in every way except one: Axicore's right eye was green and his left eye blue, while Armigus's left eye was green and his right eye was blue. When the twins faced each other, they appeared to be mirror images. When they were standing side by side, the colors of the eyes made it possible to distinguish them. Armigus had often wondered about this anomaly, something that marked no Grigori before or since. Perhaps they were different, more unique, somehow better than the others.

Sighing with annoyance, Armigus reached the door. Under normal circumstances his Anakim angel would take care of this for him, but he always dismissed the Anakim from the house when he held human beings there. The screaming and crying always spooked the Anakim, who were truly lower in the hierarchy of angelic beings in every sense of the word. They simply could not tolerate the preferences and habits of the Nephilim.

He felt the hot, sensual energy of an Emim angel before he actually saw Eno in the doorway. She slid her sunglasses into her hair and said, "Your brother asked me to come for you."

Armigus stepped aside, letting Eno push past. She was as tall as Armigus, strong and dangerous. "He'd like me to help capture Sneja's Nephil?"

"I have caught her already," Eno said, giving him a haughty look, one that perfectly represented her feelings about Armigus. She preferred Axicore, thought him a true Nephil, and always reported to him. Armigus was just a secondary master, the one with a weakness for human beings. "Axicore is moving her to Russia now, but he needs your help. He wants you to speak with Sneja—to tell her that he's got Evangeline—and to meet him in Siberia to finish the job."

"What about Godwin?"

Eno blinked, clearly surprised that he would speak to her about the subject. The Grigori dealings with Godwin were confidential, not the kind of topic to be discussing with a mercenary angel, but

Armigus wanted to win Eno's confidence. He wanted her to like him. But she only thought he was weak. He could see it in her eyes.

"You will have to speak with your brother about that," Eno said, her voice cold.

Walking to the center of the room, she paused under a glass sculpture suspended from the ceiling, its crystals catching light and scattering it over her dark skin, her black hair, the eerie yellow glow that surrounded her eyes. A cry rang through the room.

"You aren't alone?" Eno asked, raising an eyebrow. Her long black tongue appeared at the side of her mouth, thick and wet as an eel.

"I'm in the middle of something," Armigus said.

Eno met his eye and smiled, a sadistic look suffusing her face. "Armigus—do you have a human here?"

Armigus looked away, refusing to answer. Axicore didn't approve of his appetite for human men, but Eno understood his preferences all too well.

"You know, Armigus, your brother needs you now. You haven't the time for playing games. I would be happy to take care of the creature for you," she said, stepping toward him. "More than happy."

Armigus took the key to his bedroom from his pocket and placed it in Eno's hand. She was doing him a favor—he hated finishing them off, hated the stink of the blood and human flesh—and yet he couldn't help but feel as though he had been cheated. "Don't leave a mess behind," he whispered.

"You know me better than that," Eno said, smiling.

Bracing himself, Armigus grabbed his jacket and hurried out the door, closing it before he could hear the sounds of Eno's work.

At that hour, with the sun rising at the edge of the city and the sky oozing a diaphanous mist, the oak tables were completely empty of scholars. Verlaine always found such places comforting, a reminder of who he had once been when he spent his days in quiet research, preparing classes and organizing notes for his next lecture. Indeed, the moment he and Bruno had set foot in the research center, and he heard the sound of their shoes on the polished floors, he felt his entire being relax, as if, after wandering in inhospitable territory, he had at last come to a place of safety.

A commotion in the hallway drew his attention as Vera Varvara walked briskly into the room, an air of crisp efficiency about her. He leaned down and kissed her twice, Parisian style, noting that her blue eyes didn't settle on his but stared through him, as if they had never met before. He felt his cheeks go warm, and he wondered if it had been a good idea to have called her at all.

While she was the perfect agent to consult—her extensive knowledge of St. Petersburg and access to the angelological collection at the Hermitage was invaluable—he wasn't sure how she felt about seeing him again. They'd met the year before at a conference in Paris, and spent the night together after having drinks at a bar in the fourteenth arrondissement, near the academy. The next morning they agreed that it had been a mistake, that they would simply pretend that the night hadn't happened. They hadn't spoken much since then. While he'd suspected that one day her professional savvy would be useful, he'd never imagined that he would be coming to Vera about Evangeline.

Verlaine stared at Vera, watching her move. She was as beautiful and brutally elegant as he remembered, but to his surprise he could not recall what it had been like to be with her in bed, what her body had felt like next to his. He could only summon forth the sensation of holding Evangeline, her presence like a vortex of white-blue snow, swirling and dancing around him as he tried to catch it.

Vera, however, hadn't forgotten a thing: She suddenly turned to Verlaine, giving him a hard look, one that conveyed curiosity and complicity at once, and then glanced from Verlaine to Bruno. Registering that she and Verlaine weren't alone, she assumed the expression of a disinterested colleague.

"Thanks for agreeing to meet us on such short notice," Bruno said.

"It was quite a surprise to get your call." Vera shook Bruno's hand and gestured for them to sit at one of the tables. "Please, tell me what I can do to help you."

"I'm not entirely sure if you can help," Bruno said.

"Actually," Verlaine said, cutting in, "we're hoping you can give us some information."

"With pleasure." Vera moved her eyes over Verlaine until he felt his stomach turn. Details of their night together were beginning to come back to him.

Without trying to explain, he removed the jeweled egg from his pocket and turned it in his fingers as if it were a Rubik's cube. With each twist of his wrist, he struggled to forget that this egg had been in Evangeline's hands only hours before, and that the Nephilim had likely abducted her in hopes of obtaining it.

Vera took the egg from Verlaine, lifting it as if it might explode in her hand. "My God. Where did you get this?"

"You recognize it?" Bruno asked, clearly surprised by the intensity of her reaction.

"Yes." Her expression softened as she grew thoughtful. "It's Fabergé's Cherub with Chariot Egg, made in 1888 for Empress Maria

Feodorovna." Vera ran her fingers over the enamel and, with expert movements, opened the egg, moving the hinges apart so that the golden mechanism creaked. As she removed the chariot and cherub figurine, Verlaine stepped behind her and examined it over her shoulder. The workmanship was exceptional: The sapphire eyes, the golden hair—every detail of the cherub had been perfectly rendered.

"What does it say on the sash?" Bruno asked.

"Grigoriev," Vera said, reading the letters painted in Cyrillic. She paused, considering the word. "The patronymic of Grigori, meaning son of Grigori."

Verlaine couldn't help but think of Evangeline's connection to the Grigoris: As the granddaughter of Percival Grigori, she was a descendant of one of the most vicious Nephilim families on record. "Is it possible that the egg could belong to the Grigori family?"

Vera gave him a weary look. "Grigori is an extremely common name in Russia."

Bruno rolled his eyes. "It's just a piece of tsarist bling, a nicely made bauble. Nothing deeper than that."

"I don't agree with your aesthetic sensibility," Vera said. "Fabergé's eggs are exquisite objects, almost perfect in their lack of practicality, whose sole purpose was to delight and surprise the recipient. Their seemingly impermeable exterior cracks to reveal another egg and then, at the center of this egg, a precious object, the surprise. The eggs are the most pure expression of art for art's sake: beauty that reveals only itself."

Verlaine liked the way Vera stood when she spoke, her posture that of a ballet dancer midstep, one arm moving with her voice, as if her ideas had been choreographed to match the rhythm of her body. Perhaps sensing the intensity of Verlaine's gaze, she changed her stance.

"Go on," Bruno said.

"The first Imperial Easter egg was constructed by Peter Carl Fabergé for the Russian tsar in 1885, and delighted Empress Maria

Feodorovna, who had seen similar creations in her childhood at the Danish court. Fabergé was commissioned to create a new and original egg each year. The jeweler was given the artistic license to design the eggs according to his imagination, and, as you can probably guess, they grew more elaborate—and more expensive—with time. The only requirement of Fabergé was that there must be a new egg each Easter and that each must contain a surprise."

Vera took the chariot and the cherub and placed it on one of the oak reading tables. It seemed to Verlaine like a precious windup toy that might, with the twist of a key, twitch into motion.

"Some of the surprises were miniatures, like this one," Vera continued. "Others were jeweled brooches or portraits of the tsar and his family painted onto ivory. After Tsar Alexander III died in 1894, his son Nikolai II took up the tradition, commissioning two eggs each year, one for his mother and the other for his wife, Empress Alexandra. There were fifty-four eggs designed for the Romanovs in total. After the 1917 revolution, many were confiscated. Those that were not were dispersed—smuggled out of Russia and sold to collectors or passed on to the living relations of the Romanovs. Since then, they have become museum pieces and treasures for the rich. There are a number of them here at the Hermitage, and Buckingham Palace houses dozens as well. The Forbes family collected them for years, and Grace Kelly was given one—the Blue Serpent Clock Egg—for her wedding to Prince Rainier. The eggs are extremely valuable, rare, and, as a result, have become coveted displays of wealth and taste, especially after the Forbes auction. Of the fifty-four original imperial eggs, the location of eight is unknown. Collectors believe they were lost, destroyed by revolutionaries, stolen, or kept hidden in private vaults. This egg—and its cherub and chariot surprise—is one of the missing eight."

Bruno gave the egg a dismissive look. "It's not really missing if we have it," he noted.

"To the world at large—and to collectors especially—it has

disappeared," Vera said. She plucked the golden chariot from the table and turned it over. Squinting, she examined the chassis, pushing it with her fingernail. Suddenly, a gold plate slid out. "Ah," Vera said, smiling triumphantly, as she showed Verlaine a series of Cyrillic letters stamped across the plate.

Verlaine couldn't begin to decipher it. "What does it say?"

"Hermitage," Vera said. She held up the plate for Verlaine to get a better look. He saw a string of numbers etched over the length of the plate, the numbers so faint that he had to squint to see them. "After the revolution there was a committee formed to catalog the Romanov treasures. They added numbers to many of the items— sometimes even painting them onto the canvases of Rembrandts— to identify their place in the archival storage area. Often the numbers rubbed off, or the identification tags were lost, leaving a holy mess of miscataloged and forgotten objects in the archive."

Verlaine tucked the egg into his pocket and said, "You seem to know a lot about this."

"Unfortunately, my first years here were spent doing such drudge work. I would find the strangest things shoved into the archival vaults." Vera sighed and returned her gaze to the egg. "The interesting thing about this, however, is that while most of the Romanov treasures were cataloged, the Fabergé eggs were not."

"But the plate you found?" Bruno said.

"Clearly the number was inserted into the egg by someone else," Vera said.

"But why?" Verlaine asked.

Vera smiled softly, and Verlaine realized that there was truly more to what Vera was saying than he had imagined. "Come with me. There's only one way to know for sure."

They left the reading room and turned into a corridor off the main entrance of the research center, passing door after door, each one identical to the one before, until Vera stopped abruptly at an electronic keypad. Vera pressed her thumb against it and an adjacent entryway clicked open.

Her high heels clicked on the polished marble as she led them into an immense gilded Rococo space. The ceilings glittered with chandeliers, and glass cases lined the walls, holding objects donated by past angelologists: a treatise on the seraphim by Duns Scotus; a scrying stone that had belonged to John Dee; a gold model of the lyre of Orpheus; a clipping of hair taken from the dead angel in the Devil's Throat. The upper walls were lined with thousands of Russian, Byzantine, and Eastern Orthodox manuscripts collected over the course of generations, most of them relocated to the Hermitage during the cold war. Were it not for Evangeline and the urgency he felt to find her, he could imagine spending a lifetime exploring this room.

A short man in a brown wool suit greeted them. "Vera Petrovna Varvara," the man said, his reedy voice filled with weariness. After the night shift in the archives, he was clearly glad to have human contact.

Handing him the tiny golden plate, Vera said, "From the permanent collection, please."

"You have clearance for this?" the man said, examining first the gold plate and then Vera.

Vera lifted the sleeve of her dress and presented the man with her forearm. He took a pen from his pocket, switched it on, and, in one quick gesture, scanned the chip implanted in her arm. A beep confirmed Vera's identity.

"Very well, then," the man said and, turning on his heel, he disappeared behind the desk and into a darkened room. It took nearly ten minutes for him to return, leading Verlaine to imagine that he had become lost in the folds of shelving, each one connected into the other like the bellows of an accordion. He was growing impatient.

Maybe the whole idea of coming to the Hermitage had been a mistake to begin with. Evangeline could be food for vultures before the archivist got back to them. Finally the man arrived with a large manila envelope in his hands.

"This was deposited here in 1984," the man said tersely as he handed Vera the envelope.

Vera slid her finger under the seal and opened it. A reel of 8mm film slid onto the table.

"I haven't seen one of these since I was a kid," Verlaine said, "And even then, 8mm was retro."

"Eighty-four," Bruno said, picking up the envelope and looking for something that might explain it. His voice was hollow, and Verlaine knew that something about the year loomed in his memory, immense and solid as a stone monument to a massacre. "That was the year Evangeline's mother was murdered."

Evangeline arched her back until the thick straps of leather tightened over her chest. She tried to move her legs, but they, too, were strapped down. She couldn't even turn her head more than an inch. A dull pounding behind her temples caused her vision to blur. She closed her eyes and opened them again, trying to regain focus, willing herself to understand where she was and how she had gotten there, pinned like a butterfly to a board. Her memory held shapes she couldn't decipher—forms of sensation that she felt but could not identify well enough to name: the whine of a jet engine; the prick of a needle; the cinching of buckles against her skin. Making out the sterile wash of white paint on concrete, she guessed that she was in a hospital or, perhaps, in a prison. The strange pulsing sound took on the pitch and tempo of a voice before dissolving into a rain of static. Whoever was speaking could have been nearby, but she heard the voice as if it were at the far end of a tunnel, distant and echoing.

The noise suddenly ceased and, as if a door had opened in her mind, memories rushed into her consciousness. She remembered the rooftop, the black-winged angel, the duel. She remembered the fleeting freedom, that brief but exhilarating buoyancy she'd felt before her surrender. She remembered Verlaine, standing nearby, helpless. She remembered what it had felt like to be touched by him. She remembered the heat of his skin against hers as he ran his finger along her cheek, and the shiver that went through her as he touched the delicate skin that joined her wings to her back.

And then her thoughts were driven even further back to the only time in her life that she had felt as frightened as she did now. It was

1999, New Year's Eve in New York City. While the rest of the world celebrated the coming of the new millennium, Evangeline was caught in her own private apocalypse. She found a park bench and sat in Central Park, too stunned to move, watching the crowds passing by. The angelic creatures had blended into the population with such skill that—despite the eerie colored light that surrounded them— they appeared to be entirely human. Some of the Nephilim paused, noticing her, recognizing her as one of their own, and Evangeline felt her whole being recoil. It was impossible that she was one of them. Yet she was no longer human. She noted the changes in her body as if they belonged to someone else. Her heartbeat was slow and shallow, the beat barely registering against her finger. Her breathing had sunk to such a depressed level that she took one or two breaths a minute. When she inhaled, the sensation was intense and pleasurable, as if the air itself gave her nourishment. She knew that Nephilim survived for five hundred years, a little more than six times the average life span of a human being, and she tried to imagine the years before her, the days and nights of unrelenting imprisonment in a body that needed little sleep. She was a monster, the very creature her parents had worked to destroy.

Evangeline strained against the leather straps once more, but they held fast. Her wings were open and pressed flat against the table. She could feel them against her skin, soft as sheets of silk. She knew that if she could move her wings, the straps would loosen, giving just enough for her to slip free. But as she twisted, a biting pain stopped her cold: She had been pinned to the table. The nails ripped into the skin of her wings.

A figure stepped into her peripheral vision. Evangeline could turn her head just enough to see a woman in a white lab coat.

"She's a very unusual creature," the woman said.

"I thought that was what Dr. Godwin was looking for," a second voice responded.

Evangeline's skin grew hot; her hands trembled against the metal cuffs. She recognized the name Godwin. She knew it from her childhood. If Godwin was behind this, she knew she was in terrible danger. It would be better to tear off her own wings than to be subject to his will.

She pressed her forehead against the leather strap, seeking the coolness of it, but the throb of the electrodes sent a current of heat into every part of her body. The pain caused her eyes to fill with tears. She blinked them away and they slid down her temples. A bright light burst on overhead, blinding her. When her eyes adjusted, she saw a syringe poised in a hand. As the nurse inserted the needle into her vein, she took a deep breath and struggled to stay conscious. She wanted nothing more than to drift to sleep. But she couldn't let herself go. If she did, she might never wake up.

A s they walked down the narrow iron staircase and into the underworld of the Hermitage, Verlaine was subsumed by the smell of thick deoxygenated air shot through with the slightest hint of gunpowder.

"Stay close and be careful not to trip," Vera said. She moved ahead, flipped a switch, and a naked bulb illuminated the space. They had descended into a long hallway made of old limestone. Vera grabbed a flashlight from a shelf, turned it on, and walked through a narrow, dark passageway. "This passage leads to chambers where the tsars once hoarded ordnance to stave off political agitators." They turned a corner. Verlaine found the passage so tight that the walls brushed the sleeves of his jacket, leaving a film of powder behind. "You smell the gunpowder, yes?" Vera continued. "Whenever I smell it I remember the thousands of people gathered outside the palace and the crimes committed against Russians by their own army."

Vera opened a door and led them into a room.

"Now these rooms belong to the society, and for decades they've been employed as a staging area for more than three million pieces of undocumented art. The first months of my time here were spent cataloging objects for my supervisor." Stopping before a wooden door sunk into the stone, she took a set of keys from her pocket and unlocked it. "This is his private space. If he knew I was bringing you here, I would be out on the street."

In a single motion, Vera opened the door and led them into the space. Verlaine walked inside, feeling awed by the chaos of objects.

"After Angela Valko's death, her father, Dr. Raphael Valko, donated her research papers to the research academy."

"I haven't heard news of Raphael for years," Bruno said. "He left the academy abruptly in the eighties to pursue his own research. He was ancient when I met him. I imagine he must have passed away by now."

"Raphael Valko is very much alive," Vera said. Reaching beneath a shelf, she hauled out a suitcase trimmed in leather. As she opened it, clouds of dust rose into the air, spinning in the weak gleam of the flashlight. Shining the beam across its contents, she picked up a picture frame, the glass coated in a thick film of dust, and gave it to Verlaine. Wiping away the grime, he found an image of Evangeline. She stood between her parents, one hand in her mother's hand, the other in her father's. She could not have been much older than five or six years old. Her hair was long and braided; a missing front tooth created a gap in her smile. Evangeline had been a normal kid once. He wished, suddenly, that he had tried harder to protect her. He couldn't help but feel that he'd gone about everything in the wrong way—they should have captured Evangeline and Eno when they had had the chance. Looking up, he found Bruno holding a folder.

Bruno opened the folder. There was a collection of loose pages inside. A passage had been scribbled on the top page. Bruno read: *"To you this tale refers who seek to lead your mind into the upper day, for he who overcomes should turn back his gaze toward the Tartarean cave. Whatever excellence he takes with him he loses when he looks below."*

"Boethius, *Consolation of Philosophy*," Verlaine said. The passage was from what had become a veritable mantra of the angelologists, a text that referred to to a geological formation called the Devil's Throat Cavern, the mountainous cave where the Watchers were imprisoned, and where, angelologists believed, they waited still for their release. He stepped closer, to get a better look at the inscription, and saw that someone had written the words *Dad's translation* next to the passage.

"Any ideas?" Verlaine asked Vera.

"This is an early draft of Dr. Raphael Valko's translation of the Venerable Clematis's notebook, which was written during the First Angelic Expedition. The most obvious reference of the passage is to the myth of Orpheus and Eurydice—Orpheus rescued his beloved, but at the point of leaving Hades, or Tartarus, he turned back and lost her forever. But Angela Valko thought that this passage referred not just to the myth of Orpheus—and his lyre, which was recovered in the Devil's Throat Cavern, as you very well know—but to a spiritual journey, the emergence of the individual mind from the darkness of self to find a higher purpose."

"You make Angela sound like some kind of Sufi mystic," Bruno said.

"True, she was a bit unusual," Vera said. "Although a die-hard scientist, she interpreted much of her work as part of a spiritual journey, believing that the material world was the expression of the unconscious, and that this collective unconsciousness was God. The word of God brought forth the universe, and each human being has access to this original language through the unconscious. You might call her a Jungian, I suppose, but there was a history of such mysticism long before Carl Jung. In any case, Angela was interested in this passage for its verticality—the upward trajectory from the pit to the sky, from darkness to light, from hell to heaven. Each step up brought the seeker out of chaos and into a place of beauty and order."

"Like Jacob's Ladder," Verlaine said.

"Or," Vera said, turning the flashlight into a room, "a passionate collector."

Verlaine could hardly believe his eyes. There, displayed in glass cases, was an incredible collection of eggs—thousands of varieties of bird eggs: plain bird eggs glazed with paint; dodo eggs cut apart and labeled; robin's eggs preserved in formaldehyde, with the chick still curled against the shell, delicate as a bean in a pod. There were crystal eggs, jeweled eggs, eggs from the courts of Denmark and France. The assortment was singular and obsessive, qualities that piqued Verlaine's curiosity.

"The egg you showed me in the research center would fit very nicely here, don't you think?" Vera asked.

"Perfectly," Bruno said under his breath. "Where did they come from?"

"I haven't uttered a word about this to anyone," Vera said, "but I don't come down here to simply admire the eggs. I believe the fact that Angela Valko had one of Fabergé's eggs in her possession—and found a way to catalog the egg in our archives—is more than just a coincidence."

"You can't seriously think there is a connection between one of our best scientists and this collection," Bruno said.

"Quite," Vera responded crisply. "I won't bore you with my research any more than necessary, but one of my pet projects at the moment has to do with Nephilim reproduction. It just so happens that once upon a time egg births were common among the purest breeds, their offspring superior in strength, beauty, agility, and intelligence."

Verlaine's eyes fell upon an illustration from Albrecht Dürer's famous *Manual of Measurement* propped up among the eggs. He had heard of Dürer's theory of the egg line, and his obsession with the egg, with its perfect euclidean shape, as the vessel through which pure angels were born. Verlaine had dismissed the idea. It seemed to him that when angelologists couldn't prove their work with hard facts, they fell to creating airy theories. He wasn't sure whether Vera's support of such an idea granted it credence or if it proved that she was out of her mind.

Vera continued. "Many of the royal families in Europe longed for an egg-born heir, and they mated with this in mind, arranging marriages with other royal families based on their reproductive prospects. Nevertheless, as time went on, Nephilim eggs became more and more rare."

"Enter Carl Fabergé," Verlaine said.

"Indeed," Vera replied. "Clearly, the Romanovs were not immune to the ostentatious fuss over the eggs. Fabergé played on this obsession. His eggs were precious and intricate objects that, when cracked open, revealed a surprise that spoke of the secret desires of kings— the most precious surprise of all would be an heir hatched from an egg. The tradition of giving enameled eggs at Easter stemmed from the imperial family's longing for another such birth. Indeed, all the Nephilim of Russia wanted an egg-hatched heir. Such an event would be prestigious, and would guarantee instant advancement."

"If this were the case, why aren't we seeing eggs now?" Bruno asked.

"There's no concrete answer to this question, but it seems that the Nephilim lost their ability to create the eggs. There were no egg births after the seventeenth century, as far as I know, but that did not kill hope. At the court of Louis XIV, there was such a fuss about the production of an egg that the court confectioner created elaborate chocolate eggs and presented them to the king and queen at Easter. The surprise at the center of the egg was something of an inside joke, one that the royal families understood all too well. Suddenly eggs were everywhere. The fashion for eggs spread to the masses. Ordinary human families began to color chicken eggs, and factories molded chocolate eggs by the millions, some of which contained small toys inside, a direct reference to the surprise of the jeweled eggs, which, of course, referred to the coveted angelic child. Human beings have copied Nephilim habits without realizing that they were celebrating the hatching of their oppressors. It is a great irony that chocolate eggs are now so common at Easter. When you eat a Cadbury egg you don't realize that you are following this tradition without understanding its origin, or the joke."

"For Christians, the eggs symbolize the resurrection of Christ," Bruno said. "There is nothing Nephilistic about that."

"On the surface this appears to be compatible with the Christian celebration of Easter," Vera said. "But if you look deeper you will see that the egg symbol has little to do with the church. The decoration of eggs, the Orthodox practice of breaking eggs on Easter morning, the egg hunt—these are all popular practices whose real origin is obscure. Of course, there is the pagan Germanic goddess Eostre, whose feast day was celebrated in the spring, but ask the man on the street why he's coloring eggs at Easter, and he has no idea."

"Wouldn't there be Christmas eggs rather than Easter eggs?" Verlaine asked.

"Christmas is a celebration of Jesus's human birth," Vera said. "Easter, his second, spiritual, immortal birth. One birth within the next. An egg within an egg." Vera placed the flashlight on a table. "Which brings us back to our purpose in this room. Someone— Angela Valko most likely—added the metal card to the surprise at the heart of Fabergé's Cherub with Chariot Egg. She intended for whoever would discover the egg to watch the film stored in the archives."

Vera walked to a gray plastic box at the far side of the room and carried it to the table. She flipped a series of metal clasps and revealed an old film projector. Unwinding a cord, she plugged it into a makeshift socket hanging from the wall, its wires dangerously exposed. An electric buzz hummed through the projector, and, with a flip of a switch, a searing white light blazed onto the wall, cutting a perfect square of light.

"Voilà," she said. "Give me the reel of film."

As Verlaine placed the film in Vera's hand, he felt another tremor of anxiety. Perhaps it was filled with nothing more than images of lab equipment, or, worse, it had been damaged and would spit out a series of distorted and indecipherable images.

Vera locked the reel into place and fiddled with the levers until they were in the correct positions. After feeding the film into the catch and turning the wheel so that it spooled, she pressed a button, and the reels began to move. A flickering of sepia frames flashed over the limestone wall, and then, as if by some feat of magic much stronger than any charm taught at the Academy of Angelology, Angela Valko appeared before them.

Verlaine's muscles stiffened at the sight of Evangeline's mother, as if the electricity that powered the projector had funneled itself through his spine. Angela's face was serious, her blond hair tied back in a ponytail, her large blue eyes staring into the camera, and into the eyes of the people who had gathered together to try to understand the message she left behind.

Verlaine felt the irrational urge to speak to the woman on the wall, to reach out and touch the insubstantial light that flickered in the dusty air, to draw close to the illusion. She was beautiful and—Verlaine could only make the comparison now, after having seen Percival Grigori in person—a near replica of her Nephilistic father. She wore a white lab jacket unbuttoned to reveal a black turtleneck. The laboratory was sterile, orderly, with large glass windows and a polished concrete floor. Droppers, tongs, tubes, and other equipment he couldn't readily identify were arrayed on a shelf behind her. A series of beakers had been placed at hand, some filled with liquid, others with powders. Something flashed at her throat. Verlaine looked more closely until he made out a necklace—the lyre pendant he'd touched only hours before—at her throat.

Suddenly Evangeline's father stepped into the frame. Striking in his T-shirt and jeans, Luca looked nothing like the man Verlaine had imagined him to be. In the film he was young and vibrant, filled with energy and determination. He had long black hair that fell over his brow, tanned skin, dark eyes. There was an aura of care in his movements—he stepped deeper into the frame and paused to be certain everything was in place—but he had a buoyancy about him that seemed at odds with the accounts Verlaine had heard. The founder of the angel hunter unit was, as legend had it, a darkly laconic man, a warrior whose strategic mind allowed him to trap and kill angels with an ease most angelologists found unnerving.

The couple exchanged a look of complicity—as if they had planned every last detail of the film—and Luca leaned over and kissed Angela's cheek, a quick gesture, one that he might have performed without thought many times each day, but in the kiss it was clear how profoundly he had loved her.

A strange, guttural noise—half moan, half growl—caused Angela to turn. The camera, following her gaze, panned over the lab and settled on a creature. The Nephil was suspended from a metal hook, its feet dangling above the floor. Although the creature was male, the long, white-blond hair, narrow shoulders, and elegant, tapering waist gave it a delicate beauty. Bright copper wings fell around its body like the feathers of a dead bird. The creature had been stripped, perhaps beaten, most likely sedated, as it seemed to be in a state of confusion.

As a captive of the flickering image, Verlaine was horrified and fascinated at once. It was beautiful and grotesque, like a fairy caught in a spider's web, its luminous skin creating the softest glow through the glass. He recognized the honeylike liquid that oozed over its skin, sliding slowly over the creature's chest and legs, dripping from its suspended feet and pooling on the glass floor—it was the same excretion that coated Evangeline's skin when he'd touched her earlier. For an unsettling moment he imagined how Evangeline would react to such bondage. Would she struggle if the ropes burned her wrists? Would she fold her wings against her body like a shield as they interrogated her? Luca must have beaten the creature—there was no other explanation for its condition—and it remained to be seen whether he would resort to even more violent methods. A wave of nausea came over Verlaine, and he wanted, suddenly, to walk out of the room and breathe the fresh cold air aboveground.

Angela Valko began to speak. "To those who object to our methods of obtaining information, I say this: We can no longer submit to the moral code created two thousand years ago by our founding fathers that requires us to fight with approved methods. We have acted with dignity, showing restraint and judgment in our fight. As a result, our enemies have become more vicious than ever. They evolve in their methods to harm us. We must, in turn, evolve in our methods of defense. Angelologists who have worked with me, either in the academy or here at my laboratory, know that I am no reactionary. My work has been a steady accumulation of facts gleaned through observation and experimentation. I am a scientist, and I would prefer to be left in peace, to continue my work. My belief that the Nephilim can be routed only by hard work over multiple human lifetimes hasn't changed. But it is clear that the reach of the creatures has grown and that we must respond. The angelic life-forms around the globe multiply exponentially each year. The victory of the creatures over humanity is at hand, and it seems that we must stand by and watch their ascendancy. We have fought too long and too hard to lose our war against the Nephilim. I will not allow that to happen. It is to that end that I record this communication. It is not an apology for what Luca and I intend to do but an attempt to demonstrate our motives and, in the case of our deaths, which both Luca and I realize to be a very strong possibility, to help other angelologists to understand the secret structures the Nephilim are building."

Another man stepped into the frame, and Verlaine was startled to see a young Vladimir Ivanov. Verlaine calculated that he had encountered Vladimir in New York nearly twenty years after this film was made. In 1999 Vladimir's whole manner had been that of a man exhausted by life; in the 1984 film he was a man fully energized by his work. Next to Vladimir was a woman Verlaine did not recognize. She wore a white lab coat over a brown dress. She was so still, so statuesque in her manner, that Verlaine hardly registered her presence.

"That is Nadia," Bruno whispered. "Vladimir's wife, a lab tech who assisted Angela in her work. After Angela's murder, she quit her work at the academy. When Vladimir left for New York, she didn't go with him."

Verlaine turned back to the film just as Vladimir was putting his arms around the angel's chest and lifting it from the hook. The creature was unwieldy—at least two feet taller than the men in the room with it. Struggling, it hissed, its body contracting and writhing as Vladimir bound it to the chair, the ropes cinching tighter as it moved. The creature's wings hung outside of the stays, falling limp as bat wings until suddenly, in desperation, the angel thrust them open, striking Angela in the face and slamming her against the wall. Verlaine's urge to protect Angela, to pull her away from the creature, felt even stronger than before, a feeling mirrored by Luca: The camera jolted and wavered, then stabilized as Luca set it onto the table and rushed into the frame. He grabbed the creature, wrenched the wings closed, and, holding the angel steady, assisted Vladimir in binding the wings.

"Let's get on with this," Angela said, her voice hardened. The left side of her face had been scratched. She pulled a chair close to the bound angel, balanced a notebook on her lap, and tapped a pen against the paper. The metallic click of the spring pounded an even rhythm as Angela spoke.

"Interrogation of Nephil male, 1984, Montparnasse, Paris."

Angela glanced at Luca, as if to check that he was filming the exchange, and then turned her attention back to the angel. "The creature was captured on the rue de Rivoli at approximately 1:30 A.M., and injected with ketamine en route to our facilites in Montparnasse.

Preliminary observations suggest the creature to be between two hundred and three hundred years old, with the characteristics of all Nephilim. Initial attempts to interview the subject were fruitless. He remains unresponsive."

Angela looked at the angel, and Luca followed with the camera. The creature stared at his interrogator through narrowed eyes. His face was flushed with anger, and his breathing—whether from the cinch of the ropes or the strain of fury—came in labored bursts. Veins snaked over his skin, as if they might explode with the pressure of his blood.

Angela looked at him with a cold, clinical eye and said, "Are you ready to begin?"

The creature's nostrils flared. He displayed a level of belligerence consistent with Nephilim of his rank and heritage. Verlaine recognized the insouciant, indignant anger of the fallen angel. Although he had not read Milton for years, he couldn't help but think of Lucifer—the brightest star of heaven—falling to the depths of the earth, undone by beauty and pride.

"Speak, beast," Vladimir said, stepping behind the angel and tightening the ropes.

The creature closed his eyes and said, "If words were shields, my voice would rally to my defense." His words seemed to float upon his light, buoyant voice, its tone taken from the pure registers of the angels.

"Riddles will get you nowhere," Vladimir said.

"Then I will remain stationary for the time being," the creature said.

Vladimir assessed the angel and, with a swift movement, slapped him across the face. A stream of blue blood slid over his lips and chin and dripped onto his chest. He smiled a vicious, devilish smile, one filled with arrogance. "Do you really believe pain is an effective method? I have lived through things you cannot begin to imagine."

Angela stood, placed the notebook and pen on the chair, crossed her arms over her chest, and said to Luca, "Perhaps he'll be more cooperative if I speak to him by myself."

The camera moved abruptly, and Luca—setting the device onto a table, leaving Angela and the angel in view—stepped into the frame. "There is no way I'm leaving you alone with this thing," he said.

Angela placed her hand on his arm, as if to assuage his worries. "He can't do much under the circumstances. I know he has information we can use, if we can get him to talk. If you hear anything alarming, come back in." Angela glanced at the creature, who had closed his eyes, as if waiting for the ordeal to end. A look of determination passed over her features, and Verlaine knew that she was testing herself against the creature, marking her strength and intelligence against it, placing her bets on her ability to defeat it. He recognized the feeling. It was exactly this that kept him hunting.

"Go on, Luca," Angela said, opening the door. "I'll alert you if there's a problem."

The film went black and then, in a sputter of light and movement, resumed. The bright, industrial overhead bulb had been dimmed, and a single desk light glowed in a corner, casting a blue shadow over the creature. Angela Valko sat in a metal chair across from the angel. They were alone.

"Identify yourself, please," Angela said.

"Percival Grigori III," the creature said. "Son of Sneja and Percival Grigori II."

Verlaine looked more closely at the creature, trying to understand how this could be the person he had met in New York. The Percival Grigori he had known was twisted and ill, his skin transparent, his eyes a watery, weak blue. The angel in the film was beautiful, his skin glowing with health, his golden hair glossy, his expression one of superiority and defiance. In fact, there was a staggering resemblance between the angelologist and the angel. It was obvious to anyone who saw them together that they were related by blood. And yet, Angela never knew the true identity of her father. Neither one of them could guess what time would bring. Frozen in 1984, they were forever suspended in their innocence.

"Percival," Angela said, her manner softer, as if she were playing a new role, that of a woman charming a quarrelsome companion. "Can I get you a drink?"

"How kind," Percival said. "Vodka. Straight."

Angela stood and walked offscreen. Verlaine heard the clinking of glass. Soon she returned with a cut-crystal tumbler.

Percival looked from the glass to his hands, which were bound by rope. "If you please."

As Angela hesitated and then untied the ropes, Verlaine wanted to jump into the film and to stop her, to warn her against Percival, to pull her away. He felt his heart sink at what lay ahead. Angela Valko was falling into a trap.

When the ropes fell from Percival's wrists, Angela gave him the tumbler of vodka and returned to her seat. "Now it's time to answer my questions."

Percival took a sip, swallowed, and said, "Perhaps. But first I have a question of my own: Why does such a lovely young woman spend so much time in this dungeon of a laboratory? I can't imagine it offers much pleasure."

"My work has its own rewards," Angela said. "One of which is capturing and studying creatures like you. You would make a fine specimen for my students."

Percival smiled, his expression cruel. "It is very fortunate that I am not as brutal as my grandfather. He would have killed you within the first five minutes of meeting you. He would tear you apart and leave you here to bleed. I wouldn't dream of killing you in such a messy fashion."

"That's reassuring," Angela said, a hand disappearing in the folds of her white lab coat. She removed a pistol and aimed it at Percival's chest. "Because I have no such scruples."

Percival drank the vodka, turned the glass in his hand as if pondering what to do, and then, with an explosive movement, threw the tumbler at Angela. It smashed against a wall, the crystal shattering offscreen, creating chords of dissonance. "Untie me," he said.

Angela leaned back in her chair, a smile on her face. "Come now, I can't let you go. I've only just got you talking." She raised the gun, slowly, as if considering its weight in her hand, and shot. The bullet missed, yet Percival cried out in surprise and anger. "I have a reason for bringing you here. I don't expect to let you leave until I have answers."

"About what?"

"Merlin Godwin."

"I have no idea who you're talking about."

"I have proof that he's been in communication with you," Angela said. "What you need to do now is to give me the details."

"You are mistaken if you think that you pose a threat to us. Indeed, your work has helped us enormously."

"What has Godwin given you?" Angela said, her voice carefully calibrated. "I want to know everything: the experiments, the subjects, the purpose. I am especially interested to know how Merlin Godwin has gained access to my work."

Percival took a deep breath, as if considering his options. "The project is but in its beginning phases."

Although Angela maintained a clinician's equilibrium, Verlaine could see that Percival had taken her by surprise, that she had not expected his capitulation at all. He was going to cooperate. Getting what she wanted had thrown her off balance.

"Technically, we are advancing with great rapidity." Percival's complexion changed as he spoke, his white skin turning even paler, as if he'd drifted away from Angela and fallen into an argument he'd long been fighting inside his mind.

"Merlin Godwin has made trips across the Iron Curtain in recent months," Angela said. "Is this related in some way to your project?"

"It wasn't my first choice to build in the old world, but, of course, we mustn't forget the Watchers."

"Are you mining Valkine?"

"'Mining' is not how I would describe it," Percival said. "It is more like extracting dust from a hurricane. The quantities are minuscule and the conditions are wretched. And yet we need the material. It is the only way."

"The way to what?"

"Perfection," Percival said, flatly. His blue eyes seemed to sharpen as he spoke.

"Perfection is a concept," Angela said. "It is not something one can construct."

"Purity is perhaps the better word. We are recovering the purity we lost four thousand years ago. We will take back what was destroyed in the Deluge, the purity of our race that was compromised by generations of breeding with humanity, and re-create the original breed of Nephilim."

"You want to re-create paradise," Angela said, astonished.

Percival smiled and shook his head. "The Garden of Eden was created for human beings," he said. "The Angelopolis is for angels, pure creatures, the likes of which haven't been seen on earth since Creation."

"But that is impossible," Angela said. "The Nephilim were never pure. You were born of angels and women. You were mixed at your origin."

Percival said, "Look at me closely—at my transparent skin, my wings—and tell me what is and what is not possible. My family is the last of the exceptionally pure Nephilim. If my existence is possible, anything is possible. But what we can make in the future, now that is even more incredible."

Angela stood and paced the room, her shadow falling over the angel. "You are engineering an alternate world for yourselves, one that will be wholly constructed for Nephilim."

"It would be more correct to say that we have made a petri dish, and from this small biological culture we will grow a new world, one that will replace what you call human civilization."

As Angela Valko considered this, Verlaine imagined the obvious questions forming in her mind: *Why would the Nephilim do this now, after thousands of years of coexistence with human beings? What is their motivation? How could they achieve something so drastic? And what would they do with human beings?*

"This isn't a new endeavor," Percival said, reading Angela's thoughts. "We've been looking for a way forward for many, many years. The twentieth century has provided many pieces to the puzzle: War allowed us to test our formulas on human subjects; science has allowed us to look inside the mechanisms of our creation; technology has allowed us to collect and compare data." Percival folded his hands in his lap. "And we've found an ally."

"Dr. Merlin Godwin," Angela said. "You've found an angelologist to spy and steal for you."

"We've found a man who appreciates the dilemma of our race," Percival said.

"Nephilistic diminishment," Angela said. "Nephilim fertility has dwindled, immunity to human diseases has weakened, and wingspan has shortened, as has life expectancy. Of course I'm fully aware of this phenomenon. I have been studying the possible causes for the past few years."

Percival said, "Your theory on the genetics of angelic creatures has been extraordinarily helpful. In fact, Dr. Valko, it is because of your work that we will be able to rebuild our race."

"My work has nothing to do with genetic engineering."

Percival smiled again, and the frightening hunch that Verlaine had sensed earlier—that the creature could manipulate Angela as he wished—returned. "I know your theories very well, Dr. Valko. You have spent your career deciphering Nephilistic DNA. You've speculated about the role of Valkine in the production of angelic proteins. You've explored the mysteries of angelic and human hybrids. You've even found and captured me, no small feat. Your work has uncovered the codes, the secrets of production, all the answers to the questions you have. And still you don't see."

A tremor in Angela's lip was all that revealed her growing irritation. "I think you may be surprised by our capabilities," Angela said, the faintest hint of insecurity passing over her features. She stood, went to a cabinet, and removed an oblong object. "This, I believe, might be familiar to you."

Verlaine recognized it instantly: It was an elaborately jeweled enamel egg. Although similar to the one in his pocket, its design was distinctly different. The exterior was sprinkled with brilliant blue sapphires.

"That," Vera said, her eyes trained upon the egg, "is another of the missing eggs."

As Verlaine followed Angela's movements, he realized that his entire body had gone rigid.

Angela sat down, turning the egg in her hands, the gems glittering. To Verlaine's great surprise, even Percival watched with fascination.

"I thought you might recognize it," Angela said. She opened the egg. Inside there was a golden hen with eyes of rose-cut diamonds. Angela pushed the beak and the bird split apart, revealing a series of glass vials.

While Percival Grigori's expression transformed from surprise to bafflement, and then to rage, his voice remained calm. "How?"

Angela smiled, triumphant. "Just as you have watched us, we have been watching you. We know that Godwin has been collecting samples of blood." Angela lifted one after the other and read the labels. "Alexei, Lucien, Evangeline."

Were it not for the undertone of anguish in Angela's voice when she spoke her daughter's name, Verlaine would have doubted what he'd heard. *If Evangeline had been marked by the Nephilim from childhood, what would they do with her now that they had her in their possession?*

Angela returned the vials to the egg and closed it. "What I want to understand is why, exactly, you have these samples."

"If you want to understand," Percival said, "you will join us. There is a place for your work at the Angelopolis."

"I don't think that will be possible," she said, removing a small syringe from her pocket. "I have some ideas of my own about purification."

Percival narrowed his eyes as he examined the needle in her hand. "What is it?"

"A suspension that holds a virus. It affects creatures with wings— birds and Nephilim are particularly vulnerable. I created it in my laboratory by employing mutations of known viral strains. It is a simple virus, something like the flu. It would give human beings a headache and a fever, but nothing more serious than that. If it is released into the Nephilim population, however, it will cause mass extinction unlike anything you've seen since the Flood." Angela lifted the syringe to the light, revealing a green liquid. She shook it slightly, as if swirling wine in a glass. "A biological weapon, some might call it. But I think of it as a way to level the field."

A hint of cruelty shone in Angela's eyes, and Verlaine understood that she had succeeded in turning the interview around. Percival Grigori was once again in her power.

Angela hesitated for a moment, and then, taking the syringe in hand, moved toward him. Verlaine sensed with growing alarm that he should not be there, should not be witnessing Angela Valko's final interaction with her father. In the decades since the film had been made, the virus in her syringe had infected 60 percent of the Nephilim, killing and disabling the creatures with a vicious efficiency. The disease had been such a powerful force that many in the society had joked that it was a pestilence sent from heaven to help along their work.

But Verlaine knew a terrible truth that Angela did not: The personal wager she was making would fail. The angel would tell her his secrets, but there would be consequences. Soon, within days after the film was shot, Angela Valko would lose her life.

The Third Circle

GLUTTONY

D
r. Merlin Godwin noted the heaviness of Evangeline's
breath, the labored flickering of her eyes, the expression of
despair that crossed her face whenever she came back into
consciousness. The last time he saw her she had been a little girl. She
had stared at him with intransigent curiosity. He had spent twenty-
five years looking for her, all the while hoping to have her just as he
did now, weak as a dragonfly dessicated in the sun.

"Come, come, have some water," he said, when she opened her
eyes once more. Smiling, he poured water over her lips, letting it drip
over her chin. The drugs were effective. Even if the straps were loos-
ened she wouldn't have the strength to lift her head.

"Do you remember me?" he whispered, caressing her arm with
his finger. When it was clear that Evangeline had no clue who he
was, he added, his voice little more than a whisper. "It was so long
ago, but surely you recall how you came to see me with your mother."

At Angela Valko's request, Godwin had handled the scheduling
of the visits, asking only that he organize the sessions with Evangeline when the lab was empty. As a result, they had met early in the
morning or later in the evening, when the others had left the building. He had examined Evangeline himself, taking her pulse, listening
to her breathe. He couldn't help being moved at how the stolid Angela Valko, renowned for her sangfroid in the most unnerving situa-
tions, held her daughter close, steadying the girl's trembling body as
the needle slid into the vein, the bright vermilion blood drawn
swiftly into the barrel of the syringe. The clinical nature of the procedure seemed to reassure Angela but not Evangeline—she had an

instinctual fear that seemed to Godwin to belong less to a little girl than to a wild animal caught in a cage.

During each session, Angela watched the procedure with rapt attention, and Godwin could never tell if she felt anxiety or curiosity, if she secretly hoped to discover something unusual in the blood. But there was never anything at all unusual about the results when they came back from the lab. Still, Godwin had kept a sample from each session, labeling the vials and locking them in his medical case.

"Your mother insisted on the exams herself," Godwin whispered, dabbing a drop of water from Evangeline's chin. "And although she demonstrated a reasonable concern for your well-being, it's difficult to understand the motives of a mother subjecting her own child to such invasive scrutiny. Unless, of course, she was not entirely human."

Evangeline tried to speak. She had been heavily drugged. Although her voice was weak, and she could not focus her eyes, Godwin understood her when she said, "But my mother was human."

"Yes, well, Nephilistic traits can appear in a human being, manifesting like a cancer," Godwin said, walking to a table of medical instruments. A series of scalpels, the edges of varying acuity, lay in a line as if waiting for him. He chose one—not the sharpest but not the dullest either—and returned to Evangeline. "Both you and your mother appeared to be human, but angelic qualities could have—how shall I say it?—blossomed in you like a black and noxious flower. No one can say for sure why it happens, and it is quite rare for a human-born creature to transform, but it has occurred in the past."

"And if there had been a change?" Evangeline asked.

"I would have been very pleased to have seen this happen," Godwin said, his fingers rolling the scalpel. Once upon a time he had been Angela's most prized student, the first in years to be granted his own laboratory, and the only one to be taken into her confidence. What she had not considered, and what he had not allowed her to see, was the extent of his ambition. "Unfortunately, neither of you showed signs of being anything but human. Your blood was red, for example, and you were born with a navel. But if you had changed, or shown signs of changing, and the angelologists had discovered this, you would have been handled in the usual fashion."

"Which is?"

"You would have been studied."

"You mean to say that we would have been killed."

"You did not know your mother well," Godwin said, lightly. "She was above all else a scientist. Angela would have applauded the rigorous empirical study of any one of the creatures. She allowed you to be tested. Indeed, she pushed to have you studied."

"And if I were one of them?" Evangeline asked. "Would she have sacrificed me?"

Godwin wanted to smile. He bit his lip instead, and concentrated upon the cold metal of the scalpel. "It makes no difference what she would have wanted. If there had been any sign of a genetic likeness to the Nephilim, and the society was alerted to this fact, you would have been removed from your mother's care."

Evangeline strained against the leather straps. "My mother would have resisted."

"That her father was a Grigori was completely unknown at the time. Her heritage was hidden—from herself, from other agents—out of necessity. Your grandmother Gabriella understood that if it were known that Angela was an angel, such a taint would have ruined them both. The threat was not in what she was, but what she could become. Or, rather," Godwin said, meeting Evangeline's eye, "the danger was in her genetic potential—in what her body could create."

"The threat was me."

"I wouldn't say that you pose much of a threat, Evangeline," Godwin said, placing the scalpel on Evangeline's neck and pressing it against her skin.

Godwin slid the sharp edge under Evangeline's white skin until a bulb of blue blood rose, collecting into a globe. He watched it rise and fall over her collarbone, pooling and expanding in the arc of her neck. He took a glass vial from the table. Holding it to the light, he felt a surge of triumph.

Verlaine's thoughts were in a state of chaos as he walked with Vera and Bruno alongside the palace embankment, the dark water of the canal sluicing by below, glistening as if coated with a layer of oil. Two grand buildings rose on each side of the stone pathway, ornate and Italianate, and, for a moment, Verlaine had the feeling he was walking through a historical film about the Renaissance, that noblemen in velvet cloaks would step from behind the shadows. The contrast between his physical surroundings and the images playing in his mind—of Angela and Percival and the syringe filled with the virus—left him disoriented.

Out of the corner of his eye he saw Vera gesture from one building to the other. "Old Hermitage and the Hermitage Theater."

Verlaine stepped ahead, replaying the film in his mind. Of all he had seen in the Hermitage, the image of Percival Grigori haunted him most. His golden wings, his long body glistening with the amber excretion, the ropes cinching his wrists and ankles—Percival had been a sublime creature, one that Verlaine didn't fear so much as admire. Of course Verlaine had seen such angels before. He'd interrogated many in much the same fashion as Angela had. But now something had shifted inside him. Now that he had seen Evangeline up close, touched her wings and taken in the chill of her body, it was impossible for Verlaine to think that the Nephilim were simply the enemy, nothing more than horrible parasites that had attached themselves to humanity, devils marked for extermination. He felt both strangely repulsed by the aims and methods of the society and desperate for them to help him find Evangeline.

He turned to Vera. She had caught up with him and was walking by his side, her hands shoved into the pockets of her jacket.

"There is absolutely no record of this structure, this Angelolopolis, anywhere," she said, as if they'd been discussing the subject all along. "Not a single angelologist has seen such a place, nor has an expeditionary team attempted to locate one."

"That is because nobody in his right mind would consider the possibility that the Nephilim would actually construct one," Bruno said, walking behind them.

Verlaine turned back to look at Bruno. "And yet," he said, annoyed by Bruno's dismissive manner, "Percival Grigori spoke of it as if it were already under way."

"The video was taken nearly three decades ago," Bruno replied. "If they'd constructed such a thing, we would know about it."

"Grigori could have been lying," Vera offered. "An Angelopolis is a utopia of angelic creatures, something everyone hears about at school but never wholly believes to be real. The Nephilim may have wanted to build it, but that doesn't mean that it was physically possible to do so. It's a concept more than anything, an idea that has existed for the angels since the great massacre of the Flood."

"Stories of a mythical angel paradise called an Angelopolis are like Peter Pan's Never Never Land," Bruno said.

"But the film points to the fact that the Nephilim—at least Percival Grigori—were working to build it," Verlaine said. "He mentioned Valkine. They had a sample of Evangeline's blood. It seems clear to me that whatever they wanted from Evangeline in 1984 is the same motive for why they want her now."

Vera stopped abruptly and turned to Verlaine. "Evangeline Cacciatore hasn't been seen since 1999."

Verlaine looked across the water of the Winter Canal, his gaze settling upon the wide stretch of embankment.

Bruno said, "Evangeline was abducted by an Emim angel last evening in Paris. Verlaine had the honor of speaking with her beforehand. The Cherub with Chariot Egg was in her possession—that is how it came to us."

"And that is why you came to me," Vera said.

"You're our best chance at understanding this," Verlaine said, struggling to control the sense of urgency he felt. "This can't all be a coincidence. The Nephilim went after Evangeline for a reason. Angela, the egg, the film, this fairy tale of an Angelopolis—this has to be more than a wild-goose chase."

"Sure," Bruno said. "But the function of the Angelopolis, the purpose for building it, its exact location—Percival Grigori didn't give anything away."

"True," Vera said. "We need to find out what was said after the recording stopped."

"They're all dead," Verlaine mumbled. "Vladimir, Angela, Luca—even Percival Grigori."

"Actually, not all of the participants of that interview are gone," Bruno said, walking off ahead, scanning the streets for a taxi.

A frigid wind blew off the canal, and Verlaine pulled his jacket close to his body. A cluster of Mara angels stood under the stone archway, the granite façade reflecting the illumination of their sallow skin. They rarely came out in daylight; their sunken eyes spoke of hundreds of years of living in the shadows. Their wings were mottled green and orange with streaks of blue, as iridescent as peacock feathers in the blue light of dawn. There was something disconcerting about seeing the creatures standing before the lovely archway of the bridge, a kind of dislocation that took a moment to adjust to. If it had been a normal morning, and they had been in Paris, Bruno would have insisted that they take the whole lot of them in.

After what seemed like an eternity, a beat-up station wagon rattled to the curb and stopped abruptly. Bruno gave the driver an address and they climbed in. As they pulled away, Verlaine noticed a sleek black car emerge behind them. It followed them, keeping an even pace with the taxi.

"You see that?" Vera asked.

Bruno nodded. "I'm keeping my eye on it."

Verlaine leaned against the door and watched the car, waiting for Vera to meet his eye. She smiled slightly and brushed her hand over his. Her gesture was ambiguous, and he was certain she meant it to be that way.

The taxi sped past the Theatre Arts Academy on Mokhovaya Street and, after crossing Pestel, let them off on a narrow avenue lined with trees. The windows of bars and cafés were lit up, while stores were still shuttered and locked, the glass protected by metal cages.

"Drop us here," Bruno said, directing the driver to leave them near a crowded bar. They got out and walked some blocks, Bruno looking over his shoulder the whole time before stopping at a shop with weathered stucco chipping from the façade. A sign above the door read LA VIEILLE RUSSIE.

Bruno lifted an iron knocker and let it fall against a metal plate. Verlaine heard the sound of footsteps from somewhere in the house. Suddenly a peephole opened at the center of the door and a large eye peered outside. The door swung back, and the woman from the film, Vladimir's wife, who had assisted Angela Valko, appeared before them. Nadia—smaller, grayer, and slightly bent—was dressed in a black velvet dress, a ruby brooch pinned at her cleavage. Verlaine looked at his watch—it was nearly seven in the morning.

"Isn't it a bit early to be going to the opera?" Bruno said, bowing slightly.

"Bruno," she said, pushing a swirling mass of gray hair over her shoulder.

Bruno bent to kiss her, his lips brushing each cheek. "You knew we were coming."

"Parisian angelologists aren't as conspicuous as they used to be," she said, waving them into a darkened corridor. "Nevertheless, I have friends in the Russian branch of the society who identified your presence at the research center and telephoned me. Come in, come in. You should be careful. I may not be the only one who knows you've arrived in St. Petersburg."

The interior of the house was distinctly French. They walked through a corridor and into a drawing room paneled in dark wood and red velvet, with Second Empire wallpaper, its panels clotted with flowers climbing the walls. A great chandelier hung from the ceiling, the crystals muted in the half light. Nadia led them through into a smaller chamber, the walls dripping with Russian Orthodox icons. The paintings were of every size and shape and hung so close together—the edge of one frame cutting into the next—that it appeared the walls were covered in a brilliant, gilded armor.

When Nadia noticed Verlaine examining the paintings she said, "My father loved Orthodox icons and opened up the back room of his antique shop in Paris to Russian painters when they needed support. In exchange for paint and brushes, he accepted their work. At the time, this was a more or less even exchange. Now, as you can imagine, they hold a certain historical, as well as a sentimental, value. These images are a record of an era that has disappeared. When I see them I recall what it was like to be in exile, the long lunches in the garden with my parents and their friends, the low murmur of Russian, with its elegant, yet biting, resonance. These icons form a museum of my youth."

As if remembering that she was not alone, Nadia turned and led them onward, taking them through a succession of narrow rooms filled with birdcages and marble busts. A cabinet of butterflies stood against a wall with hundreds of colorful specimens pinned to boards inside, a copper plaque naming the collection as belonging to Grand Duke Dmitri Romanov. When Verlaine drew closer to examine them, the rows of powdery wings cast a sinister sensation over him, a kind of illusion of perspective. Suddenly he realized that the specimens were actually feathers from the wings of angels. He saw the bright yellow wings of Avestan angels, those beautiful but toxic creatures whose wings dripped with poison; the iridescent green wings of Pharzuph, the dandies of the angel world, whose feathers blanched blue and purple in a certain light, like the scales of a fish in an aquarium; the lavender and orange wings of the Andras scavenger angels; the pearlescent white wings of the Phaskein enchantress angels, whose voices invoked daydreaming and listlessness; the flat green wings of the Mapa parasite angels, who occupied the souls of human beings, feeding off the warmth of the living. Verlaine himself had a Linnaean catalog of many of these varieties stored in his mind—only he'd never had the nerve to preserve them. The thought of killing and cataloging the creatures both fascinated and sickened him.

"The Grand Duke Dmitri Romanov was a very special man," Nadia said, noting Verlaine's interest. "With the help of a Russian chemist, he made a preservative that could envelop an angel's feather and fix it, a marvelous feat, something along the lines of being able to encapsulate the contours of a scent or of an illusion. Dmitri gave these feather samples to my parents, who knew him during his time in exile. Indeed, that was the same period that Dmitri assisted his lover, Coco Chanel, in the creation of her perfumes, most notably her famous No. 5. Some people say he gave her the idea to use a secret ingredient: the wing fibers of a Phaskein angel. Ms. Chanel had connections with many Nephilim, and so this is not startling information. More interesting is that she managed to keep her perfumes in production for so long, and that the secret ingredient is used still in limited-edition batches of the perfume. It is the favorite scent of Nephilim everywhere. It was no coincidence that Chanel was embroiled in intrigues during the Nazi occupation. She had connections with Nephilim that went back to the Russian Revolution."

Verlaine was at a loss for how to interpret this information. The imperial family's Nephilistic lineage was well-known—their downfall was celebrated by the society as a great victory—but he had never imagined how this might manifest among their descendants. *If Dmitri Romanov was a Nephil, what in the hell was he doing collecting feather specimens from fellow angelic creatures? What sorts of people were Nadia's parents that they had associated with him? How did his connection with Chanel, and the Nazis, play into his family history?* He wanted to press Nadia to tell him more, but a look from Bruno signaled that he should let it drop, and so he followed Nadia in silence to the far end of the room.

After unlocking a wooden door, she ushered them into a larger space. It took a moment for Verlaine to get his bearings, but soon he realized that they had just walked through the back door of the antique shop. An enormous brass cash register sat on a polished oak table, its gleaming keys reflected in a large plate-glass window that opened onto the street. The scent of tobacco hung heavily in the air, as if the residue of decades of cigarette smoke coated the walls.

Verlaine maneuvered through the room. It had been filled to capacity with curiosities: a barometer, a mannequin displaying a large muscovite headdress, and Baroque chairs upholstered in silk. One wall had been hung with mirrors in gilded frames. There were porcelain figurines, oil paintings of Russian soldiers, an engraving of Peter the Great, and a pair of golden epaulets. Verlaine noted the irony of a French-born Russian woman selling prerevolutionary Russian antiques to post-Soviet Russians in twenty-first-century St. Petersburg. Painted across the glass window in inverted letters were the words: LA VIEILLE RUSSIE, ANTIQUAIRE.

"Forgive the clutter," Nadia said. "After my parents died, I took over La Vieille Russie. Now the entire stock of the antique shop is stored here."

Another woman entered and stirred the dying embers in the fireplace, adding wood until a glow of warmth and light filled the room. Verlaine realized that the antique shop doubled as a guest apartment: There was a daybed and a cupboard with boxes of tea and jars of honey. Mismatched chairs, piano benches, stools, and trunks were scattered through the shop. Nadia gestured that they should sit.

Vera nudged his arm and nodded to a wall and whispered, "Look, it's another missing egg."

Verlaine turned his gaze to a framed oil painting behind Nadia. It was a portrait of a child, painted in creams and browns and golds. The thick application of paint gave the flesh a glossy texture. The child was five or six years old, dressed in a white smock trimmed with lace. Verlaine's gaze lingered a moment on the large blue eyes, the abundance of curly brown hair, the rosy hue of the little hands that—to his amazement—held a pale Fabergé egg.

"The girl in the portrait is me," Nadia said. "Painted in Paris by a friend of my father's. The egg was Alexandra's beloved Mauve Egg, given to her in 1897, in the happiest period of her marriage."

Verlaine looked from the old woman to the painting. Although there was a resemblance in the eyes, little else connected her to the image. The painted Nadia displayed a childish innocence that was reflected in the trinket cupped in her hands. Rendered with quick impressionistic brushstrokes, the details of the egg were difficult to make out. Verlaine could see the Mauve Egg with what appeared to be hazy portraits on the surface. Looking from the painting to Nadia, he found that he was helpless to gauge the significance of finding this, the third in a set of eight treasures that had been lost for nearly a century. He felt as desperate, and as childish, as Hansel following a path of shiny pebbles.

"You will eat something," Nadia said. "And then we will talk."

"I don't know if we have time for that," Verlaine said.

"I remember how hard Vladimir worked," she said quietly. "He would be out on a mission for days at a time without eating properly. He would return to me exhausted. Eat, and then you can tell me why you've come."

As if her words brought him back to his body, Verlaine felt a sharp shock of hunger, and he realized he hadn't so much as thought of food since before his encounter with Evangeline. *How strange it would feel,* he thought, *to be like Evangeline, a creature suspended above the physical needs of human beings.* Even hours after seeing her he felt a sharp need to be near her. He had to find her, and, once he did, to understand her. *Where was she now? Where had Eno brought her?* He saw Evangeline in his mind, her pale skin and dark hair, the way she had looked at him on the rooftop in Paris. The brittle exterior he had developed in his work cracked a little more with every thought of her. He needed to steel his resolve if he was to have any hope of finding her.

Nadia cleared a set of encyclopedias from a slate tabletop and, opening a trunk, removed a stack of porcelain bowls and a handful of silver spoons, which she wiped with a cloth as she laid the table. The woman who had lit the fire returned some minutes later with a tureen of kasha and then a platter of cured salmon. She poured water into a samovar by the tea cupboard, turned it on, and left the room.

The very smell of food made Verlaine ravenous. As they ate, refilling their soup bowls until the tureen was empty, he could feel his body become warm, his strength and energy returning. Nadia took a dusty bottle of Bordeaux from an armoire, opened it, and filled their glasses with wine the color of crushed blackberries. Verlaine took a sip, tasting the fruit and tannin prick his tongue.

He could sense Nadia was watching them, studying their gestures, assessing their body language. She was someone who understood the work of angelologists, who had seen the best of their kind in action. She was deciding if she could trust them.

Finally, she said, "I understand that you were with Vladimir during his last mission."

"Bruno and I were with him in New York," Verlaine answered.

"Can you tell me if he was buried?" Her voice was so quiet he had to strain to hear her. "I've been trying to get information from the academy, but they won't confirm anything."

"He was cremated," Bruno said. "His ashes are being held in New York."

Nadia bit her lip, thinking this over, and said, "I would like to ask a favor of you. Could you help me get them transported to Russia? I would like to have them with me."

Bruno nodded, and in the austerity of the gesture, Verlaine could almost taste the regret over what had happened to Nadia's husband.

She stood and left the room, returning with a pear tart, which she cut into slices and served on gilded dessert plates, releasing the scent of caramelized sugar and cloves. She dispensed the tea from the samovar, pouring it into teacups shaped like tulips.

"Nadia, there is a specific reason that we came to you," Bruno said.

"I gathered that there was something on your mind." She straightened in her chair as Bruno gave her the Cherub with Chariot Egg wrapped in cloth.

Nadia slid a pair of reading glasses onto her nose and, pulling the cloth away, examined the egg, her hands shaking. Her face became flushed; her eyes brightened. Verlaine could see that she was struggling to contain her reactions.

"Where did you get this?" she asked at last, her voice filled with excitement.

"It was found among Vladimir's effects by your daughter and, by various twists and turns over the past twenty-four hours, came into our possession," Verlaine explained, glancing at Bruno, to see how much information he could divulge.

"We believe that Angela Valko gave it to Vladimir," Bruno said.

"Perhaps with the intention that he would hold it for Evangeline," Verlaine added.

"They brought it to me, at the Hermitage, and I was able to help them identify it as one of the missing Fabergé eggs," Vera said.

"Now I understand why you are here," Nadia said, weighing the egg in the palm of her hand.

"You recognize it?"

"Of course. It was in my parents' possession for many years. It was the companion of the egg you see in the portrait."

"Then you understand its significance?" Verlaine asked.

"Perhaps," Nadia said quietly. Standing, she walked to a shelf filled with dusty books and removed a leather-bound album. "You should know, however, the egg alone is not significant. It is a mere vessel, a kind of time capsule, something that carries significance inside it, preserving it for the future."

She pressed the pages flat on a table, gently, so that they were clearly visible. The pages were filled with dried flowers, each blossom fixed by a square of clear wax paper. Some pages contained three or four of the same variety of flower, while others featured only a single petal. Nadia moved the pages under a lamp and the colors sharpened. The rows were neat and meticulous, as if the position of each item had been carefully considered before being assigned its place. There were examples of iris, lily of the valley, whole rosebuds closed tight as a fist, and a number of speckled orchid petals that curled like tongues. There were also flowers that Verlaine didn't recognize, despite the tags pasted below identifying them in Latin. Some petals were as delicate and transparent as the wings of a moth, their fanning tissues pale and dusted with powder. He was tempted to touch them, but they were so lovely and ephemeral, so delicate, that it seemed they would turn to dust at the slightest contact with his finger.

The flowers formed the original content of the album. On top of this, however, a second layer emerged, more modern, less picturesque, and more haphazard than the first. Notes had been written directly on the pages between the rows of pressed flowers, messy jottings that sprawled at odd angles in a slanted script. Mathematical equations were scrawled in the margins; chemical symbols and formulas written carelessly, as if the notebook had been kept at hand during sessions of laboratory experimentation. There was little order to the notes, or none that Verlaine could discern, and strings of numbers often bled over one sheet and onto the next in complete defiance of the edges.

Nadia flipped through the book until she found a loose yellowed page with sentences scrawled across it in French. "Read this," she said, giving the album to Verlaine.

And we explained to Noah all the medicines of their diseases, together with their seductions, how he might heal them with herbs of the earth. And Noah wrote down all things in a book as we instructed him concerning every kind of medicine. Thus the evil spirits were precluded from harming the sons of Noah.

They sat together, silent, considering these cryptic words. Verlaine could feel the direction of their minds turning toward a new path, as if the album were a clearing in a forest of brambles, one that allowed them to move forward.

Suddenly Nadia closed the book, causing dust to rise into the air. "I am the child of average people," she said, narrowing her eyes, as if challenging them to contradict her. "People whose lives became wrapped up in extraordinary events. Thus my life has been the vehicle for much larger forces, what Vladimir used to call the forces of history and what I call simple human stupidity. My role was but a small one, and my losses have meant little in the scheme of things. And yet I feel them profoundly. I have lost everything to the Nephilim. I hate them with the pure, well-considered hatred of a woman who has lost all that she loves."

Nadia finished her tea and set the cup on a table.

"Tell us," Bruno said, taking Nadia's hand. His gesture was filled with tenderness and patience.

"Perhaps my life would have taken an altogether different turn if it hadn't been for Angela, who made me her assistant. Without Angela Valko, I would not have met Vladimir, the man whose love changed my life, and I would never have learned how vital my parents' contribution had been to the cause of angelology."

The image of Dmitri Romanov's collection of wings appeared in Verlaine's mind. "They were involved with the Romanov family?" he asked.

"Before the revolution, my father and mother worked in the household of the last tsar of Russia, Nikolai II, and his wife, Tsarina Alexandra. My mother was one of the many governesses for the tsar's daughters—Olga, Tatiana, Maria, and Anastasia. She had come to Russia from France at eighteen years of age and met my father, a stableman who cared for the horses of the tsar's military regiment, the Yellow Cuirassier, soon after. My parents fell in love and married. They lived and worked in Tsarskoye Selo, where Nikolai and Alexandra took refuge from the more festive life of the royal court in St. Petersburg. The imperial family preferred to live a quiet, domestic existence, albeit one filled with luxuries that ordinary people could hardly imagine.

"My mother—who had been born and raised in Paris—taught the grand duchesses French. She once recounted her memory of assisting the girls with an introduction to the children of a high-ranking French diplomat. The meeting was unusual—the children of kings rarely met the children of diplomats—but whatever the reason for the introduction, my mother was summoned to the dining room and asked to stay near the grand duchesses, to assess their language skills and observe their manners. My mother remained with the duchesses, listening to them speak. She was impressed with the girls' social graces, but she was even more taken by the treasures displayed throughout the room. Of particular interest were the jeweled Easter eggs given each year to the tsarina by her husband. Positioned in primary locations, they glittered in the sunlight, each one unique but retaining a uniform opulence. She could not have known at the time that in a number of years Nikolai would abdicate and their life at Tsarskoye Selo would end. Not in her wildest dreams would my mother have believed that a number of these eggs would end up in her care."

Verlaine stole a look at Vera, wondering how all of this was striking her. It seemed that her dubious theories about Easter eggs and royal egg births could be supported by the tsarina's collection. But Vera's expression was as impassive as it had been upon his arrival at the Hermitage in the hours before dawn. Her feelings were stored away behind the cold pose of scholarly expertise.

Nadia didn't appear to notice their reactions at all. She continued, her gaze focused upon something in the distance. "The revolution of 1917 and the murder of the royal family in the village of Ekaterinburg on July 17, 1918, turned my parents' world upside down. In the brief window of time between the tsar's abdication in March 1917 and the revolution in October and November of 1917, the tsarina, knowing that they were in danger, endeavored to hide some of her more precious treasures. The jewels stayed with the family until the end—indeed, when the family was gunned down, the bullets lodged themselves between diamonds and pearls—but the larger treasures stayed behind. My parents were simple people, hardworking and loyal to the Romanovs, qualities much admired by Alexandra. And so the tsarina entrusted the location of the hidden treasures to my parents."

"But the palace at Tsarskoye Selo was pillaged," Vera said, cutting Nadia off. "The royal treasures were confiscated by the revolutionaries and brought to warehouses, where they were photographed, cataloged, and often disassembled before being sold outside of Russia in an attempt to raise capital."

"Unfortunately, you are correct," Nadia said. "My parents were helpless to protect the tsar's belongings, and so they took what they could carry and fled the country, traveling to Finland, where they remained in the service of a Russian in exile until the end of the First World War. Soon after they settled in Paris where, some years later, they opened an antique store called the Russia of Old."

"They carried all of this?" Verlaine asked, gesturing to the clutter around them.

"Certainly not," Nadia replied. "These objects have been acquired over a lifetime of collecting. But my parents did smuggle out a number of treasures. They risked much in doing so."

Verlaine held up the jeweled egg that had brought them to Nadia. "This egg financed your parents' life in France," he said.

"Yes," Nadia said. "The jeweled egg you hold in your hand and the rose-strawberry guilloche enameled Mauve Egg in the portrait— these are just two of the eight eggs my parents brought out of Russia in 1917. The other object was less flashy but no less valuable." Nadia gestured to the album and then took it between her gnarled hands. "My parents originally believed it to be a remembrance album. These kinds of albums were fairly common in the late nineteenth and early twentieth centuries. Young women would press flowers received on special occasions, especially flowers from suitors—corsages, Valentine's roses, and that sort of thing—as souvenirs. They were in fashion among girls of the upper classes as keepsakes. The four grand duchesses may have collected all of these flowers themselves. It is a curious book, and my parents never fully understood it. What they did understand was this: that the tsarina had prized it. Because of this, they held on to it, refusing to give it up. Over the course of their lifetimes, my parents acquired and sold many imperial treasures. It was how their business began and how their reputation was made. But my mother never sold the eggs, and she never sold the album. Before her death, she gave this book to me."

"Your parents may not have understood the significance of this book," Vera said, her voice hard, her eyes glistening with interest. "But surely you must have your own theories about the flowers."

There was a moment of hesitation, as if Nadia considered the danger of revealing what she knew.

"Nadia," Bruno said, his voice gentle, as if speaking to the child in the portrait rather than to the old woman. "It was Evangeline who gave the Cherub with Chariot Egg to Verlaine. It was Angela Valko's daughter who led us here."

"I guessed as much," Nadia said, an edge of defiance in her voice. "And that is the reason why I will help you unlock the egg's meaning."

E vangeline blinked, trying to identify the strange images coming at her, but she could see only faint gradations of light: the flickering of colors moving above; the flash of white at her side; the darkness beyond. She swallowed and a sharp pain tore into her neck, bringing her back to reality. She remembered the stab of the scalpel. She remembered Godwin and his expression of triumph as he filled a glass vial with her blood.

Scanning the ceiling, her gaze followed a swirl of moving color. A projection emanated from a machine—it looked to be a kind of microscope—at the far side of the room. Godwin stood under this kaleidoscope blur, his pale skin absorbing red then purple then blue. A line of text appeared at the bottom of the projection. Evangeline squinted to read it: *"2009 mtDNA: Evangeline Cacciatore, age 33, matrilineage of Angela Valko/Gabriella Lévi-Franche."*

Following her gaze, Godwin said, "Years ago, I examined samples of your mother's DNA. I also examined your mitochondrial DNA, although, strictly speaking, this wasn't exactly necessary: The female line is preserved completely in the mitochondrial DNA. You, your mother, your grandmother, your great-grandmother—all the women in your family have an identical mitochondrial genetic arrangement. It is quite beautiful, conceptually. Each woman holds within her the same sequences of DNA as her most ancient female relative; her body is a vessel carrying this code forward."

Evangeline wanted to respond but found it difficult to speak. The drug was wearing off—she could wiggle her fingers and feel the pain of the incision—but the residue made each word a challenge.

"Don't try so hard," Godwin said, moving closer, until he stood directly above her. "There is no point in speaking. Nothing you could say would interest me in the least. It is the one thing that I love about my work—the body expresses everything."

Evangeline pressed her lips together and, forcing her numb tongue to form words, said, "My mother let you take my blood—why?"

"Ah, you are curious about motives. For me the psychological component of my work with you—the reasons for extracting your blood, the feelings of your mother when she subjected you, her only child, to such exams—is uninteresting to me, to say the least. My work is a razor, cutting through the unnecessary padding of human existence. Feelings, emotional attachments, maternal love—this means nothing at all here in my lab. But, as you are interested in questions of 'why,' let me show you something that might fascinate you."

Godwin walked to his microscope and, after a clinking of glass plates—the changing of slides under a lens—a new image appeared on the ceiling.

"These are the very unsophisticated images I captured of your blood, and your mother's blood, thirty years ago. It is amazing that I could work with such images at all, they are so imprecise. Technology has changed everything, of course." Godwin walked to the table and stood by Evangeline's side. "You cannot see the details, but if you were to look closely, you would note the vast difference between your mother's blood and your own. Your mother was not an angelic creature. She was the child of Percival Grigori and a human woman. The angelic genes were, in her case, recessive, and she always gave the impression of being human. She looked like her father, but her appearance was just a shell for a wholly human organism. This can be seen in the genetic sequence." Godwin stepped sideways, so that he was under the second image. "Your blood, however, was instantly recognizable to me—and to your mother as well—as something quite different, something special. It is not at all like your mother's mixed blood. Nor is it like your grandmother Gabriella's human blood."

"But you said that my DNA was identical to theirs," Evangeline said, squinting to see the image.

"Your mitochondrial DNA is identical," Godwin said. "But it is not your mitochondrial DNA that interests me. No, it is the genetic inheritance you received from your father that made you what you are."

Evangeline closed her eyes, trying to understand what Godwin meant. She could see Luca walking at her side, filled with restless energy. He had done everything in his power to take her away from the Nephilim, to protect her, and for this she had always seen him as a man with extraordinary powers. But, in reality, her father was an ordinary human man, with ordinary human characteristics. Godwin must be mistaken. What she had inherited from Luca could not be measured in her blood.

From the moment Bruno saw her in the film—her quiet, thoughtful demeanor obscured by the brighter, more vivid personality of Angela Valko—he suspected that she had all the qualities of the perfect witness, one who watched and listened with great care, filing her experiences away. As Vladimir's wife, she was both inside and outside of the action, allowing her to bear witness from the sidelines. The trick would be to handle the situation the right way. Verlaine could hardly contain his impatience with the situation, while Vera remained aloof, pretending that Nadia was some minor player. Verlaine he understood, but Bruno didn't know if he could trust Vera yet, and so he monitored her reactions carefully. The best agents were often the most duplicitous.

Nadia pointed to the inside of the album cover. There was a copper plate with an inscription embossed at its center, the words twisting through the patina with swirling flourishes: *To* OUR FRIEND, *with love,* OTMA, *Tsarskoye Selo.*

"You see this?" Nadia said. "OTMA was the collective name for the four Romanov grand duchesses: Olga, Tatiana, Marie, and Anastasia, all of whom were brutally murdered with the tsar and tsarina in 1917. Apparently the girls used to sign cards and letters with this collective name, and when their brother, Alexei, was young, he referred to his pack of older sisters as OTMA." She paged through the album and pulled out a black-and-white photograph.

All four of the girls struck Bruno as remarkably beautiful, with their wide expressive eyes and white linen dresses, their pale complexions and curled hair. What a crime it was to have murdered such lovely creatures.

"Anyone who knows even the rudimentary facts about the Romanov family could tell you the meaning of OTMA," Nadia continued, running her finger over the copper plate. "But understanding the nickname Our Friend is a bit more complicated."

"Complicated by what?" Verlaine asked, his manner filled with impatience.

Bruno shot Verlaine a warning look—*Cool off and let the woman speak*—before turning back to Nadia. "Do you have any ideas about who Our Friend was?"

Nadia eyed them, cautious, and turned to Vera, who was studying the album with care. "It did not refer to just one person. The tsarina Alexandra used this moniker as a code name for her spiritual advisers. When writing to her husband, she never committed her guru's name to paper but tried to mask him in order to avoid scandal. Alexandra used the name Our Friend for the first time with a man called Monsieur Philippe, who came into their life in 1897. He was a French mystic and charlatan who entranced the empress— Alexandra was a woman prone to mystical spells and esoteric beliefs—and he became a kind of court priest."

"Like John Dee to Queen Elizabeth," Vera said.

Bruno held Vera's eye for a moment, impressed. John Dee was an obscure angelologist who had conducted some of the first angel summonings on record. He was starting to like Vera.

"John Dee was not a spiritual adviser so much as a court renaissance man," Nadia said. "But that said, the analogy is appropriate. It was only one of the many similarities between the Russian and British royal families. They were intricately linked."

"The tsarina was the granddaughter of Victoria and Albert of England," Vera said. "The tsar Nikolai himself was the cousin of King George V of England on his mother's side. And Nikolai's father was Alexander III, a Romanov."

"Exactly right," Nadia said. "All of these branches of the imperial family had been heavily infiltrated by the Nephilim, and all of the children of these families—save a select few who by genetic fluke had human characteristics, the Grand Duke Michael II for example— were Nephilistic by birth. Their reproduction was watched with great interest by all of Europe's angelologists, as the children of these families set the course of our work and, of course, history. The story of how Alexandra and Nikolai tried desperately to produce a son and heir to the throne is a common tale, one that can be found in any history book. They had daughter after daughter, each one beautiful and intelligent but considered a nonentity as far as the succession went: The Romanov daughters were unable to become regent.

"As royal governess to Alexandra's daughters, my mother was given a window into a more hidden dimension to her household. The empress was a formidable creature who dominated Nikolai from the very beginning of their marriage. While Nikolai was weak—he had small white wings that resembled the unimpressive plumage of a goose—Alexandra was a particularly pure breed, like her grandmother. Her mauve wings were strong and full, with a span of over ten feet; her eyes were deep-set and steely blue; her will was indomitable. Alix, as she was called by her husband, was extremely proud of her inheritance and her gifts. She spent hours and hours grooming her great pink wings. She would use her leisure time teaching her daughters to fly in the private garden of their country estate in the Crimea. All of this is to say that she was an extremely determined woman. Alexandra would stop at nothing to create an heir."

"And Our Friend was involved in all of this?" Bruno asked.

"In a word, yes," Nadia said. "But not in the manner you are imagining. Monsieur Philippe's primary attraction for the empress was the predictions about her future heir. He used prayer and a form of hypnosis to win her trust, and when she became pregnant, he told her that the child would be a boy. Alexandra announced her pregnancy and dismissed the court doctors. The whole of Russia waited. In the end, no child was delivered. It was kept quiet, but the servants and doctors gossiped that the tsarina had a phantom pregnancy: She had believed M. Philippe so strongly that her body produced all the symptoms of a normal gestation.

"But the biggest disappointment came years later. Another holy man, a seer and mystic like M. Philippe—with his knowledge of medicines and tinctures and potions—entered Alexandra's life. That man came to be their closest adviser, her primary doctor, priest, and confidant. He, too, was referred to in many letters as Our Friend. This man eventually became notorious as the peasant who ruined the great Romanov dynasty and changed the course of the twentieth century."

"Grigory Rasputin," Vera said, her eyes bright with recognition.

Nadia turned to the first page of the album, where two Cyrillic words were scribbled in ink.

"Can you read it?" Verlaine asked.

"Of course," Nadia said. "Your colleague is correct: It is the name Grigory Rasputin."

Bruno took the album and looked at it more closely. "This album belonged to Rasputin?"

Nadia smiled, and Bruno knew their pathways had converged for a reason. "Rasputin was one of the most intriguing and, in my opinion, misunderstood men in the history of Russia. Father Grigory was the center of what we would now call a cult—he created a circle of largely upper-class female devotees, who gave him money, sex, social standing, and political power in exchange for his spiritual guidance. Rasputin came to St. Petersburg in 1903 and by 1905 had total access to the Empress Alexandra and, through her, to Nikolai and the children. Rumors have it that he seduced the tsarina, that he played sexual games with the grand duchesses, that he spent lavish amounts of state money for his own pleasure, and that he was actually ruling

Russia during the crucial period of World War I, when the tsar left to command the military. All of these accusations were false, except for his influence on governmental policy. Alexandra believed Rasputin to have been sent by God. As such, she allowed him to choose state ministers from his friends. He duly filled the government with incompetents and sycophants, ensuring the Romanovs' downfall. For the Russian people, Rasputin's access to power was a mystery. They called him a magician, a hypnotist, a demon. He may have been all three, but the true reason for his power had little to do with magic or hypnotism. What the gossips of Moscow and Petersburg didn't know about Father Grigory was that he was the only man who could keep the heir, Alexei, from dying of hemophilia."

"The Romanovs found Rasputin to be an effective doctor?" Bruno asked.

"He wasn't a doctor by training," Nadia said. "There has been much speculation about what, exactly, he did specialize in. His power over Alexei certainly had much to do with a kind of medical treatment. Hemophilia was a deadly disorder at the beginning of the twentieth century. The disorder affected the blood vessels, which, when ruptured, could not heal, and thus the smallest bruise could lead to a hemophiliac's death. Alexandra was a genetic carrier of the 'bleeding disease,' as it was called, inheriting it from her grandmother Queen Victoria. Women were carriers, but it only became manifest in men. Victoria's sons and grandsons withered and died like cut flowers because of their inheritance. The tsarina felt horrible guilt over transmitting the disease to her son. She knew it to be a deadly disorder, requiring real medical care, and yet she trusted Rasputin, who was never trained as a doctor, to heal her son."

"Why?" Bruno asked.

"That is at the heart of this album," Nadia said. "He had methods that went beyond the perimeters of medicine. Of course, much of his power also stemmed from the force of his personality," Nadia conceded. "He was a mystic, a holy man, a cunning and manipulative social climber, but there was—at the center of it all—an incredible mastery of human nature. Nothing he did was by chance. Later, once he had made the friendship of the tsarina, and had learned that his power over her would be absolute if he could heal her son, things changed. He needed an effective medicine for hemophilia, and he desperately tried to find one. I believe he saved Alexei with his formulas."

Bruno glanced at the album. Nadia had opened it to a page filled with numbers.

"I have access to all of the records of the imperial treasures," Vera said. "And I've never seen anything about this album."

"It isn't exactly common knowledge," Naida said. "After the 1917 revolution, a committee was formed to make an official inquiry into Rasputin's life, his influence on the tsar, and his murder. They interviewed people who knew him and collected firsthand accounts from his followers, patrons, friends, and enemies. A file was created about Rasputin. This file went missing during the Communist era—most people believed that it was burned with so many other tsarist-era documents."

"I have colleagues who believe the burning of the imperial papers a crime against humanity, as egregious as Stalin's purges," Vera said.

Bruno shot Vera a look, wondering if she too believed the historical record more important than living, breathing human beings. It was this kind of thing that made Bruno feel allergic to academics.

"Perhaps your colleagues would be assuaged to learn, then, that the Rasputin file was spared," Nadia said, her voice terse. She was clearly unhappy at the idea of papers being more valuable than human lives. "I was working in the Soviet archives in the eighties when I discovered it, buried in a room full of moldering surveillance records. It was not long after Angela Valko's death. Vladimir had relocated to New York and I here to St. Petersburg—Leningrad at the time—where the tight restrictions on my existence felt like a salve to the wounds I had sustained during my work in Paris. So I took the file and, after copying everything, gave it to a friend, who smuggled it to France. It was put up for auction at Sotheby's in Paris in 1996 and was purchased by a Russian historian. The original file is now in the hands of this man, who has made its contents public, even going so far as to create an investigative television series on Rasputin's life."

"You didn't imagine that it could be important to our work?" Bruno asked, wondering how loyal Nadia was to the society.

"At that point I was finished with angelology," Nadia replied. "I wanted nothing to do with this dead Russian mystic. I was not alone, of course. After Stalin came to power you would be hard-pressed to find anyone in Moscow or Leningrad willing to talk about Rasputin and the tsar. But my reasons were far more personal than the sour aftertaste of history. It was Rasputin and his album that put Angela Valko in danger. The power of this man, and his reach beyond death, was too strong—even now I fear what could happen as a result of this album."

"You believe that Rasputin is to blame for Angela Valko's death?" Verlaine asked, incredulous.

"When my mother died, bequeathing the eggs and the album to me, I showed the pages of flowers to Vladimir, drawing his attention to Rasputin's name. He knew it was extraordinary, and so together we took it to Angela. She believed that the album was the most surprising link between ancient and modern methods of fighting the Nephilim to be discovered in the twentieth century. In my presence—indeed, using me to translate the contents of Rasputin's writings—she identified this volume as a kind of medical recipe book. She believed it to contain the most precious, most dangerous of chemical compounds—a formula from the ancient world. It could be a poison or, depending upon your point of view, a medicine."

"Was it Angela who added this?" Vera asked, squinting as she pulled out the passage about Noah tucked in the leaves of the book.

"Indeed," Nadia said. Taking it from Vera's fingers, she read: *"We instructed him concerning every kind of medicine. Thus the evil spirits were precluded from harming the sons of Noah."*

Bruno couldn't believe what he was hearing. *Could Angela Valko really have interpreted a book full of pressed flowers in this way?* The famous passage from Jubilees was considered to be one of the great textual conundrums surrounding Noah and the Flood. It posited that a medicine was capable of killing off the Nephilim, and that Noah created and used the medicine, but every first-year student of angelology knew that the Nephilim had survived the Flood. In fact, they continued to thrive in the postdiluvian world.

"Did Angela believe that Rasputin was trying to kill the Nephilim?"

"We all speculated about his motives. Vladimir believed he was from a Nephil family, and that this was why Alexandra trusted him. The name Grigory is a common one, often shortened to Grisha, a name popular among Russians. But there has been evidence that Rasputin's mother had a hint of Nephilistic blood, and that she gave her son the name Grigory in homage to the great Grigori family, known throughout Europe in the nineteenth century. Rasputin's physical strength, the hypnotic power of his blue eyes, as well as his reputed sexual domination of female devotees—these were all traits that would lead one to believe so, although this theory is difficult to prove, as his lineage is pure peasant stock. Even his surname had a vulgar connotation in Russian. It displeased the tsar so much that he officially changed Father Grigory's family name to Novy, or 'the new one.'"

"But even if Rasputin attempted to create such a quote-unquote medicine, he failed," Bruno said. "The Nephilim still live."

"You are right," Nadia said. "Whatever his intentions and

capabilities, he did not succeed. Nor did Angela. But you, with this album, might."

Vera stood and, taking the album in her hands, said, "In my first years with the society I tried working with my fellow Russian angelologists. It was simply impossible. They are a territorial bunch, wary of new ideas and dismissive of research that doesn't dovetail with their own. And so I turned to the only person I knew who could help me, an old family friend named Dr. Hristo Azov, an angelologist working on the Black Sea coast of Bulgaria. Soviets were allowed to travel to the Black Sea when I was a girl, and my family spent holidays there. Azov supported my early work. He is a brilliant man, and his research quite startling."

"Do you think Azov would be interested in looking into this?" Bruno asked, realizing even as he spoke that Vera was two steps ahead of him.

"Of course," Vera said. "Despite the distance, Azov has been a close contact for the past few years. He's advised me in every aspect of my research. I'm sure I could arrange to see him immediately." She looked at her watch. "It's nearly lunchtime. If I start now, I could probably be there tonight."

"You will report back the second you learn anything," Bruno said.

"Of course," Vera said, kissing each of them good-bye. She extricated herself from the situation so gracefully that Bruno had to admire her. If only he could get out of there with such skill.

Taking the album in hand, she looked to Nadia. "I'm sure that you don't want to let this out of your sight, but Azov can't help us unless he sees it."

"You will take it then," Nadia said, hesitant. "But you must be extremely careful. This album has been hidden for many years. If the Grigori know you have it, they will want it. And I believe you understand what they will do to get what they want."

Vera looked momentarily concerned and then, finding a plastic bag in the corner, she slipped the album inside and walked into the labyrinth of Nadia's home. Within seconds Bruno saw her through the dusty glass, hurrying along the street, her blond hair filled with midday sunlight.

The blow struck Verlaine before he'd fully stepped out into the street. The world seemed to waver and tip; he hit the cobblestones hard and rolled as the sharp wooden sole of a shoe sliced into his hand. A warm, wet substance dripped over his forehead and into his eye. He blinked, trying to clear his sight. He was blinded by blood.

In the seconds he lay on the cobblestones, he put together the facts of the ambush: The car they'd spotted at the Neva must have followed them. The creatures had waited outside the antique store, preparing to attack the moment he and Bruno stepped out of Nadia's door. It had been planned and executed perfectly.

Wiping his eyes with the sleeve of his jacket, he saw that there was not one but two Nephilim. As he moved his gaze from one to the other, he realized that they were identical in every aspect, from their lush blond curls to their Italian leather shoes. The twins seemed eerily familiar to him. He recognized their build, their features, even the way they dressed. And yet it was impossible that he'd seen them in Paris. Nephilim rarely did their own dirty work.

He jumped to his feet and kicked at the closest twin, aiming for the solar plexus. He felt his shoe connect, but it had no effect. His target—it must be a Grigori, he realized; there was no other family that looked quite like them—simply smiled, as if Verlaine were nothing more threatening than an insect. Bruno fought, taking on the second Nephil, but it pinned him to the ground. Verlaine patted his jacket, feeling for the egg. For the moment, it was safe.

Then, quick as a flicker of light in the corner of his eye, he saw Eno. She stepped from the shadows, her skin translucent in the early afternoon light. Her wings were hidden under a sable cape, but he knew that if she were to open them, they would span the width of the street.

Time seemed to stop as Eno walked coolly to Verlaine and kicked him in the stomach. He tried to stand, but she pushed him back to the ground and, feeling his pockets, took his gun, which she looked at with disdain and threw aside. She paused and felt his jacket a second time. Verlaine knew even before she removed it that she'd found the egg. He struggled to grab it from her fingers, but the other two creatures held him down. Bruno jumped up, gun in his hand, and fired at Eno, who turned on her heel and ran. The twins climbed back into a car and drove off, disappearing as quickly as they'd attacked.

"Come on," Bruno said, brushing himself off. "We'll follow them."

"We'll be more efficient if we split up," Verlaine said, spying Eno in the distance.

Bruno eyed him, wary. "Think you can handle her?"

"We'll soon find out." A moment of doubt came over Verlaine. Bruno had warned him that taking her on alone was suicide. Yet she was the kind of creature every angelologist dreamed of hunting. She would either be the biggest catch of his life, or she would kill him.

"Okay, move," Bruno said. "Stay on her. She'll know you're following, but it doesn't matter. The important thing is to put the pressure on. I'll go after the car. They're sure to meet up with Eno at some point."

Verlaine picked up his gun, tucked it into his pocket, and ran, knowing he had to catch her, corner her, stun her, and restrain her, skills Bruno had drilled into him year after year. Verlaine had done it time and time again, first on the Golobium, working his way up to the Gibborim, and then, finally, to the Nephilim. He had learned to match the pace of the creature, choose the precise moment to reveal his presence, and then, when he had maneuvered it into position, capture it. And yet he had never tasted the sweetness of a creature like Eno.

She turned onto Nevsky Prospect, a wide thoroughfare lined with boutiques and galleries, and ducked into a shop, its polished window filled with leather luggage, scarves, and handbags. Pausing outside the door, he wondered if he should go in after her or wait. Neither choice presented itself as a good option. She knew he was following her. If he went inside, she'd run. If he stood outside, she might find a way to escape through another exit. Verlaine leaned on the glass and squinted. Beautiful, well-dressed women filled the shop. Eno stood at a glass display filled with wallets and accessories. She dialed a number and brought her phone to her ear, all the while examining the pattern of a silk scarf—a white foulard with black flecks that matched, as she tied it around her neck, her white beret, and black cape. After a few minutes she turned off the phone, slid it into her bag, paid for the scarf, and walked back out onto the street. Verlaine hid and watched her walk away.

If Eno had detected Verlaine, she didn't alter her behavior in the least. She stepped off Nevsky Prospect, toward the Neva, her pace quickening. Verlaine increased his speed, his determination to catch her growing stronger each second. Her stiletto heels made her seem enormous among the human beings around her. He walked faster and faster, until finally he broke into a run, the cool wind blowing through his hair. It was not a question of whether he could catch her—he was determined to apprehend her no matter what it took. Rather it was a question of how far she would go to evade him. If he knew anything at all about the Emim, he knew that Eno would keep going.

Even as he followed her, something in him pulled back. He saw himself at a remove, as if he were outside of the scene, looking on his movements from high above the city: a man in a bloodstained yellow sport coat pushing his way along the crowded bridge over the river, dodging traffic as he crossed the street at the Hermitage.

Verlaine glanced at the great block of the Winter Palace rising before him once again. The buildings seemed even more massive in the afternoon sunlight than they had when he'd arrived before dawn. It seemed like a lifetime ago when he'd held out the egg, unaware that it was more than an ornate bauble.

When Eno turned down a tree-lined side street, Verlaine saw his opening. Although the labyrinthine ancient quarter behind the Winter Palace wasn't as sheltered as he would have liked—not a dark alley or an enclosed courtyard or a deserted tunnel in a subway station—it would have to do. He didn't have much time to make his move. If he was going to get her, it had to be now.

As if sensing his intention, Eno increased her pace. He matched her gait, gaining on her from behind, his entire body tingling with anticipation. After all of the years of tracking angels, he still found the hunt exhilarating and terrifying. Eno's effect upon him—the mixture of fear and disbelief that left him jittery and anxious—was similar to what he'd felt the first time he had chased a creature, years before. He moved closer and closer, until he was dangerously, recklessly near her, so close that he could smell her thick scent—a musky smell that marked her kind. He'd first heard the scent described as ambroisal—it is in some of the earliest recorded descriptions of the creatures—but to Verlaine it was a rotten odor, like a decaying animal, an odor that distinguished the lesser breeds from the more refined scent of the Nephilim. He felt the air chill between them and he grew tense, overwhelmed by the proximity. Her pale skin glowed; her features were sharp, aquiline. When she looked over her shoulder, he saw that her eyes were amber, more golden than anything in the natural world. The very traits that painters had used to represent angels from the Renaissance onward were imprinted upon her face:

She had wide symmetric eyes, a broad forehead, and high cheek-bones, the characteristics that had come to be the hallmark of an-gelic beauty. It was no mystery why angel hunters kept chasing her. Eno was ravishing.

As they rounded a corner, Eno stopped and faced Verlaine. Her golden eyes rested on his, challenging him to come closer. A delicate white membrane had fallen over her eyes, creating a milky sheath, like the eyes of a reptile. She blinked and the film retracted. For a terrifying moment he felt that she would kiss him. A shiver of elec-tricity passed through him, a kind of recognition that Verlaine didn't want to admit feeling, but the truth of it hit him squarely in the chest: Eno was one of the most frightening, most seductive creatures he'd ever seen.

He needed to hit her just hard enough to stun her, so he could get a cuff around her neck. He touched his back pocket, making sure the device was where he always kept it—it was so thin and flexible that it rolled up to the size of a coin—and then grabbed her by the arm, pulling her back hard and kicking her feet out from under her. She landed on the sidewalk, hitting the pavement, her bag falling at her side. Verlaine grabbed it, threw it from her reach, and dug his knee into her chest, pinning her to the concrete. He'd knocked the breath out of her—he could hear her gasp as she struggled to breathe. Verlaine held her wrists together with one hand and grabbed the collar from his back pocket with the other. But as he pressed the metal to her neck, she pushed him away with such ease, twisted from under him and jumped to her feet, a smile changing her icy features to the radiant beauty of a Botticelli. "You'll have to do better than that."

Verlaine lunged, landing a blow to her stomach. She countered by dragging her fingernails across his face, then swept his legs out from under him. In a blur of movement, he hit the sidewalk. He heard the sharp sound of Eno's boots tapping against the cobble-stones as she fled.

He jumped up and started after her. She was fast, but Verlaine kept pace with her until she opened her wings. They glistened, vibrating with energy. She lifted off the ground and flew through the streets, gaining speed with each passing second.

Verlaine looked around for something that might help him catch her. There was a rusty Zid motorcycle parked nearby, its wires hanging loose. The engine was vastly different from his Ducati, but in a matter of seconds, he'd hot-wired the bike, thrown his leg over the leather seat, and was speeding after Eno. He held tight to the bars as he swerved through streets and turned back onto the wide boulevard. He tried to get his bearings. He was driving west, toward the Neva. A minaret rose against the purple sky.

A dull, throbbing pain seeped through his skull. The cut had scabbed over and, when he turned his head, he felt it break open. Warm, fresh blood seeped across his skin.

Suddenly, Verlaine saw Bruno up ahead in the backseat of a taxi. He was follwing the twins, trailing their sedan, gaining momentum by the second. Verlaine could see that he was close enough to assist Bruno and, with the right balance of velocity and control, could cut the twins off. Glancing up, he saw Eno, her black wings stretched against the sky. She was guarding the twins from above. If Verlaine went after the taxi, it would draw her down so that he could fight her.

A rumbling caught Verlaine's attention. He turned and found a pack of black MV Agusta motorcycles behind him, moving in formation. Bruno leaned out of the the taxi's window, gave a quick wave of his hand, and the Agustas swarmed the twins' sedan, their motors buzzing as they swerved in and out of its path.

The sedan spun around, screeching to a halt, and Bruno's taxi followed. Verlaine pulled over and dropped the motorcycle.

"Nice timing," Bruno said, looking Verlaine over and giving a low whistle. Verlaine must have looked as bad as he felt. He'd be black and blue, no doubt, with his head stitched together like a football. As he stepped toward Bruno, he realized that the bump to his head was making him unsure on his feet.

The pack of Russian angelologists dismounted their motorcycles and flanked Bruno and Verlaine. He'd never met their colleagues in Russia, but he'd heard about them often, mostly in jokes about their use of heavy gear. They wore black gloves with steel knuckles embedded in the leather and black steel helmets with angel wings painted in silver on the sides. He counted nine Russian angel hunters, giving them a total of eleven angelologists. Under normal circumstances the numbers would have been more than sufficient. But it was clear after his encounter with Eno that this wasn't an average hunt, and Eno and the twins weren't average targets.

Just when Verlaine was beginning to feel confident that they could handle the situation, a new creature jumped from the twins' sedan. It was one of the Raiphim, an angelic order indigenous to Russia. From the lexicon of angels Verlaine owned, he knew that the Raiphim were phoenixlike monsters who rose again and again from the dead. They were known as "the dead ones" for their pale pink eyes and their ability to return to their bodies after death. He had never seen one up close. He found them ghoulish, their pallor that of bloodless flesh.

Verlaine blinked as the passenger side door opened and a second Raiphim emerged. One of the Russian hunters ran at the first creature, aimed, and kicked, trying for the chest. A second hunter stunned it from behind. The beast collapsed onto the pavement, gasping for breath, as a third angel hunter leaped onto the felled creature and slapped a collar around its neck.

"Easy does it," Bruno called. "They come back stronger and meaner if you kill them."

Verlaine saw, from the corner of his eye, that the Russians had cornered the second Raiphim. A hunter lunged forward and grabbed one of its stalky wings. The creature struggled and fell backward, its wings whipping through the air. In the frenzy, it sliced a gash across the exposed skin below the hunter's motorcycle helmet. He gasped and fell to the pavement, holding a gloved hand to the wound. The creature moved in, sensing weakness, and—just as he was about to come down on the wounded man—Verlaine stepped between them, trying to hold him off. The monster struck Verlaine and his mouth filled with fresh blood. He spit, trying to clear the taste. The creature was coming at him a second time when one of the Russian hunters slapped a collar around its neck. As if a switch had been flipped, the angel fell to the ground, its wings folding under it.

The twins stood at the center of the road, watching the fight with cool detachment. They were exact replicas of Percival Grigori—not the decrepit Percival Verlaine had known in New York City ten years before but the young and healthy Percival from Angela Valko's film. He studied them, perplexed, wondering who they were and how it had happened that there was no record of them anywhere. According to Bruno—and to the rest of the hunters who relied on profiling—if a creature didn't exist in their database, it didn't exist at all.

Whoever these Nephilim were, Eno was serving them. She stepped forward, protecting them, her wings outstretched. The twins allowed her to shield them, standing at a remove, watching the angel hunters with growing alarm.

"They're looking for something," Bruno said, scanning the crowd.

Verlaine glanced over the plaza, hoping to find a backup team of angelologists ready to fight. They were at the very heart of St. Petersburg, across from the Hermitage, a location that complicated matters. There would be police there any minute, and Verlaine couldn't be sure that they would be friendly. The sky began to glow pink with twilight in the background, smoky and dim. Lights around the square were coming on, throwing a pale, eerie glow over the Winter Palace, its stone creamy as white chocolate.

Bruno was right: Eno was looking for something. Wiping blood from his eyes, Verlaine tried to anticipate what she would do next. If she were waiting for other Emim, it would be next to impossible to fight them. If they hoped to find Evangeline, they would need to take Eno down carefully, without killing her. They approached in tandem, one man on each side, Verlaine centering his attention on Eno.

"If you manage to get the egg," Bruno whispered, "get on the motorcycle and get the hell out of here. Don't stay to help and don't look back."

Motioning for the hunters to follow him, Verlaine closed in. When Eno didn't back away, Verlaine made a grab for the egg, hazarding a guess that it was in a pocket of her cape, and hit the jackpot. He scooped it up, feeling its cold weight in his hand, and made his way toward his motorcycle. As he threw his leg over the bike, he felt a cold shadow fall over him, an icy sensation that penetrated his clothes and chilled him to the bone. Suddenly, quick as a viper striking its prey, Eno pulled him to the ground. He pulled his gun from his belt, aiming it at her chest and—although she was moving and he couldn't be certain of his shot—pulling the trigger. A burst of electricity knocked the gun from his hands, eliminating all hope for a second shot, but he could tell from the strength of the surge that he wouldn't need one.

He had stunned her. She clasped her arms over her chest, moaning in pain. A female angel hunter—Verlaine guessed her to be one of their elite by the skillful way she reacted—threw him a collar. Verlaine opened it and went for Eno's neck. He had been trained to act quickly, to disarm while the creature was stunned, to lock the collar in one strong gesture. Once it was in place, the angel would sink into a state of drowsy submission, allowing the angelologist to take it into custody with ease. Verlaine followed this procedure perfectly. Yet, as he moved to secure the collar, Eno struck back. He fell, knocking the wind from his lungs. The collar slid from his hands, skittering across the pavement. Verlaine couldn't breathe. He was paralyzed.

In a violent strike, Eno pinned Verlaine to the ground, pressing the stiletto of her boot into the curve of his neck, as if to puncture his throat. She knelt over him, placing her hands over his chest, her wrists meeting above his heart. A shock of electricity moved through him, and a low, grating sound filled Verlaine's hearing. It wasn't a sound he recognized, and it was impossible to tell if the noise was something generated in his own mind—the mental clatter of terror ringing in his ears—or if Eno was causing this bizarre music to move through him. Although he had studied the Nephilim's use of vibration to stun human victims—it was one of their many tactics to derange the senses before a kill—Verlaine had never heard of an Emim angel having the power to do so.

Verlaine struggled, pushing against her, feeling her wings take hold of him as she pressed her hands harder onto his chest. He could feel a sharp, vibrating pulse pounding over the beating of his heart. He had seen the victims of angelic electroattacks. Their bodies were charred to black cinders. A wave of fear and panic struck him. Eno was going to kill him.

Heat slithered over his skin, as if he had fallen into a pit of boiling oil. He might have screamed—he heard his voice in his ears, but had no sensation of using it. Somewhere in the distance there were footfalls, gunshots, the echo of Bruno's voice. A brilliance subsumed him, and in a burst of heat, the strength of which overwhelmed his body and mind, Verlaine lost consciousness.

The Fourth Circle

GREED

Burgas, Black Sea Coast, Bulgaria

Vera watched the sky as the plane descended. The flight from St. Petersburg to Burgas had been four hours of relentless turbulence, the Cessna twisting in sharp currents of air. Nevertheless, she had fallen asleep the moment the plane took off. The dips and jags of the plane blended into the liquidity of her dreams. She couldn't remember what she dreamed but felt a weightlessness at the back of her mind, distant yet vivid.

The airport was a small, regional outpost with a single jet parked on the tarmac. She took in the concrete building, the swaths of muddy lots around the airfield, the barbed wire spiraling at the top of the chain-link fence. She had never been to Azov's Black Sea outpost before and had seized this opportunity to see for herself what the great expeditions to Bulgaria—the first taken in the twelfth century and the second during the Second World War—might have been like. She found that the airport looked tired, run-down, as if it were recovering from a long, abusive winter. The sky, however, was filled with a lingering spring light. Vera slid on her sunglasses and followed the other passengers.

She was greeted at the end of the runway by a pair of security guards and ushered through a mesh gate, where a black Mercedes jeep waited, ostentatious and anonymous at once. She hadn't been asked for her passport: Her presence in Bulgaria would not be registered. Officially, she had never entered the country.

A woman with black hair and deeply tanned skin greeted her from the driver's seat. She introduced herself as Sveti and told her that Bruno had called hours before about Vera's arrival and her requirements while in Bulgaria. She said, "If you're hungry, help yourself."

Vera opened a wicker basket filled with cucumber and tomato sandwiches, an egg and feta cheese pastry Sveti called *banitza*, stuffed grape leaves, bottles of Kamenitza beer and Gorna Banya mineral water. She couldn't imagine eating much after her morning with Nadia but nonetheless spread a cloth napkin on her lap and took a sandwich.

"We are currently outside of Burgas," Sveti said, pulling away from the airport, the tires kicking gravel as she turned onto a paved road. "About twenty-five minutes from Sozopol. Once we arrive I will take you to the Angelological Society of Bulgaria Dive Center, where we will meet with Dr. Azov. Our outpost has been here for years, but somehow we've managed to stay off the radar. He's been doing work nobody could dream existed. And yet the rest of the world has never come calling before. You are the first foreign angelologist in ages to visit us."

Vera stared out the window as they drove through the city of Burgas, gas stations and a McDonald's marking the way. They passed dour concrete apartment buildings, a Lukoil station, and any number of makeshift fruit-and-vegetable stands. Traffic was sparse, and Sveti took full advantage of the open road, driving faster and faster. As they made their way south, the two-lane highway swung out to the water's edge, skirting the jagged coastline. They passed a shipping yard filled with industrial barges and clusters of houses that seemed ready to tip into the water. The Black Sea glinted in the sunlight, an enormous pool of green-blue, still and calm as a sheet of glass. The peculiarity of the color, Sveti informed her, was due to a certain variety of algae that bloomed in the spring. Normally the water was a steely gray, a shade more in keeping with its dark name.

"We're nearly there," Sveti said, turning off the highway and onto a winding road that overlooked the water. A village rose before them, perched high on a promontory.

"Sozopol was once called Apollonia," Sveti said. "The Greeks traded from the port, and it became an important outpost on the Black Sea. Obviously much has changed since then: the Romans came, and then the Ottomans, and then the Russians. I've been visiting this place since I was as a child, when Sozopol was a small fishing village where families vacationed every summer." Sveti slowed on the winding road. "Then the village itself was contained on an arm of land that reaches into the Black Sea. Since that time there has been massive development. Hotels and clubs have sprung up on every vacant piece of land. A modern section of the town has taken over the opposite side of the bay. It used to be a kind of paradise. Now, well, now it is like everything else: all about business. At least it is still quiet in the spring."

They drove along a harbor, past sailboats and fishing vessels, reams of net hanging from the sides. Sveti stopped the jeep, cut the engine, and jumped out, gesturing for Vera to follow. She stretched, feeling the sunlight on her skin. Suddenly the cold drafts of the wind from the Neva seemed a world away.

Vera glanced up at the village. It rose behind the harbor, displaying a warren of narrow streets. She studied a house poised upon the hill. The construction appeared to be ancient—the first floors were built entirely of stone, windowless, as if to resist the onslaught of water, with a wooden second floor that overhung the stone base. There was a small terrace laden with strings of drying peppers, bundles of herbs, and wet laundry. An old woman stared down at them, a pipe hanging from her lips, her hands crossed over her chest, incurious as to what was happening below.

Within minutes of their arrival a motorboat arrived at the water's edge. Vera and Sveti climbed aboard, took seats, and held tight to a metal railing on the boat's edge. The driver turned the wheel and the boat angled away from Sozopol as they headed into the calm waters of the Black Sea.

"The research center is on St. Ivan Island," Sveti said, pointing to a landmass in the middle of the bay, where a lighthouse sat at the highest point.

"The island was inhabited by Thracians between the fourth and seventh centuries B.C., but the lighthouse—or an early version of it—wasn't constructed until the Romans arrived in the first century B.C. The island was considered holy, and has always been revered as a place of mystical discovery. The Romans would have found temples and monastic chambers built by the Thracians. To their credit, they preserved the nature of the island: A temple of Apollo was built and St. Ivan has remained a place of contemplation, ritual, worship, and secrets." Sveti said, "We'll dock in a few minutes, which leaves me just enough time to give you an update. As I understand it, you are well acquainted with Dr. Azov, but perhaps it is best if we start from the beginning."

"No need," Vera said. "I know that Azov has occupied the center on St. Ivan Island for over three decades—since before I was born. His outpost was created in the early eighties, when a body of research pointed to the presence of well-preserved artifacts under the Black Sea. Before this, angelologists stationed in Bulgaria worked near the Devil's Throat in the Rhodope mountain chain, where they monitored the buildup of Nephilim and, of course, acted as a barrier should the Watchers escape. But as information came to light about the significance of the Black Sea—of Noah and the sons of Noah, in particular—Azov petitioned for an outpost here as well."

"Clearly you've followed his work," Sveti said. "Yet I wonder if you or your colleagues are aware that we are, at this very moment, working on the most exciting recovery project of the decade."

"I assume that almost anything with Dr. Azov behind it would be of that nature," she said.

Sveti smiled, as if pleased to have found a fellow Azov admirer. "I don't have to tell you, then, that Azov is doing something that no one in the history of our field has done before. This center was founded so that we could conduct on-site exploration of artifacts pertaining to Noah and the Flood."

Vera looked past Sveti to the island. She could make out the details of the lighthouse, its smooth stone spiraling around and around until it reached a series of windows at the top. Looking back toward the shore, she saw the village rising in the distance, as if emerging from the sea.

"So this is where the Nephilim got their second start," Vera said.

"Over the years there have been many conjectures about what might lie underneath our waters—the lost civilization of Atlantis being one of them—but the most interesting theory, popular since the fourth century, is that Noah's Ark landed on Mount Ararat, on what used to be the coast of Turkey."

"But that's a thousand miles away from here," Vera said.

"True," Sveti said. "And it's no longer even close to the edge of the Black Sea. Scholars have always believed the actual recovery of objects from the ark to be impossible for this reason. A little over a decade ago, however, academics at Columbia University, William Ryan and Walter Pitman, published a book that changed the nature of investigations about the Flood. They believed that the myth of the Flood—which can be found in nearly every major mythological system, from the Greek to the Irish—had originated from a cataclysmic event that occurred roughly seventy-six hundred years ago. They posited that, as glaciers melted, water from the Mediterranean breached the sill of the Bosporus, and a deluge of water gushed over the land, wiping out ancient civilizations and creating what is now the Black Sea."

Vera remembered when the book was published. Azov had mailed her articles about the controversy. "Serious scholars of the region agreed that the Bosporus had been breached, but they thought the scale that Ryan and Pitman proposed was completely off the mark. If I recall correctly," she added, "their theories were attacked as unsubstantiated."

"They were at the time. But then Robert Ballard, the American oceanographer and nautical explorer who'd made his name by discovering the *Titanic*, began to explore the Black Sea with submarines and advanced equipment. Even skeptics had to wonder if they weren't onto something. What the world at large did not know was that Ballard was actually working under the advisement of Dr. Azov. And, as it turns out," Sveti said, handing Vera a finely wrought topographical map, "there is something much, much better than the ark below the Black Sea."

"So the Ryan-Pitman theory of the Flood is correct," Vera said. "The land under the Black Sea was once inhabited."

"Exactly," Sveti replied. "Only, after years of research, we now believe that the Flood did not occur in one grand cataclysmic deluge, as the mythology from the Bible to Gilgamesh describe. Rather the water rose in small increments over a vast span of time. The Bosporus broke bit by bit and the waters flowed into the basin over a period of decades, subsuming the villages as it rose."

"Forty days and forty nights were more like forty years," Vera said.

"Or even longer," Sveti said. "In our explorations we've discovered that the first wave of flooding caused a massive migration from here to here." Sveti moved her finger along the map in Vera's hand. "You can see the present-day shoreline of the Black Sea drawn in a solid red line. The dotted line you see about two inches inside—and then the next dotted line you see two inches from that, and the third three inches from that—these are ancient shorelines." Sveti pointed to the innermost dotted line, then the middle one. "The second wave of the Flood caused another migration—and the construction of new villages—and so the pattern continued over the course of many decades. Many of the oldest villages on the Black Sea coast, such as Sozopol and Nessebar to the north, were built generations after the settlement of the present shoreline. The villages under the sea are, obviously, ancient. Thousands of years older than anything we can find above water."

"I see the scholarly significance of this discovery," Vera said. "But what does it have to do with Noah and his sons?"

Sveti smiled, as if she had been waiting for that precise question. "It has everything to do with them." She took the map from Vera and folded it. "As you will soon see."

As the boat veered toward land, Vera climbed to the prow, feeling the wind rushing against her body as she tried to get a better view. The island was covered in long wild grasses that shivered in the breeze. Seagulls swooped and circled, as if scouring the scrub for mice. From such a close proximity, the lighthouse seemed to tilt away from the land, a trick of perspective that allowed her to see a man standing at a small red door, gazing out at the boat as it approached. The driver cut the engine, and the boat slowed and slid alongside a long wooden dock.

She climbed out of the boat and followed Sveti over the dock and up the uneven terrain. The lighthouse loomed ahead, its stone surface ragged with age, rubbed and eaten through by saltwater and wind. A great iron casement sat at the top of the tower, protecting the enormous spotlight from the seagulls. A helicopter was perched on a paved circle, its bulbous plastic windshield awash in sunlight. The man Vera had noticed earlier was gone, but the red door had been left ajar.

"Come," Sveti said. "Follow me. Azov will be waiting inside." She turned and led her up the winding, rough-hewn steps of the light-house, following the spiral to the very top.

Vera could hear voices behind a door. Sveti pushed the door open, the bottom scraping against the stone floor, and they walked into a bright, circular observation room, which had windows that gave a panorama of sea. The afternoon sunlight was brilliant and warm, glinting off the emerald water. A scattering of fishing vessels floated in the distance. The lighthouse was removed from the real world, peaceful, and she tried to imagine what it would be like to wake up every morning in that room, to rise and look over the sea as the sun rose.

Azov sat at the head of a table piled high with mollusk shells, slabs of wood, and a glass jar filled with odd-shaped beads. He was in his midfifties, with gray-flecked black hair and a matching beard. He watched Vera with affection as she stepped into the room. Standing, he switched off a radio, and gestured for Vera to sit.

"I have to admit," Azov said, smiling at Vera, "that I was surprised to get the call that you were coming on official business. We've been all but ignored by your colleagues. The society in Berlin has extended some support, but other than that, nothing."

"Scholars in Russia are always interested in making progress against the Nephilim," Vera said, struggling between the loyalty she felt toward her employers at the Hermitage and the deep respect she had for her mentor. "We are working toward the same end."

"A prudent answer, my dear," Azov said, clearly proud of Vera's diplomacy. "Come, give me a kiss. I'm thrilled that you have finally come to visit me here, where I am most in my element."

Vera stood and went to Azov. As she kissed his cheek she felt anxious to seem every bit the accomplished angelologist she had become. She turned to the artifacts piled on the table. "These must be your finds from the bottom of the Black Sea."

"Correct," Azov said, picking up a piece of pounded copper. "These objects are from a settlement that was begun within the first four hundred years of the postdiluvian period, during Noah's lifetime."

"That seems like quite a few lifetimes," Vera said.

"Noah lived to be nine hundred and fifty years old," Sveti said. "By the end of this period, he would have been middle-aged."

"We located the village a little over twenty years ago," Azov continued, "and have been doing underwater excavation since then. It hasn't been easy, as we don't typically have the kind of equipment and resources that high-profile exploratory divers have, but we've managed to pull up a number of intriguing objects to support our most recent hypothesis."

"Which is?" Vera asked.

"That Noah was not only charged with protecting the various species of animals, as is believed in biblical lore, but that he was protecting the plant life of the planet as well. His collection of seeds was extensive. When the rain stopped, he cultivated and preserved these plants for future generations, making certain that the precious cellular energy of ancient times was carried forward," Azov said.

Vera toyed with the latch on her satchel, wondering if she should wait to give Azov Rasputin's album. She was keenly aware that the plants pressed inside represented a similar kind of energy, and that Azov would find them fascinating.

Sveti stood, went to a cabinet, unlocked it, and removed a fat spiral notebook, the pages wrinkled, as if they'd been drenched in water and dried in the sun. "There are multiple tales of what happened to Noah after the water levels descended," she said. "By some accounts he planted grapes and produced wine. By other accounts he became the most significant farmer in history, planting all the seeds himself. Others believe he distributed the seeds to his sons, and that they took them to different continents, where they planted and cared for them."

"The regeneration of the world's flora and fauna would have taken thousands of years," Vera said. "I thought it was just a myth that he did it alone."

"Of course," Azov said. "But within myth there is often a seed of reality."

Azov stood and, taking Vera's hand, led her to a giant glass case against the wall. The case was empty save for pieces of driftwood of various sizes resting upon the shelves.

Azov pointed to the pieces of wood. "These are tablets that we believe belonged to Noah. They were discovered by Ballard's team on an underwater ridge off the coast of the Black Sea, on what was once the shoreline of an ancient freshwater lake that existed before the Bosporus broke. The settlement there was later subsumed by a second level of flooding, perhaps as large as the first flood, and was destroyed. We posit that Noah left the settlement too quickly to take the tablets. He may have lost them during the second flood, or he may have left them on purpose; there is no way to be certain. He traveled to the border of what is now Turkey and Bulgaria, and here he planted the seeds and raised the animals that he had carried in the ark. It was here, on our coastline, that the new world began."

"Or was dispersed," Vera added.

"Exactly," Azov said. "Noah's sons—Shem, Japheth, and Ham—migrated to different regions of the world, founding the tribes of Asia, Europe, and Africa, as we all know from our beginning tutorials in angelology. We also know that Japheth was killed by the Nephilim, and his place on the boat was taken by one of their own, thus ensuring that the creatures continued to exist after the Flood."

"What was not known," Sveti cut in, "is that Noah kept records of everything—the Deluge, his journey on the ark, records of his sons' wives and children, even records of the propagation of the animals he herded. He had seen one world pass away and another begin. He had been chosen by God to live while the rest of the world perished. It only makes sense that he would write about what he had experienced." She opened the notebook she'd pulled from the cabinet. "My work before I began this project was in ancient languages, and so it has fallen to me to assist Azov in his attempt to understand the contents of Noah's tablets. This page," she said, indicating a script that Vera found inexplicably familiar, "is a copy of the words found on that tablet there." She pointed to a fragment of wood lying in the case. "It is a record of the seeds Noah carried onto the ark."

"These are Noah's memoirs?" Vera asked.

Azov slipped on a pair of plastic gloves before reaching into the case and removing the tablet. "This piece of wood," he said, "is one of over five hundred tablets we recovered from a village submerged 350 meters below the surface of the Black Sea. They were bundled together and stored in a casket. Carbon dating shows that it is nearly five thousand years old."

"I'm sorry, but it is really difficult to believe," Vera said, slipping on the pair of gloves Sveti offered before taking the wood from Azov. "Any organic material would disintegrate rapidly under water."

"On the contrary," Azov said. "The composition of the Black Sea created ideal conditions for preservation. It is essentially a dead sea. Although it was once a freshwater lake, saltwater from the Mediterranean spilled into it, creating an anoxic climate. The organisms that might eat wood or other degradable materials are absent. Artifacts that would have disappeared within a millennium are still intact, as if frozen in time. It is an archaeologist's dream."

Vera ran her gloved fingertips over the crevices. The tablet was light, made of a hard durable wood, with strange symbols stamped into it. Glancing at Sveti's notebook, she realized that the symbols had an uncanny resemblance to the scribbling in Rasputin's album. It took all of her restraint to refrain from confirming the match immediately. "So you are saying that you believe these tablets are not simply from that period of Noah's life, but that they were written by Noah himself?" Vera asked.

Azov said, "These tablets were discovered among the items in the settlement, and we're certain that the settlement was Noah's home after the Flood."

"What is your proof?" Vera asked.

"Carbon dating, the location of the settlement, identifiable personal belongings. And, most important, the tablets themselves."

Vera turned the slab of wood over. It looked like something out of an Egyptian tomb. "If this is as old as you claim, it is simply incredible that it exists at all," she said. Carved into the grain were more symbols, many of them partially washed away. "What is this alphabet?" she asked, trying to mask the growing excitement in her voice.

"It is a language called Enochian," Sveti said. "It was given to Enoch by God, and Enoch used it to write the original story of the Watchers and the Nephilim. It is a common belief that a pre-Deluge lexicon—a universal language that contained the original power of Creation—existed. Some believe it was the language God used to create the universe, and that it was the language used by angels and Adam and Eve. If Noah was the last human being to carry antediluvian traditions to the new world, it makes perfect sense that he would have been versed in the language of Enoch."

"Noah was a direct descendant of Enoch," Azov added. "Which could explain how it was transmitted."

Sveti continued. "Enochian script was revealed to an angelologist named John Dee in 1582, and was called *Sigillum Dei Aemeth*. His assistant, Edward Kelly, transcribed the script at the instruction of an angel, and went on to fill many volumes with it. It was considered by most angelologists to be a revealed language—authentic, but impossible to trace historically. Enochian script seemed, in the sixteenth century, to literally come out of nowhere. Of course, there are those who believe John Dee simply made it all up. Linguists have analyzed the language and concluded that there is nothing particularly remarkable about it. But if these tablets are authentic, they would not only verify Dee's script as the language used by Enoch's descendants, they would also support Dee's claim that the language was not composed but revealed by God. The magnitude of such a discovery would be enormous."

Sveti paused, as if detecting objection in Vera's face, but in truth Vera was fascinated by what she had just heard. She had studied John Dee's historical role in angelology extensively—from his angel conversations to his extensive classical and biblical library—and knew that he was the only known human after Mary who survived the act of summoning an archangel. But, like everyone else, Vera had always believed Dee's Enochian script to be a hoax.

Sveti continued. "This list of the seeds Noah carried on his ark is most likely a fragment of a larger catalog. The entire record must have been enormous, ranging in the hundreds of thousands."

Vera thought of the pages of flowers in the album, thousands of petals pressed behind paper. "Why the interest in Noah's plants in particular?" she asked. "Have you connected the seeds in this list with flora in existence today?"

Azov looked circumspect, as if weighing whether he should disclose a long-held secret. "As you know, Vera, I have devoted my life to the mysteries of Noah and his sons. At the heart of this is an obsession I am reluctant to admit to—my own El Dorado, if you will." He glanced at Sveti, as if looking for support, and continued. "I have been trying to replicate the medicine of Noah, the one cited in the apocryphal Book of Jubilees."

She had expected Azov to offer some insight into the vagaries of antediluvian geography; she had hoped that he might give her some understanding of the flowers in Rasputin's album. Never had she imagined how momentous this visit would be for her career, for angelology itself, possibly for all of humanity. "Thus the evil spirits were precluded from harming the sons of Noah," Vera said, reaching into her bag for Rasputin's album.

"It is the most cryptic—and therefore the most ridiculed—text in the ancient canon," Azov replied. "Of course, the project has been a challenge from the beginning—there is no description of the formula in Jubilees, and only a few references are made to the medicine in ancient literature, but I believe in it."

"Perhaps," Vera said, pulling out the album full of flowers, "you are not alone."

Azov studied the pages of the album, pausing to puzzle over the equations written in the margins, his expression changing from confusion to wonder. He narrowed his gaze. "Where did you find this?"

"It was given to me by a retired angelologist named Nadia Ivanova," Vera said. She could see his excitement growing as she explained the jeweled egg that had led them to the 8mm film featuring Angela Valko, which in turn brought them to Nadia and Rasputin's album of flowers.

Azov shook his head in disbelief. "I was beginning to think I was a lunatic for spending the last thirty years working on this, and then something happens and I see a glimmer of reason to what I'm doing, and I know I'm on the right track. You know that Nadia's husband, Vladimir, was a friend of mine."

"He was in Angela Valko's film," Vera said. "I had no idea you two knew each other."

Azov smiled. "Angelologists behind the Iron Curtain relied on very old friendships, some made before the revolution. My network is made up of the children and grandchildren of tsarist agents. Vladimir was a good friend. He was able to transmit messages to me even before the fall of the Berlin Wall, through a network of old contacts. But what strikes me most powerfully about what you've just told me is this: I briefly worked in the service of Angela Valko. I know her research well. Indeed, I contributed in some ways to her findings."

Vera was silent, her surprise upon hearing this information overwhelming.

Azov continued. "Unfortunately, the Soviet Union didn't allow me to travel, and so I never met her in person. But we were in continual contact for a couple of years in the early eighties. She was extremely particular about what she wanted, and I found the instructions strange, to say the least. When she was murdered in 1984, I feared my contributions to her work were to blame. Her father, Raphael, assured me that everyone in the society was grappling with the same guilt. The reach of her influence and collaboration was that vast."

"You knew Raphael Valko as well?" Vera asked.

"I know him still," Azov said.

How Azov's society connections had eluded her all these years was something that Vera wanted to understand. She'd always thought of him as a genius in exile, and yet he seemed to be at the very center of everything that mattered in angelology. "It is most likely that, when she contacted you, Angela Valko was working to decode the contents of this album."

Azov opened the album and turned through the pages, his eyes falling over the flowers. "I knew that she was creating a chemical compound," he said. "She didn't disclose the nature of the compound, only that it required ancient ingredients. I was so young then, and my work in the field had just begun. Looking back, I suppose my willingness to participate in her rather unusual experiments made me useful to her."

"Now that you have the full story of why she contacted you," Vera said, "what do you think?"

Azov removed the folded piece of paper upon which Angela Valko had scrawled the famous passage from Jubilees. "This passage has been dismissed so often in the past that it was difficult for Angela to believe its importance. I'm the one who made her take it seriously. Jubilees is one of the books of the Bible that the founding fathers considered to be in the canon of angelological studies. The Book of Jubilees—like the Book of Enoch—was not included in the Bible, although scrolls were circulated among theologians and it had influence upon the texts that eventually became the Bible. The discovery in Qumran of the Dead Sea Scrolls revealed that Jubilees was read and revered just after the time of Christ. It is essentially a list of holidays and religious commemorations, but there is one very important element to the text that has great significance to my work, and one passage in particular that relates to the battle between humans and Nephilim."

Sveti recited it as if on cue: *"And Noah wrote down all things in a book as we instructed him concerning every kind of medicine. Thus the evil spirits were precluded from harming the sons of Noah."*

"It refers to the Book of Medicines," Azov said. "At least, that is a modern name for it, one invented by angelologists. But it is an accurate description for the writings mentioned in Jubilees. They contained Noah's observations and his reflections about the destruction of human civilization during the Flood. As you have seen, Noah wrote of his mission to preserve the earth's fauna and flora. He recorded the technical details of protecting and mating the animals, the process of planting and harvesting the seeds. Sveti and I have also found allusions to a medicine, or elixir, that disarms the Nephilim. That is why the Jubilees passage is something we take very seriously."

"Disarms?" Vera asked. "How exactly does one disarm them?"

"It's my supposition that the medicines mentioned in Jubilees would produce the effect of human vulnerability in Nephilim. They would lose their angelic powers. They would be prone to human illness and human mortality. And they would die as human beings die."

"That sounds more like a poison than a medicine to me," Vera said.

"The formula given to Noah was of divine origin," Sveti said. "The logic involved is not one we would recognize."

"And you've made this text the basis of a lifetime of research?" Vera said, unable to mask her incredulity.

"It's true," Azov said, smiling slightly, "that the information in Jubilees is obscure at best. The Book of Medicines is—for all intents and purposes—an angelological Holy Grail."

"There have been many angelologists who abandoned important work for this," Sveti said. "If one's motives are not kept in check, pursuing the writings of Noah—the Book of Medicines mentioned in Jubilees—can result in pure madness. In this respect, chasing after Noah's formula can be as dangerous as our enemy. This is why the pursuit is officially discouraged at the academy."

"So the truth was deliberately hidden to keep scholars away from Jubilees?" Vera asked.

"In a word, yes," Azov replied. "The academy once sent scholars to the great libraries in search of Noah's writings. They offered rewards for information. This alone guaranteed a deluge of quite convincing fakes. Raphael Valko once told me he saw dozens of them passing through the academy in his days as a student. There's a long tradition of this cycle. In the Middle Ages there was an abundance of copies and, eventually, fakes coming out of convents and monasteries. So the council halted the practice of pursuing it, and Jubilees was ignored for centuries. Then, in the sixteenth century, the occultist John Dee claimed he had a copy. He'd always believed that Enochian would be the medium for the Book of Medicines, and he conveniently claimed to have had the language dictated to him by angels. Whether he actually discovered the Book of Medicines or forged it is open to debate. Consensus has tended to rest on the latter, though the debate is moot because no copies from Dee's library— fake or otherwise—have turned up."

"The search was revived in the late nineteenth century after the

Book of Enoch was rediscovered," Sveti added. "Scholars believed that if Enoch could be rehabilitated, there was a chance that we could re-create the Book of Medicines—whether by revisiting Jubilees or by excavating a copy of the work itself."

"There is one thing all who see the Book of Jubilees can agree upon," Azov said. "That the passage Angela Valko slipped into the album is one of the most tantalizing in all of our ancient sources on the Nephilim. Whereas human beings were susceptible to sickness and disease, and human beings died before their one hundredth year, the Nephilim were not prone to sickness. Human women died in childbirth while the Nephilim reproduced without pain and lived to be five hundred years old. The advantages of angels over humans were legion. The Book of Medicines was meant to level the playing field."

"And now I have brought you the volume that Angela Valko considered to be the real McCoy," Vera said. "Tell me, am I correct in deducing that the symbols written on these pages by Rasputin are of the same alphabet as the script on Noah's tablets?"

"You are correct," Sveti said, smiling. "How an uneducated, drunken charlatan like Rasputin came to discover Enochian is a mystery I can't even begin to solve. But I believe it is worth considering this volume to be a possible iteration of Noah's Book of Medicines."

"You believe it's authentic, then?" Vera asked, feeling her ambition grow by the second.

"Come with me," Azov said, gesturing for Vera to follow him. "We'll answer that question together."

They made their way down the lighthouse, following the twisting stairway of the tower. At the bottom of the stairwell, they took a rocky path down the slope of the island, descending between two hills. On the left sat the crumbling stone structure, perhaps of the Roman temple Sveti had mentioned earlier. Vera looked over a crest of rock to the dock and saw that the motorboat was gone. She glanced across the bay, taking in a vista of the dusky blue water, searching for the boat. It wasn't anywhere to be found. She would be at the mercy of her hosts if she wanted to leave the island.

Sveti led them into the single-story remnant of what had once been a much larger building. The space was low ceilinged, with slits in the wall that allowed shafts of weak light to fall into the room. An impressive number of air tanks, diving suits, lamps, and fins were stacked up along one wall. A mattress lay on the floor, a wool blanket folded neatly over it, with a hot plate and a miniature refrigerator nearby, attesting to Azov's presence in the room both day and night. The crumbling walls had shed a fine dust over the floor, leaving them slippery. The entire structure had the appearance of a ruin, the light fixtures crude, as if the building had been wired for only the most basic functionality.

"Our large diving center is farther south," Azov said, gesturing to the air tanks. "This equipment is for personal use. When I want to go down myself, I take the boat and my diving gear and spend time with the lost world. I can't visit the ancient settlement often— we need to be dropped by boat about thirty-two hundred feet off the coast of Faki. But simply going below the surface of the water is unimaginably relaxing." Azov sighed. "Not that I have much time for such things. Come, I'll show you my collection."

He led them through a narrow hallway and into a cold, windowless room. Sveti lit a match and brought it to a series of taper candles whose brass holders rose from a rectangular wooden table, the surface of which displayed various tools and glass vials. Soon the room glowed with a warm light. Along the wall, rising from floor to ceiling, stood an elaborate metal case with thousands of tiny drawers.

"My filing system," Azov said.

"For what?" Vera asked, wondering what would fit into such small spaces.

"For our collection of seeds," Azov replied. "We have recovered close to two thousand varieties." He went to the cabinet, opened a drawer, and removed a cloth sack, which he tipped gently onto the table. The contents were as small and white as pearls. "These are an ancient variety of vegetable. And these," he said, taking another small sack from a drawer, "are peonies, but unlike any peony seen in the modern world. I grew one fifteen years ago—the flower was as big as my head, pale purple with streaks of yellow on the petals, utterly beautiful."

"Surely these seeds would have been completely destroyed if they were among the objects of the settlement," Vera said. "Even anoxic water would damage them. You could not have found these in proximity to the tablets."

Azov said, "The seeds were not recovered from the settlement. We found them inland, stored in a dry, cold space under the ground, a place that may have been built by Noah as a storage center for them but was later used as a Thracian burial mound. We found a map of the storage rooms among the tablets. After the water rose and Noah was forced to leave the first settlement, he traveled into what is now northern Greece but was once Thrace. By that time his sons had begun their migrations, founding the new civilizations of the world, and Noah was a tired old man nearing his thousandth year. Noah's journey inland, meanwhile, had consecrated the land he'd moved through as sacred—priests, monks, and holy men walked that path for centuries after his death to pray and purify themselves. This island was used as the starting place of such pilgrimages. The bodies of saints have been transported and laid to rest on the island. In fact, Saint John the Baptist's body was entombed here. His headless body lies in the sanctuary of the monastery."

"But keeping the seeds safe has been our primary purpose," Sveti said. She gestured toward the filing system. "Azov can pursue his study without threat of intrusion, and he has his work cut out for him: Many of these seeds remain unidentified."

"Have you grown all of them?" Vera asked, trying to mask her almost childlike desire to see such an exotic garden.

"Some of them, yes; others, no," Azov said, "The seeds are limited. I watch over their storage; I make sure they are not exposed to light or water; I keep potential thieves away—and that is all. There are many of us appointed as guardians of one kind or another. Our work is relegated to simply standing at the gate, keeping the Nephilim—and others who wish to do harm—away. I couldn't bear the idea of inadvertently killing the seeds, or, worse, losing them to the enemy due to incompetence. Recovering and protecting them is one thing; growing them is another."

"You've clearly succeeded in creating a working system to classify them," Vera said. But is it really possible that the seeds could be viable after more than five thousand years?"

"In geological numbers, it isn't such a long time," Azov said. "It has been a mere seven thousand years since the Black Sea flooded. Any basic history of botany will show that prehistoric plant life flourished hundreds of millions of years before this, and these seeds were remarkably durable. The atmosphere we breathe developed because of the oxygen released by massive groupings of leaves. Many species of dinosaurs existed solely by eating plants, and so we must conclude that the majority of the planet was covered in vegetation. The cache of seeds we've recovered is surely only a tiny fraction of the actual pre-Deluge flora, most of which died. It is miraculous that these seeds remain, but when you think of the amount of plants that went extinct, you will see that these seeds are the exception. The seeds that remained viable were the strongest seeds, the most resistant to the elements."

Vera followed Azov and Sveti into another cramped room. Azov's laboratory was a mixture of modern equipment and an old-fashioned angelological research center—an antiquated computer sat among plants on a glass-topped desk, emitting a soft glow over a set of bronze scales. There was a statue of Mercury and a series of glass containers, a velvet divan stacked with papers, and a bookshelf stretched across an entire wall. Vera could see, at first glance, herbal encyclopedias; books of chemistry; French, German, Greek, Latin, and Arabic dictionaries; the collected works of Dioscorides. The hunch she'd had upon first walking into the room was confirmed: This was the home of a workaholic of the first order.

As if reminded of the task at hand, Azov said, "Vera, the album. Sveti, did you bring the seed list?"

Vera gave the album to Sveti, watching her reaction carefully, as if something in her expression might tell her the meaning of the Enochian symbols etched onto the page.

"You understand it?" Vera asked.

"I do, for the most part," Sveti said. "Written around these flower specimens are ingredients and proportions varying in number and volume." She stopped at something Vera had missed earlier, a mostly blank page with what appeared to be a heart drawn at its center.

Intrigued, Vera asked, "What is this symbol?"

Azov took a pen from his desk and drew a similar heart on a piece of paper. "This shape was derived from the shell of the silphium seed, which was tapered at one end and cleft at the other. It eventually became known as a symbol of love, a heart, one of our most powerful modern symbols. Indeed, the heart's association with romantic love could be said to have stemmed from the use of silphium as an aphrodisiac in ancient Cyrene." Azov glanced at the album, as if to verify the symbol, and continued. "When I was in contact with Angela Valko, there was one plant in particular she was looking for, but she was never able to name it. I wonder if this heart symbol was the element she was trying to decipher."

"Surely she would have known that the heart symbol's origin lies in silphium," Sveti said.

"Angela was a skeptic," Azov answered. "Silphium is one of the most intriguing plants of the ancient world. Many modern botanists refuse to verify it, claiming that there is no proof that it even existed."

"I get the feeling that you don't agree," Vera said.

"The plant has been extinct for over one thousand years, but you are right, Vera. I have no doubt that silphium existed. Whether it was the cure-all it was purported to be in ancient Mediterranean cultures, I cannot say. Indigestion, asthma, cancer—silphium was allegedly used to treat all of these maladies. Perhaps most important, the plant was believed to both aid in contraception and, as I mentioned, act as an aphrodisiac. It was considered so precious that it formed an important part of trading between Cyrene, now Libya, and other coastal countries, so much so that glyphs and coins were created bearing its image."

Sveti examined the album page once more. "It is intriguing in this context, because silphium appears to be the single nonfloral ingredient in the formula, and the only one that is extinct." She flipped through the pages of rose petals. "For example, there are over one hundred varieties of roses in the book. Clearly the formula would have required a distillation of rose oil."

"But rose oil is so common," Vera said. "Roses can be found everywhere."

Azov said, "Now, yes. But after the Flood there would have been only a few seeds keeping the plant from complete extinction. Humanity has—over the millennia—cultivated and revived the rose. If we hadn't, we would be living in a world without roses. The same can be said for all of the flowers listed in Noah's catalog of seeds. It is through the human preference for flowers that many of these remain with us. It is a wonder that silphium, which was once so important, nearly died out."

"Nearly?" Vera said. "I thought it was extinct?"

Azov smiled. "It is extinct," he said. "Except for one or two remaining seeds."

Vera stared at Azov, taking in the meaning of what he had said. If they had this plant, it would be possible to create the formula—whatever it was. "Is the silphium among your seed collection?"

"It's here," Azov said. He opened a tiny drawer and removed a metal box. He unfastened the catch and lifted a silk pouch. It was ominously airy, as if nothing at all were stored inside. He upended the pouch and a single seed—yellowish brown with specks of green—rolled onto the table. "There is only one left in my care," Azov said. "The other seed was given to Dr. Raphael Valko in 1985."

"Do you think he knew about this album, and about this formula in particular?" Sveti asked.

"It's hard to say," Azov muttered, as he paged through the book. "The scope of Angela's work was no secret to him, and he certainly knew that she and I were in close contact before her death. But Raphael never mentioned her when I delivered the seed to him."

"I fail to see what Raphael Valko has to do with any of this," Vera said. "Though I have to confess, I am dying to meet him. Especially if he has some connection to this elixir."

"The real question is: Can we mix this potion?" Sveti asked.

"And if such a potion will do anything at all to the Nephilim," Azov said, returning his gaze to the album. "If we take the flower petals from behind the wax paper and grind them together in the correct proportions, and in the order designated in Rasputin's equations, we would have the base for a chemical reaction. That leaves silphium, which we might be able to grow, although in minute quantities."

"More difficult is the last ingredient," Sveti said, pointing to a page in the album. "This calls for a metal that was not even verified to exist during Rasputin's lifetime."

"I know what it is that you're going to say," Vera said. "It is a metal that was used in great quantities before the Flood but had virtually disappeared after the death of Noah. It was given various names by Enoch, Noah, and others in the ancient world who had contact with it. It was rediscovered and classified by Raphael Valko, who renamed it Valkine." Vera thought this over for a moment and said, "There hasn't been a piece of Valkine available for more than sixty years."

"If you exclude the Valkine lyre that was recovered in New York in 1999, then you're right. The last person to have even a tiny amount was Raphael Valko himself. He came across significant quantities of the substance at the beginning of the twentieth century, when he took possession of one of the celestial instruments, a beautiful lyre that was believed to have been the very instrument Orpheus played. Before he found the lyre there were speculations about the substance that made up the instruments. Some angelologists believed they were made of gold, others of copper. No one knew for certain. And so Valko took a file and scraped shavings from the base of the lyre, ana- lyzed the metal, and came to understand that it was an entirely unique material, one that had never been studied or classified. He named it Valkine. While the lyre itself was packed up and sent to America for safekeeping during the war, the shavings were his. He kept them for some years, and then, the story goes, he melted them down and made three lyre pendants."

"Dr. Raphael Valko fashioned the pendants. He must have more of the metal, even if it is just a trace amount," Vera said.

Azov stood and slid on a brown leather jacket. "There's only one way to find out for sure," he said, putting his hand on Vera's shoul- der and leading her from the room.

The Fifth Circle

FURY

Verlaine's ears rang with a steady, grating buzz. He opened his eyes and saw an indistinct space, foggy and insubstantial, its gray walls bleeding into a gray ceiling, giving him the impression that he'd awoken in a cave. His whole body was consumed in heat, so much so that even the crisp cotton sheets under his shoulders burned his skin. He couldn't figure out where he was, how he had ended up on such a hard mattress, why his whole body throbbed with pain. Then it all came back: St. Petersburg, the black-winged angel, the electricity moving through his body.

The outline of a woman appeared at his side, a shadowy presence that seemed both comforting and menacing at once. He blinked, trying to make out her features. For a second he was in his recurring dream with Evangeline. He felt the icy coolness of her kiss, the electric attraction as he touched her, the strength of her wings as they wrapped around his body. He was disoriented by her presence, confused about whether he had seen her at all, afraid that—when he awoke completely—she would be lost to him again. But his eyes were open and she was at his side. The beautiful creature he had been longing for had come back to him.

Verlaine blinked again, trying to focus on his surroundings. "You might want these," a voice said, and Verlaine felt the metal of his wire-rimmed glasses against his skin. Instantly the world contracted into focus, and he caught sight of the Russian angel hunter he'd seen just before he lost consciousness. Without her helmet she looked softer than he remembered—less the professional killing machine and more a regular person. The woman had long blond hair and an expression of concern on her face. Bruno stood nearby, looking almost as bad as Verlaine felt. His hair was matted and his cheek had been scraped raw. Seeing Bruno's injuries brought Verlaine back to his own. Every breath hurt. He remembered the chase through St. Petersburg, he remembered Eno and the wretched Nephilim twins. He swallowed hard, the pain going down with it. He wanted to say something but couldn't find his voice.

"Welcome back," Bruno said, moving close to squeeze Verlaine's shoulder.

While Verlaine had discerned that he was in some kind of medical facility, he had no idea if he was in Russia or France. "Where am I?"

"Somewhere between Moscow and Yaroslavl, I'd guess," Bruno said, checking his watch.

Bruno's face was encrusted with dried blood, his clothes streaked with dirt. Verlaine gave Bruno a questioning look, trying to understand what was happening.

"We're on our way to Siberia," Bruno said. "By train."

"What happened to you?" Verlaine asked, trying to pull himself up in bed and feeling a spike of pain.

"Run-in with the Russian Raiphim," Bruno said.

"Sounds like a good name for your memoirs," the blond woman said.

"This is Yana," Bruno said. "She's a Russian hunter who has, coincidentally, been tracking Eno for nearly as long as I have. She has also agreed to relinquish one of her transport cars for your recovery."

Yana wore tight jeans and a tatty pink turtleneck sweater—a markedly different aesthetic from the leather and steel of her hunting uniform. There was a wary, tired air about her as she stepped away from the bed. She leaned against the wall and crossed her arms, as if she were anxious to get back to work. Her English was heavily accented as she said, "Feeling okay?"

"Fantastic." Verlaine's head felt like it might explode. "Just perfect."

"Frankly, you're lucky to feel anything at all," Yana said, looking him over with an air of professional interest, as if comparing his injuries with those she'd seen in the past.

Verlaine tried to sit up and the pain localized to a sharp, searing burn on his chest. "What the hell happened?"

"You don't remember?" Bruno asked.

"Up to a certain point, I remember everything," Verlaine said. "I must have lost consciousness."

"You must have lost your mind to go after Eno like that," Yana said. "Another minute and you would have been completely scorched."

Verlaine remembered the sensation of electricity moving through him and shivered. "She tried to kill me," he said.

"And she very nearly succeeded," Bruno said.

"Lucky for you we were able to stop her before that happened," Yana added. "You were burned, but it's localized."

"Are you sure about that?" Verlaine felt as if his entire body had been slow roasted over a bonfire.

"If you recall the bodies at St. Rose Convent, I think you'll count yourself as one of the lucky," Bruno said.

The attack on St. Rose had left a deep impression in Verlaine's imagination. Dozens of women had been charred to death, their bodies so badly disfigured that they were unrecognizable. He knew exactly what the creatures were capable of doing to a person.

"The electrical current threw your heart into a seizure for a good three minutes," Bruno said. "Yana performed CPR. She was able to keep you alive until her colleagues brought her a portable defibrillator."

"You came back from the dead," Yana said. "Literally."

"I guess I have one thing in common with the Raiphim," Verlaine said.

"Although that doesn't explain why you survived the attack," Yana said. "Forgive the expression, but you should have been burned to a crisp."

"Lovely image," Verlaine said, pulling himself up in bed. The skin over his chest prickled with pain, but he tried to ignore it and go forward, one small movement at a time. He remembered Eno's strength, the heat of her touch.

"This might have had something to do with it," Bruno said, pulling a necklace from his pocket and holding it above Verlaine.

He took the pendant and looked it over. It hadn't been altered by Eno's attack in the least. The metal still shone as if alloyed with sunlight. He knew that Bruno was connecting the dots and probably already understood how Verlaine had come to have the pendant. Gabriella had been Bruno's close friend, and although his mentor wasn't about to talk about the pendant in front of Yana, it was clear that Bruno was not happy that Verlaine had hid it from him all these years.

Verlaine leaned up to fasten the necklace around his neck, and winced. Yana—more out of impatience than anything resembling compassion—lifted it from his fingers and secured the clasp. "There," she said, giving him a pat on the chest and sending a fresh jolt of pain through his body. "You're safe from the bogeyman."

The door opened and a doctor arrived, a short, hefty woman with thick glasses and perfectly styled hair. She leaned over the bed, yanked the sheets down to Verlaine's waist. A thick, white, gauze bandage had been taped over his chest. She worked her fingernails under the edges, lifting the tape and pulling it gently away.

"Here," Yana said, taking a small mirror from her bag and giving it to Verlaine.

He looked in the mirror and saw the reflection of a battered man, a line of fresh stitches over his eye, a series of bruises staining his skin. The image was so unfamiliar, so startling, that Verlaine straightened his spine and threw back his shoulders. His burned skin chafed, and he wanted nothing more than to fall back asleep, but he refused to be the person in the reflection. He held the mirror level with his chest and saw that it was blackened, with raw patches of red and pink oozing a clear liquid. An impression of Eno's hands was branded into his skin.

"You now carry the telltale mark of an Emim's attack," Bruno said.

Yana examined the outline of the fingers seared upon Verlaine's chest. "The shape of the burn is very particular. It is something I have long been interested in. A creature must position its hands a certain way to draw down the electric charge—the thumbs touching and the palms angled outward. Do you recognize the shape?"

"Of course," Verlaine said, feeling sickened by the sight. "They're wings."

He was used to injuries—he'd been hurt innumerable times over the course of the past ten years—but an assault like this wasn't one he would forget. The creature had marked him forever.

The doctor stepped away and returned with a tray stacked with ointment, scissors, bandages, and cotton swabs. Verlaine breathed hard, bringing the air into his lungs slowly as the doctor used cotton to clean his chest.

"The nerves are dead where the flesh is black. The pain you feel is from the less severe burns around the edges of the wound." The doctor paused, studying the shape of the burn. "I haven't seen one of these in a while," she said, brushing an ointment over his skin and pressing on a new bandage. "This application will help enormously with the pain. In the old days it would have taken weeks, perhaps months, to fully recover from this."

Verlaine felt a coolness suffuse his skin. The effect was immediate and intense. "Amazing," he said. "The pain is fading."

"Your skin is rapidly healing itself," the doctor said, leaning close to Verlaine. "The ointment is a nanoemulsion that stops bacteria from setting in while creating the conditions for rapid skin cell production. A layer of new skin forms immediately over the burn, helping to keep out air and reduce pain. It's a rare commodity: We have only a few doses. It was developed by angelologists for angelologists. It is unbelievably effective." She ran her hand over the surface of the wound, as if to prove her point.

"Effective or not, we need this angelologist," Yana said, unable to conceal her impatience. "How long does he need to rest?"

The doctor held Verlaine's wrist and took his pulse. "Your heartbeat is normal," she said. "How do you feel?"

Verlaine wiggled his toes and then moved his ankles. The ringing in his ears and the searing pain across his chest were gone. "Tiptop," he said.

As she took the tray and headed for the door, she said, "Then he should be able to leave the train at your scheduled stop. Tyumen is about thirty-five hours from here. I would suggest taking it easy until then." Glancing at Verlaine, she said, "That means: no more dates with the devil. Although I doubt you'll take that advice. Agents like you never do."

Verlaine threw his legs over the side of the bed. He steadied himself and stood. He was with Yana on this: There was no way he was going to stay in some godforsaken hospital cot.

After the doctor left the room, Bruno said, "There's some good news in all of this. We managed get the egg back. And, most important, to capture Eno."

"Where is she?" Verlaine asked.

"In a safe place," Yana said, her gaze boring into him as if daring him to ask more.

Bruno winked at Verlaine and said, "Yana insisted that we take her to a specialized prison in Siberia."

Verlaine said, "Leave it to the Russians to have an angel gulag."

"We are taking her for observation," Yana said. "You're lucky I agreed to allow you to accompany me."

"And you think that you're capable of getting information out of Eno?" Verlaine asked.

"There's no other way," Yana said. "Once Eno is taken into custody in Siberia, she'll be forced to talk."

"Have you witnessed such questioning before?" Verlaine asked Yana.

"The specialists at the prison have very particular methods of extracting information from their prisoners," Yana replied, her voice quiet.

Verlaine moved through a mental list of what had happened in the past twenty-four hours, trying to shake the feeling that he'd landed in an alternate universe, a kind of strange, lifelike game that was both real and unreal at the same time. He was on a train moving through the vast and frozen Siberian tundra in pursuit of a half-human, half-angel creature that he now knew—after ten years of doubt—he loved. After all that he'd seen he had thought he couldn't be surprised anymore. He'd been wrong. Things just kept getting stranger and stranger.

A zov's chopper embodied just the sort of mixture of cultural references that inspired scholars like Vera to go to work every day. According to Sveti, the Vietnam-era machine had been lost by the Americans—abandoned by a crew after it crash-landed in Cambodia—and ended up in Azov's possession by dint of various trades and handshakes over the past three decades. It had been confiscated by Communists, repaired in the USSR, and sent on to their Bulgarian allies during the seventies. By the time Azov got his hands on it, the cold war had ended and Bulgaria had joined NATO. Now, watching Sveti grip the cyclic control between her knees, Vera wondered what kind of realigned world children born today would grow up to live in.

Azov gave a nod and Sveti flipped switches, checking the monitors on the dash before taking them into the air. They lifted away from the earth, shouldering the wind. Vera watched the land recede as they climbed higher, the contours of the lighthouse losing verticality, the sea growing uniform until the water below seemed little more than an adamantine sheet against the muted shoreline. The sun was setting, casting the world in a darkening purple light. She strained to see the fishing villages nestled into the cove, the squat gray shacks like rocks basking in the rarefied light. The beaches were deserted—no umbrellas blooming from the sand, not a boat floating in the bay, only endless stretches of rocky coastline. Vera tried to imagine the settlements buried under cubic tons of dark water, the remnants of ancient civilizations frozen in the suffocating chill of a lightless underworld.

The helicopter tipped as Sveti flew them over a stretch of shoreline and then cut inland, the blades overhead banging their slow and
steady rhythm. They swooped over baked clay rooftops, narrow
highways, and empty fields, leaving the Black Sea behind.

Suddenly, from the corner of her eye, Vera saw something else flying in the distance. For a moment it seemed little more than the sil-
houette of a hang glider hovering in the air, a slash of red against the
purple horizon. Then a second figure appeared, then a third, until a
swarm surrounded the helicopter, their red wings beating in the air,
their eyes fixed as they circled inward.

"You didn't mention that St. Ivan Island is being guarded by
Gibborim," Vera said, glancing at Azov.

"It isn't—they must have followed our jeep from Sozopol," Sveti
said, steering the helicopter inland as one of the creatures swung
against the windscreen, its red wing brushing the plastic and leaving
a streak of oil behind.

"We can't fight them up here," Azov said under his breath. "We'll
have to outrun them. We'll have help on the ground if we can just
make it to the airport."

"Hold on," Sveti said, as she manipulated the stick, swerving the
helicopter.

It swayed and jerked, dipping like a ship on choppy water, but the
creatures stayed with them. Suddenly the craft faltered and tipped,
throwing Vera forward against her shoulder straps. She looked out the
window and saw that two Gibborim had attached themselves to the
runners. With their wings open, they were dragging the helicopter
down toward the rocky shore.

Sveti bit her lip and bore onto the controls. It wasn't until they
approached the electrical wires and Sveti was angling the runners
toward a bank of transmission towers that Vera realized their pilot
intended to force the creatures off by scraping the bottom. Sveti

feinted right, then left, and then lowered the chopper down. The Gibborim hit the wires, their wings tangling as the helicopter ascended once more, sweeping back out over the bay.

Within minutes the shipping yard at Burgas came into view. Massive pyramids of salt grew along the shore, white and rocky. Sveti steered inland again toward the airport, stationed just miles from the water. The runway stretched into the distance, and the Cessna piper sat abandoned on the tracks like a metallic insect anticipating flight.

As Sveti moved down lightly onto the tarmac, they were approached by a group of uniformed men who seemed almost bored as they escorted the trio out of the craft, around passport control, through the exit of the airport. Stepping out once again into the cool night, Vera found the sky had gone inky blue: The runway beyond the chain-link fence was shrouded in shadow. She scanned the landing field, looking for Gibborim.

A man in jeans and a black T-shirt strolled by, and Vera felt something cold and metallic thrust into her hand—a set of keys strung onto a leather strap. The agent—she knew that the man could only have been sent by Bruno—gestured to a Range Rover and, without a word, kept walking.

Azov gave Vera a look of surprise. He was clearly not used to having equipment and personnel show up without a word. Vera hadn't experienced such assistance either—she had never been out in the field before—but she knew that Bruno would take care of them. She gripped the keys, deciding that she was going to make the most of everything they gave her, use every resource and every bit of her talent to get to Dr. Valko.

She climbed into the driver's seat without a word. Azov climbed in beside her, leaving Sveti to take the backseat. The jeep was a new stick shift, with four-wheel drive and less than a thousand kilometers recorded on the dial. The leather steering wheel was cold from the night air. A manila envelope sat on the dash. Vera tossed it to Azov, threw the car into gear, and sped away from the airport.

Azov unzipped his backpack and pulled out a stack of plastic cups and a bottle of liquor. "Rakia," Azov said, as he raised the bottle, offering it to Vera.

She accepted and took a long drink. It wasn't as potent as vodka and not nearly as smooth, but she relished the feeling it produced in her body, a slow declenching of her muscles, a gradual loosening of her mind as she handed the bottle back to Sveti.

Azov dug in his backpack again and pulled out a map outlining the route from the Black Sea to the mountains, now obscured by nightfall. "Dr. Valko lives in Smolyan, which is roughly a five-hour drive from here, near the village of Trigrad. These roads are far from ideal, but at least we're not going to meet Gibborim on the way."

Azov was right about the Gibborim—they attacked only while in flight, fixing their victims midair—but Vera also knew that if Bulgaria was infested with those kinds of creatures, there would surely be others.

As she turned onto the highway, following Azov's directions, she tried to calculate when they would get to Dr. Valko. According to the clock on the dashboard, it was just after 9:00 P.M. If they made it to Smolyan within the next five hours, they would be showing up at the home of an old man in the middle of the night. "Even if you're still on good terms with him, he isn't going to be thrilled to see us in the middle of the night."

Azov said, "It's true that we'll need to approach Raphael with care. He is enormously protective of his privacy and his work. Essentially, he cut off all contact with the outside world after Angela died. We'll have to convince him to speak to us. But it's worth the effort."

"Actually, we have little choice but to try," Sveti said, taking a swallow of the rakia.

As Vera drove up into the mountains, she was aware that her attitude toward Dr. Raphael Valko was like any other young angelologist—she was starstruck by the very mention of him. Dr. Valko was a legend. She had never dreamed that she might meet him in person.

Perhaps sensing that she wanted to know more, Azov said, "Valko lives within spitting distance of the Devil's Throat Cavern for a reason."

"He's mining Valkine?" Vera asked.

"That would certainly be useful for our purposes," Sveti said.

"Everyone has their own ideas about what he's doing up there," Azov said. "He's up there with only the most essential modern conveniences. No telephone line, no electricity. He heats his house with wood and carries water from a well. He's nearly impossible to get to. I'm in the same country as the man, and I've been to his fortress—it is the only way to describe what he's built in Smolyan—only a handful of times, always to exchange and discuss seeds. By reputation he is an explorer and a man of science, but in person he's more like a Bulgarian goat herder—difficult to rile and terrifying in his vengeance toward those he believes would cross him. He's tough as nails, even at one hundred years old."

Vera looked at Azov, astonished. "He's one hundred years old?"

"Yes," Azov said. "The first time I met him, in 1985, he looked every bit like the seventy-six-year-old man he was. Later, after we began sharing the antediluvian seeds, he had the appearance of a man no older than fifty. Now he lives with a woman who is forty-five. She became pregnant with his child ten years ago."

"He is ninety years older than his daughter?" Sveti said. "It's completely impossible."

"Not if he's been using the seeds for his own purposes," Azov said.

Vera said, "There were rumors in the nineties that Valko was supplying his second wife Gabriella with vials of a liquid distillation from the plants in his garden. Well into her eighties she was actively fighting the Nephilim, going out on missions, enduring the hardships that agents half her age struggled to endure. She died during a mission. Nobody understood how she had the strength to even participate. She seemed to defy her body. The seeds you gave Raphael Valko are the only explanation. He must be growing his own antediluvian garden up there."

"Whether he is mixing their oils or growing the seeds into plants, it is impossible to say. You should remember that the seeds Valko has cultivated are the very same ones that Noah grew before the Flood, and Noah—as you know—lived to be nearly one thousand years old. It is impossible to know what nutritional substances the plants contained or what their effects would be, but it is obvious that Valko has used them to his advantage."

"Have you considered that he may have already found the formula for Noah's medicine?" Vera asked.

Azov sighed, as if he had considered the question many times before. "The truth is that any number of things could be happening in Raphael Valko's workshops. He is the man who discovered the location of the Watchers' prison in 1939. He is also the man who organized and sustained the society's resistance during the Second World War. Dr. Raphael Valko is not a man who leaves anything to chance. I'm certain that whatever he's doing up there in the Rhodopes, he's approaching it with the same single-minded drive that has always allowed him to succeed where many others have failed."

"Aren't you afraid that one of these days you will go up there and find him dead?" Vera asked.

"Not in the least," Azov said. "But I'm very much concerned that he'll turn us away when we get there. There's no guarantee that he'll help us with this concoction at all. Although he's connected to the society through various unofficial channels—myself included—he left angelology decades ago. There's every chance that he won't want to provide the missing element—the Valkine—even for something as alluring as the elusive medicine of Noah."

Vera drove onward, moving into the foothills of the Rhodope Mountains. While her inclination was to get to the village of Smolyan as fast as possible, the terrain worked against her. As they climbed higher and higher, the roads cut through increasingly steep passes, forging a sloped conduit overhung by rock on one side and a steep drop into an abyss on the other. She forced herself to glance at the ravine, the precipice opening over a tumbling darkness that, with one wrong turn, would take them over the edge. Even in daylight, when she could anticipate the tight hairpin turns, the drive would have been daunting. She kept the gear low and powered up the Range Rover, keeping a slow, steady speed.

Cresting the peak of a ridge, the jeep was suddenly awash in the light of a full moon, which illuminated a forest of birch and oak and pines sloping off beyond them. The road plunged down into canyons cut by streaks of moonlight and up to the mountaintop villages and then down again through more narrow passes, so that it seemed to Vera that they were making their way through an elaborate topiary maze, one that might lead nowhere. After hours of driving, they reached the summit of what must have been the highest peak in the region. Vera saw nothing above them but a vast canopy of stars. The village of Smolyan crouched in a scoop of land, hidden in darkness.

Azov directed Vera to turn onto a darkened gravel road that twisted and turned downward until a small Orthodox church appeared. A tower hovered nearby, its ironwork clock looming over the village. It was nearly three o'clock in the morning. At Azov's instruction, Vera continued down the road, passing the ancient ramparts and arriving at a square lined with evergreen trees. She cut the engine. Nobody spoke, but a new sense of hope had been born. It was as if they all felt that a solution was possible, that once they made it to Valko they would overcome the seemingly impossible odds.

"We're here," Azov said. "Let's just hope Raphael will see us."

Bruno leaned into the soft cushion of his seat and stared out the window at the starlight playing over the snow. The clattering of the train's wheels punctuated his thoughts with a sharp, staccato rhythm. He tried to imagine the thousands and thousands of miles of open space stretching to the Pacific, the permafrost and ancient forests, the bogs of peat, the stark, immaculate mountains. The train traveled over five thousand miles between Moscow and Beijing. The landscape seemed so alien, so far removed from the modern Russia they had just left, that he could almost imagine the distant era of the Romanovs, with its palace balls and sledges and hunting parties and regiments of elegant soldiers on horseback. Secrets could be buried forever in such a vast and inhospitable landscape. Perhaps Rasputin had entombed some himself.

Turning, he stole a glance at Verlaine. His skin was pale, his hair a knot of dark curls, and his shoulders slightly hunched. Even if the doctor's salve had helped ease the physical pain of the attack, the psychological effects of Eno's electric shock had had a terrible and indelible effect on him. Bruno couldn't help but worry. Bruno's feelings had changed in the past several hours from anger at his own bravado—he should have known better than to encourage Verlaine to go after Eno alone—to relief that his most promising hunter was alive. He was so thankful that he couldn't be angry about the pendant.

A trolley moved through the compartment with coffee and tea. Bruno attempted to hold his china teacup steady in his hand as the server poured, but the saucer shook, spilling hot liquid over his jeans. Once this cup had been filled, Bruno smelled the rich scent of the black tea and tried to ease his mind by sorting through everything that Nadia had said before the creatures had attacked. It seemed to Bruno, as he turned over the details in his mind, that there was no clear method for how to act. Nadia had never fully explored the information in Rasputin's journal. Indeed, she had seemed content to let the pages remain a curiosity from the past. It was up to them to learn what Rasputin had intended by his book of flowers.

Bruno felt Yana's hand on his shoulder. "Come on," she said.

They walked through a seemingly endless caravan of train cars, Yana sauntering ahead, leading the way. Bruno noticed her gun, tucked discreetly into a brace under her jacket. With a pang of admiration, he remembered her savvy in taking down Eno in St. Petersburg, handling the Emim with unbelievable skill in a studied, almost clinical manner. Bruno wondered what hindered his own ability to fight Eno. Maybe he unconsciously subverted his own efforts. Maybe something inside him wanted her to be free. Maybe women hunters didn't have these problems.

Yana paused before a steel door at the rear of the final passenger car, and, after fumbling through a ring of keys, inserted one into the lock. Turning to Bruno, she said, "The last ten cars are our storage and transport cabins, reserved for prisoners on their way to Siberia. In addition to the infirmary, there are cars equipped to hold the various species of angelic creatures, each one designed to counter the creature's particular strength. Nephilim are kept in a car filled with a high-frequency electric current that renders them comatose. Eno is in a freezer car, a space reserved for the most violent angels—warrior angels such as Gibborim and Raiphim, as well as Emim like herself. As you're well aware, the lower temperatures slow the heart, diminish the power of the wings, and bring the level of violence to a minimum." Yana smiled and pushed the door open. "Eno is in bad shape. You may not even recognize her."

They stepped into a narrow, lightless passage that opened to the holding cars. As they walked, Bruno stopped at each car to examine the creatures. There were three angels bound together in one cell—a Leogan, a Nestig, and a small red Mendax, three creatures whose words could never be trusted. They didn't notice Bruno, so busy were they muttering among themselves. At the end of the train, at the front of the last car, there was a plate-glass door covered in ice.

"This is my week's transport," she said, pride in her voice.

"Impressive," Bruno said, careful to not reveal the extent of his admiration.

"Eno is an extraordinary catch, one that I've been hoping to make for years. I don't think I could have managed her alone, and so I have you to thank." Yana stopped before the frozen door. "Come and look at our angel."

Yana unlocked the door and Bruno stepped into the compartment, his skin prickling from the cold, his breath rising and fogging in the air, his shoes slipping on the frost-covered floor. It took a moment for his eyes to adjust. He saw Eno's bare leg, its blue-gray skin a curl of fog; he saw her face, drawn in sleep, her eyes closed, her violet lips. Her head had been shaved, and thick veins snaked over her skull, pulsing and blue, living. Now that her beauty was stripped away, Bruno could perceive, with visceral poignancy, how inhuman she was. As he knelt beside her, he heard her breath sticking in her chest, as if the freezing air had lodged itself into her lungs. He ran a finger over her cheek, feeling the old electric attraction to her. The train jerked and Eno opened her eyes. Their reptilian sheaths retracted. As she trained her gaze on him, he saw that she knew him, that she wanted to speak to him, but all her strength was gone.

She opened her mouth and her long, black tongue fell from her lips, its end forked like a snake's. Bruno felt an irrational urge to draw her close, to feel her breathing on his neck, to feel her struggle under him. From the way she looked at him, he could feel her rage. Their game was over. Bruno had won.

Yana said at last, "Do you have any clue how difficult this Emim is?"

Bruno let his gaze linger a moment longer. Half of his life had been spent hunting Eno. Yana had no idea how well he understood how difficult and dangerous she could be. "Unfortunately, I do," he said, following Yana back into the corridor of the train.

"You think she'll talk?"

"Maybe," Bruno said. "Now that she's isolated from the Grigoris, we have a better chance."

Yana took a cigarette from a pack and offered it to Bruno. He didn't smoke under normal circumstances, but the past days were not at all normal. He took a cigarette, lit it, and inhaled, feeling his mind clear.

"I have to admit, this is the first time a foreign angel hunter has assisted me with a hunt," she said, blowing the smoke from her cigarette away from Bruno.

"Your team isn't very large, is it?" Bruno asked.

"It's become more active in the past five years, but that is only because the oil companies have brought a lot of action back to this part of the world. Old Nephilim families—families that left Russia after the revolution—are building mansions and setting up corporations here. The new oligarchs have worked in tandem with the Grigori family to create massive wealth. Before this rush of new blood, it was just me, the occasional lost Anakim angel, and Siberia's godforsaken winters." Yana threw her cigarette onto the metal floor of the train car, its embers melting a nebula into the frost. "All this is to say that if you're looking for Nephilim in western Siberia, I know how to find them. I have files on every creature that has passed through here in the last fifty years."

"You have an enormous field to cover," Bruno said, marveling at her ability to manage such a large operation.

"I've heard about the methods you have in Paris. They are nothing like the way we do things here. Eno was special. I can't afford to expend that kind of effort on all the creatures. Most of the time my concern is getting them to the prison. Once they're there, I'm out of the picture. I can't imagine spending time in the panopticon itself."

"Panopticon?"

"The prison is modeled on Jeremy Bentham's panopticon," Yana said. "It has the classic circular structure of the original, which allows the guards to monitor each angelic creature. That said, the prison has, out of necessity, been adapted to meet our particular needs."

Bruno tried to imagine such a place, its purpose and size. He felt a sense of professional jealousy rising at the thought of the number of angels that were kept there. "Can you get me inside?"

"We certainly can't just show up," Yana said. "This prison is the biggest, and most strongly guarded, angelological holding area ever built. It is also located in Chelyabinsk, a nuclear waste area that has the distinction of being the most polluted patch of land on the planet. Russian angelologists and the military are on every inch of the grounds. Although I'm on the payroll, and have limited access to the prison, my clearance has been invalid since the beginning of perestroika. To access the interior circles of the prison, you'd have to get help from someone else."

Bruno studied her, trying to gauge whether her ignorance was genuine. "Merlin Godwin is at this prison?" he asked. It was a long shot, he knew, but since Godwin was the one person from Angela's film who remained unaccounted for, he needed to give it a try.

"Of course," Yana said. "He's been the director of the Siberia Project for more than twenty years."

Bruno considered his options: He could keep everything that he'd seen in Angela Valko's film and everything he'd learned in the Hermitage a secret. Or he could trust Yana and ask for her help. "Have you heard of something called the Angelopolis?"

Yana's face froze and drained of color. "Where did you hear that word?"

"It's something more than just a legend, I see," Bruno said, his curiosity rising.

"Quite a bit more than that," she said, taking a deep breath to steady herself before speaking. "The Angelopolis is a mystery for all of us who haven't been given security clearance to the interior realms of the prison. It is the subject of much gossip—that the prison is the site of a massive experiment, that it is a sort of sci-fi genetics laboratory, that Godwin is cloning lower angelic life-forms to be used as servants for the Nephilim. There is no way to know for certain what is going on inside. As I said, security around the perimeter is intense, and that's putting it lightly. I've been working here for two decades, and I've never even made it past the first checkpoint." Yana lit another cigarette as she considered her thoughts. "What do you know about it?"

"Not much," Bruno admitted. "I know that Dr. Merlin Godwin was working with the Grigoris at some point, and may still be, but that's about as far as it goes."

"Have you looked up his profile?" Yana asked

"No, unfortunately, I haven't," Bruno replied.

Yana rolled her eyes, as if to say that there was no point in going any further without doing what every angel hunter knew to be the first step.

"Honestly," Bruno said, feeling his skin burn. "I haven't had the chance."

Yana pulled a laptop from her backpack and opened it on the floor in the corridor.

"Our network isn't as high-tech as the one you have, I'm sure, but I have access to it. If there's anything here about Godwin, we'll know."

Bruno watched as Yana logged into the Russian society's network and began searching through an angelological database that seemed to spit out everything from enemy profiles to security events to society personnel.

Yana played around for a few minutes. Then, after a flurry of typing, a profile for Merlin Branwell Godwin appeared on the screen, as clear and concise as Eno's profile had been on his smartphone. "Here we go."

"Found something?"

"Read it for yourself," she said, holding out the laptop for him. "You can choose to read it in French, English, or Russian, take your pick."

Bruno clicked on the profile and read the report in English. Born in Newcastle in 1950, Godwin had taken a degree in chemistry from Cambridge University and, in 1982, come to the academy where he worked closely on a number of classified projects. He'd received prestigious awards and distinctions. But the strings of biographical information didn't catch Bruno's attention nearly so much as the picture that appeared alongside the text. Godwin was a thin man with bright red hair, a long sharp nose, and piercing black eyes.

"It isn't much," Bruno said at last.

"There's never anything meaty in the general files," Yana said, giving him a sly look. "Almost anyone can access this kind of information."

She resumed her typing until various windows began flashing by in such rapid succession that Bruno could hardly keep up with them as they appeared and disappeared on the screen. Suddenly she stopped. "It's weird. Another piece on Merlin Godwin does exist, a classified dossier created in 1984, but it has been deleted."

"How is that possible?"

"Someone with clearance went in and erased it," Yana said.

"Erasing a classified file isn't exactly easy to do."

"Clearly someone went through a lot of trouble."

"Could there be another way to access it?"

"Nothing is ever completely lost on this network," Yana said. "This document was probably stored inside the classified archive, and it was most likely encrypted, which would mean that there's a trace somewhere." Yana turned back to the laptop. "Let's see what I can do."

With a click, the streams of Cyrillic gave way to legions of binary numbers falling across the screen. A report appeared; he made out the name Angela Valko written at the top. As he watched Yana begin to read, he knew that she had found something of interest. He could only hope that it would be extraordinary.

Smolyan, Rhodope Mountains, Bulgaria

It seemed to Azov that they had risen high above the inhabited world to a remote and hidden place where, with one step, he would disappear into a mountain pass, never to be seen again. Everywhere they turned, they found silence. He looked over his shoulder, watching the street with wary attention. He'd monitored the road and was certain that they had been alone the entire drive, and yet he couldn't help but feel that someone was watching them, that they were surrounded by danger at every moment.

The moon shone against the stark stone walkways. Shuttered shops and cafés sat in pools of darkness, their awnings drawn. Ancient buildings rose from rough jags of hewn stone. As he led Vera and Sveti away from the square, it seemed to Azov as though the entire foundation of the village had been carved directly from the rock, each building retaining the swirls of mineral in the marble. Looking over the village, he saw gorges and valleys falling away in tiers, each new depth like a sheet of linen absorbing the inky night.

They moved through a warren of streets, each one twisting as it rose. At a dead end, Azov stopped, looked behind, and turned back. He had been to the house before, but in daylight; the labyrinthine structure of dark narrow streets had temporarily confused him. Within steps, however, he found his bearings. "Here it is," he said, stopping abruptly before a tall and narrow black door framed by a crumbling stucco façade. The house was one of a row of village houses, three stories high, with pale blue shutters closed to the street. Azov picked up a brass knocker and brought it down upon a sheet of metal.

"Identify yourself."

The voice, familiar as it was, startled him from his thoughts. He looked up to find a man with glasses and long white hair wearing what seemed, from the shadowy street, to be a military greatcoat. He held a gun in his hand.

"Tell me exactly what in the hell you're doing outside my door at three thirty in the morning," the man said.

"Dr. Valko," Azov said, his voice calm. "It is Hristo Azov, from the angelological outpost on St. Ivan Island. Forgive me for coming to you like this without warning, but we need to speak with you. It's urgent."

Raphael Valko squinted, as if trying to make out the faces of each member of the group. He paused as he saw Azov, his expression softening as he recognized his colleague. "Azov," he said. "My friend, what are you doing here?"

"I think we'd better speak inside," Azov said, looking over his shoulder as a cat ran from the shadows.

"I've been hoping you would return," Valko said. "But I expected some warning—a letter, perhaps, or a messenger. It isn't wise to come here so openly. You're risking your life, but also mine." He lowered the gun and said, "Come with me. It's best to get out of the street. Anyone, or anything, could be watching."

They followed Valko into a pinched cobblestone passageway. He stopped, unlatched an iron door, and led them into an immense, flowering courtyard. The dimensions of the courtyard were the exact inverse of the narrow alley: It was an enormous square filled with lanterns and lined with high stone walls, creating a veil of privacy. If Azov had not visited Valko's home before, he would never have been able to guess that such a marvelous private courtyard existed inside. Every inch of the garden was filled with greenery. Fruit trees grew along the wall, their branches heavy; flowers of every variety and color bloomed in earthenware pots; vines slithered along trellises, tendrils curling in the pale moonlight. The fragrance of gardenias and roses and lavender filled the air. A stone fountain gurgled at the center of the courtyard and, as they stepped deeper and deeper into the paradise of colors and scents, Azov felt utterly at ease. Here, in this secret garden, in the midst of an unnatural fecundity, he was among friends.

Even from a distance Azov could make out plants in what appeared to be a greenhouse at the far end of the courtyard. An ironwork frame held sheets of glass that rose, as they gained height and volume, into an elaborate Victorian cupola. The structure cut upward in lapidary panels, sharp and crystalline against the night sky. To Azov's surprise, a bank of solar panels had been installed beyond the greenhouse, angling toward the south. The interior lights were hazy, as if a mist of water swirled through the warm air. As they walked closer he saw leaves pressed against the glass, and his mind turned to the thousands of seeds he had collected and preserved. St. Ivan Island, and the work he did there, seemed a million miles away.

Valko unlocked the door to the greenhouse and they stepped inside. The cool mountain air transformed into a blanket of humidity filled with the scent of flowers. UV lights burned from bulbs overhead. A dull hum radiated from a solar-powered generator.

The tables were filled with every variety of plant. A forest of fruit trees grew in fat ceramic pots. Azov paused to examine a tree and saw a fruit that had the shape of a pear but the deep purplish red of a cluster of grapes. He leaned close and inhaled, smelling the fruit as if it were the trumpet of a lily. The scent was spicy and full, more like the aroma of a tea composed of cinnamon and cardamom than a piece of fruit. "Smell this," he said, calling Vera over. As she took in the aroma, her gaze fell upon a strange-looking tree. "What is this?" she asked.

Valko smiled, clearly pleased to have captured their attention. "Everything you see in this greenhouse is a plant that has not existed for thousands of years. The flowers blooming on that table, the vegetables growing at the far end of the greenhouse, the fruit you have just smelled—none of these things have blossomed since the time of the Flood. In my original plans, the greenhouse alone was to be vast, with over two thousand varieties of antediluvian seeds."

As Azov looked more closely, he saw that the plants were both familiar and strange, retaining the basic qualities of the flora one saw every day, and yet—as he touched the leaves—he knew that he hadn't seen these particular varieties before. The leaves were glossier, the fruit more fragrant. Apples hung from the branches, each one perfectly round, with skin that shone brilliant pink. Valko plucked an apple from the tree and gave it to Azov. "Taste it," he said.

Azov turned the apple in his hand. Up close the skin was solid pink, flawless and shiny as a rubber ball. The stem was an iridescent blue.

"Don't worry," said Valko, "it's too late to get thrown out of Eden."

Azov took a bite. The taste was startling and strange. He had expected a burst of sweetness, something approximating the many varieties of apple he had eaten in the past. Instead his mouth was filled with a strange and unpleasant taste, a medicinal, herbal astringency that reminded him of spiced liquor. He almost dropped the apple but caught sight of the flesh: It was the same glowing blue as the stem, phosphorescent, as if lit from within.

Valko took the apple from Azov's hands and placed it on the table. Removing a Swiss army knife from his pocket, he cut the apple in half, the juice streaking the blade. He carved the apple into slices and handed Vera and Sveti a crescent. Azov watched as the others tasted it, detecting the same reaction as he'd had seconds before—unequivocal repulsion.

"This very well may have been the fruit that caused the exile of Adam and Eve. But then again," Valko said, stepping past the apple tree and stopping before a beautiful citrus tree, its leaves lush and glossy. Between the leaves grew clusters of tiny, bright yellow fruit that looked like miniature lemons. "If I were to trade paradise to taste a fruit, it would have to be this one." He plucked one of the clusters and offered it to his guests. Vera pinched a lemon free and held it under a neon light. It was no bigger than the nail of her thumb, the peel supple and pliable to the touch. "No need to peel it," Valko said. Vera put one in her mouth.

Azov followed her example. As he bit into the fruit, sweetness filled his tongue, a rich taste that seemed to be distantly related to citrus but had been overlaid with strawberry and cherry, and with darker, more subtle tastes, such as fig and plum. He looked at the tree, wanting to pick a cluster of the lemons.

"How were you able to get so many of the seeds to grow?" Sveti asked.

"I developed a solution of fertilizer and plant hormones in which I soaked the seeds until they began to sprout. In the protection of the greenhouse, most of them thrived. I have kept a record of every blossom on every tree and every fruit that has ripened." Valko's delight was apparent as he gestured to his work. "When I close the door to this greenhouse, shutting myself inside with these ancient forms of life, I can almost imagine what the world looked like before the Flood."

Azov looked carefully at Raphael. His skin was pale and carved with wrinkles, his white hair had been pulled back into a ponytail, and a fine white beard curled to his stomach. What Azov had believed to be a greatcoat revealed itself, under the lights, to be a midnight blue gown that swept to the ankles and made the old scientist look like a magician.

Azov wanted to simply move through the garden, examining the plants. "These new varieties are even more strange and wonderful than I had imagined," he said at last. "Have you lost any of the seeds?"

"A few," Valko said. "But not as many as I had initially anticipated. Now that I have the solar energy panels, I have been very successful in growing nearly all of them, and have made enormous progress with my various medicines."

"Medicines for whom?" Vera asked, her voice trembling. Azov found her excitement charming—he'd delighted in her intelligence and curiosity since she was a child.

"For my own consumption, mainly," Valko replied.

"Is that wise?" Azov asked. Although he hadn't mentioned it to Vera and Sveti, he had been tempted to dabble in the medicinal arts but had ultimately resisted. The potential dangers of mixing such medicines outweighed the possible benefits.

"Most are tinctures of ingredients that are perfectly safe when ingested in small quantities," Valko explained. "I have had only one case of serious toxicity, and that was because I ground the seeds of a cluster of prehistoric grapes into a tea. I should have simply eaten the fruit, I suppose, but I wanted to know if the seeds contained properties associated with longevity, concentrated amounts of undiluted polyphenols that are found in diluted quantities in the seeds of modern fruits. It turned out that the seeds were more powerful than I could have imagined. And, in fact, despite the fact that I got sick a time or two, there were extreme benefits as well. I am an old man, and yet this garden has given me a second youth. I feel and look younger and younger each year."

Azov studied Raphael closely. At one hundred years old, his vitality was nothing short of astonishing.

"Once I felt the effects of the seeds, I mixed them with the extract from the hemlock plant. It is an extremely powerful concoction."

"It's a lethal concoction, Raphael," Azov said.

"Not quiet lethal," Valko replied. "With the right dosage, it is a classic example of the *pharmakon*."

"That's Greek," Sveti said, glancing at Vera to make sure she followed. "It refers to a substance that is both a remedy and a poison at once."

"Well put, my dear," Valko said. "The seeds have the power to kill me, but the seeds also have the power to prolong my life. This is the basis of homeopathy: At one dosage a substance may do great good. At a different dosage, it kills you. Certainly most medicines and vaccines work on this principle. It has been the North Star of my work. But enough about me and my fountains of youth. Come inside now and tell me what brings you here."

The Sixth Circle

HERESY

Surveillance Report, June 9, 1984, submitted by Angela Valko

This is the first such report I have filed in the history of my time as an angelologist, and I do so with some degree of discomfort. But the horrific nature of my suspicions, and the extent of Dr. Merlin Godwin's involvement in activities detrimental to our security, require that I report what I have witnessed. I submit this document with the hope that my observations can be of use to the preservation of our work.

My concerns about Godwin began on the night of April 13, 1984, when I came across Dr. Godwin in the street. My husband, Luca, and I were on our way to dinner in a restaurant on the rue de Rivoli when we recognized Godwin. He was ahead, strolling along alone. He wore a three-piece suit and carried a briefcase. We decided to catch up with him, to say hello and invite him for a glass of wine, but before we reached him he was joined by a tall, female creature with the standard angelic traits.

My husband, who was as intrigued as I by this pairing, and whose instinct as an angel hunter pushed him to discover their destination, decided it best to follow. We did, keeping our distance behind Godwin until he stopped on the rue de Temple, where he and the creature entered a restaurant. They took a table near the back, away from human beings. We didn't dare follow them inside. Dr. Godwin knows me well—he began his career as my intern—and would recognize me instantly.

Luca called a colleague—Vladimir Ivanov, a man who would not have been recognized by Dr. Godwin—and sent him into the restaurant to observe them up close. Vladimir entered the restaurant and sat at the bar, observing, and, within an hour, Godwin and his companion left the restaurant. Vladimir returned to us a short time later, relaying the following surprising information: Godwin had spent the hour in conversation with the woman, whom Vladimir confirmed to be an Emim angel. In his opinion, Godwin was working with the creature. He had spoken of his work at length and, most surprising of all, at the end of their rendezvous, Godwin gave her the briefcase.

Luca and I discussed this at length, speculating about the contents of the briefcase, and in the end decided that we should continue to watch Godwin before making an official report. Consorting with the enemy is a serious offense, but we reasoned that there might be some explanation for his association with the creature. We decided to simply watch and wait.

This was not difficult to do. Godwin has recently been given a laboratory next to mine, and so I had the opportunity to observe him with ease over the course of many weeks. I found nothing out of the ordinary. He works seven days a week; he is solitary; he keeps a strict routine. When I checked in on his work during our weekly appointments, I could find no fault in Dr. Godwin's experiments.

In the meantime, Luca began to look through profiles of previously hunted and captured creatures. He identified Godwin's companion as an Emim named Eno. I will not go into further detail about the significance of this name here, but suffice it to say that her identity impressed Luca and me and made us all the more wary of Godwin's behavior.

On the night of May 30, at eleven o'clock, I saw him leave his laboratory and hurry down the hallway. Again he was dressed in a suit and again he carried his briefcase. I followed him into the elevator and he held the door. He was deferential, bowing in a gentlemanly fashion. I believe now that Godwin must have known more about me than I suspected. For many years I had assumed his slightly awkward manner toward me grew from an inability to speak to women, and that he was too inexperienced and naïve to assert himself in the presence of an attractive colleague. I believed this trait to be a sign of innocence. I would soon see how very wrong I was in this assessment.

As we stood together in the elevator, I noticed him slipping a copper key card into the pocket of his jacket, so that a corner of the metal was visible. Perhaps it was Luca's influence, but I found myself calculating how I could take the key, what diversionary maneuver I could make to steal it, and what I would do with it once I had it. If Godwin had any secrets—if he were giving our secrets to the Nephilim, as I suspected—then there might be proof in his laboratory.

We walked together through security and left the building. He hailed a taxi and, his gaze never meeting mine, asked if I'd like to share it. Seizing the opportunity, I climbed into the taxi with Godwin. We spoke of office politics, of new policies being implemented for scientists, and of other innocuous subjects, but all the while I was watching the corner of metal poking out of his pocket.

I told the taxi driver to stop and, as I was getting out of the car, I pretended to trip, falling heavily into Godwin's arms as he held the door open for me. This feint took him off guard and, in the confusion, I plucked the key from his pocket and slid it up my sleeve. Even as I made my apologies for my clumsiness, Godwin climbed into the taxi and disappeared into the night.

I returned to the labs at once and entered Godwin's office with ease, using his key. The layout was identical to mine, only instead of equipment for the experimental work he'd been presenting to me during our meetings, I found masses of files stacked up on every flat surface of the lab. I began to look through them, trying to find something that would help me to understand Godwin's association with Eno.

What I discovered shocked me to the core. The folders were

stuffed with photographs of angelic creatures in erotic positions, pornographic shots of female and male Nephilim, sadomasochistic couplings between humans and angels, every kind of sexual perversity imaginable. As I moved through the stacks, the photographs became increasingly violent, and soon there were stills of people being tortured and raped and killed by Nephilim. The pleasure the creatures took in human suffering was evident in these photographs, and even now, with some of these images before me, I cannot believe that they exist. Even more unbelievable, however, was a thick book featuring images of the victims after they had been used for pleasure and discarded—the bodies were bruised, bloodied, dismembered, and photographed like trophies. The graphic nature of these images was like nothing I had seen before, and I understood how sheltered I had been from the everyday behavior of the Nephilim, from what horrors they are capable of performing.

As a fellow scientist, I would like to give Godwin the benefit of believing, if possible, that these images are part of his work. If Godwin were exploring the nature of angelic sexuality, he might bring an academic reserve to his participation in the underworld of angelic sex and violence, a coldness in relation to the events that he has photographed. However, I truly do not believe this to be the case, for reasons that will soon be evident.

I spent many hours in Dr. Godwin's lab that night. Aside from this trove of horrors, I found a number of items that were of intense interest to me, both personally and professionally. The first was a document written by my mother, Gabriella Lévi-Franche, that appears to be a collection of her field notes from 1939–43, the years she worked as an undercover agent while attending the academy. The volume is bound in red leather, in the official manner, signifying that the account was produced and published with the sanction of the council. Until that evening, this period of Gabriella's life was a mystery to me—she had never told me the details of her wartime

work, had never spoken of it to anyone, so far as I had been aware—
and so it was with curiosity and trepidation that I opened the red
book and looked inside. How Godwin came to possess this book,
and what his interest was in my mother's experiences, is a question I
cannot bring myself to answer in this report. I can only record here
that the revelations of Gabriella's report were deeply shocking to me
and have repercussions that will seep into every aspect of my life.

As for the second discovery, I am relieved to say, it had a professional importance that almost obscured the pain of the first discovery. On the shelf, prized in the fingers of a silver holder, was an egg.

I recognized it immediately as one of the eggs created by Fabergé
for the Romanovs. I spent many childhood afternoons paging through
books about the Romanovs—the family was of intense interest to
angelologists—and my mother had a large collection of books about
the tsar. The egg in Godwin's laboratory was one of the eight missing eggs. Instantly, picture-book images of these eggs appeared in
my mind, crisp and glistening with bright lithographic colors: the
Cherub with Chariot Egg; the Empire Nephrite Egg; the Hen Egg;
the Emperial Egg; the Nécessaire Egg; the Mauve Egg; the Danish
Jubilee Egg; and the Alexander III Egg. Sitting on the shelf was the
Hen Egg, its blue enamel surface alive with sapphires. I took it down
and, turning it in my hand, found the mechanism and pressed it.

The egg sprang apart. Inside was a hen surprise, and inside this
precious miniature, wrapped in a muslin cloth, were three glass vials
full of liquid, each labeled in Godwin's thin scrawl. Holding a loupe
to the writing, I was able to make out the names ALEXEI and LUC-
IEN, but the third word was written in such a messy scrawl that I
refused to accept the word my eyes deciphered: EVANGELINE. I removed the tiny stopper of this third vessel and brought it to my
nose. The smell was distinctly sanguine, sweet and metallic at once,
but still I could not believe that Godwin had kept a vial of my
daughter's blood.

After returning to my own workspace with a number of the most illustrative photographs—as well as Gabriella's red book and the Hen egg—I phoned Vladimir Ivanov, who aside from working closely with Luca, has aided me in a number of projects relating to Russian Nephilim. I asked him to bring his wife, Nadia, my assistant, who I knew to be an expert on tsarist antiquities, including Fabergé's eggs. Vladimir and Nadia joined me straightaway. As I began to run tests on the blood, Nadia explained that the egg in Godwin's possession— with its golden bird hatching from the center—symbolized the hunt for the savior, the new creature that would arrive to liberate our planet. Glancing through the stack of photographs, Vladimir explained that the violence of the images was not at all unusual—the Nephilim reproduced through such extreme practices—but that he had never seen it documented with such attention. I listened as I analyzed the blood, trying to understand how the elements before me fit together.

The vials made an especially fascinating trio. By far the oldest of the three was the Alexei sample—much of the blood had dried out and crusted black against the glass—but it was also the most straight-forward: Nephilistic through and through. The contents of the vial marked LUCIEN, on the other hand, defied categorization. The color was a far richer blue than the Nephilistic cerulean—more like the indigo prized by the elite of Rome—and bore none of the typical traces of human physiognomy. Had I not been so anxious about the sample taken from my daughter, I would have begun to run more complex tests on it. But it was the third and final vessel—the vial labeled EVANGELINE—that commanded my full attention.

It was clear that the crimson blood was human, and yet, at the same time, there were abnormalities atypical of Nephilistic contam-ination: The level of iron was extraordinarily high, and there was no potassium present at all, which would be strange under any circumstance—no human being can live without potassium present in the blood. I myself had authorized Merlin Godwin to run tests on Evangeline's blood—we had been monitoring her for years—but he had never disclosed such obvious abnormalities to me. In fact, he had always claimed that her blood was human, without the slightest taint of Nephil characteristics. The conclusion I am forced to draw from this revelation is particularly shocking to me: Godwin has been taking samples of my daughter's blood covertly and using the blood for his own perverse purposes.

Vera followed Valko into a squat stone building at the west end of the courtyard, Azov and Sveti following close behind. Inside, she found a large room illuminated by gas lamps and filled with ropes, boots, and belts with rock hammers. Windbreakers and backpacks had been piled on a couch, and a large map of the Rhodopes hung on the wall, its surface filled with colored pins. From the state of disorder it was clear that visitors were a rare phenomenon. As she looked over the mess, she realized that she was exhausted. The few hours of sleep she'd had on the plane weren't enough to sustain her. The mission was beginning to wear on her.

"My explorations have taken me to nearly every part of these mountains," Valko said, seeing Vera's interest in the map. "I left the Paris academy after Angela's death because, quite frankly, I couldn't bear to be reminded of her. But I've come to realize that there was another reason I left: I needed to go back to the source of my work, the inspiration for all of my efforts."

Running his finger over the map, he stopped at the Devil's Throat Cavern.

"My major discoveries have always occurred when I returned to the original dwelling places of the Nephilim—the Alps, or the Pyrenees, or the Himalayas."

"Or the Rhodopes," Azov said.

"Correct. The places most important to the creatures are always located in the remotest regions of the earth, away from human eyes."

A door opened and a girl walked into the room. She appeared to be between ten and twelve years old and wore jeans, tennis shoes, and a pale yellow sweater that matched her bobbed blond hair. She had blue eyes and the distinct patrician features of Dr. Raphael Valko. Vera guessed her to be the daughter Azov had mentioned. Looking her over more carefully, she detected a scar running along the side of the girl's face, a wide pale track of healed stitches crawling along the line of her jaw, past her ear and into her hairline. The girl set a cup of tea on her father's desk and looked at the others, as if curious to see so many visitors.

"Thank you, Pandora," Valko said.

Vera wondered if this was a tea made from the plants Valko had grown from Azov's Black Sea seeds. Not that Valko seemed the sort to acknowledge others' contributions. He had invited them inside to hear their reasons for coming to Smolyan, but not even Azov had managed to get a word in edgewise.

Sensing a gap in Valko's monologue, Vera cleared her throat and said, "There is something I am hoping you can help me with, Dr. Valko."

"I gathered as much," he said, taking the cup and drinking. "You've come a long way to speak with me. I hope that I can help."

"Vera has found documents pertaining to the medicines of Noah," Azov said.

Valko seemed unnaturally calm, as if he were in a trance. "My daughter would have been very interested to speak with you about this matter, if she were alive."

"So Angela did have an interest in this concoction?" Vera asked, standing and walking to the door, where she gazed out over the garden. The first light of dawn suffused the sky above the courtyard. She reached into her satchel for the Book of Flowers—which overnight had come to seem more her own than Rasputin's or the Romanovs'—and stepped back into the room.

"Interest?" Valko said, smiling slightly, his gaze resting on the book. "I should say it was more than that. My daughter's connection wasn't theoretical. Her involvement brought her deep into the secrets of the nature of angelic life on this planet. In the end she succeeded in learning things that put her in danger."

"You think that this information led to her death?" Azov asked.

"Most probably," Valko said, an air of sadness in his manner. "But in the beginning it was an exhilarating, if highly doubtful, quest. Rasputin's journal came to Angela almost out of the sky."

"Nadia mentioned that Vladimir simply presented it to her one day," Vera said.

"Of course, the ease with which it arrived in her life made her suspicious—it could have been a fake; it could have been created to trick her—but in the end she believed that Rasputin's work was authentic, that he was one more magus seeking the formula cited so cryptically in the Book of Jubilees—Noah, Nicolas Flamel, Newton, John Dee. The chain of seekers is long."

"And so she came to believe in the quest," Sveti said.

"Perhaps more pertinent is the question of why Rasputin would attempt to create a potion so universally believed to be of harm to the Nephilim—to the very family he served," Azov said.

"Ah, you've hit at the very root of Angela's skepticism," Valko replied. "But her doubts were quickly assuaged by consulting the Nephil family tree."

"*The Book of Generations*," Vera said. She'd seen the society's copy of the infamous collection of genealogies just once, during the same conference in Paris that had exposed her to Seraphina Valko's powerful photographs of the dead Watcher, the very conference where she had met Verlaine. The Nephilim genealogies were considered to be rare and precious resources.

Valko emptied his teacup, placed it on the table, and said, "You see, Alexei Romanov's hemophilia was passed down from Alexandra's family. The tsarevitch inherited the blood disorder from Queen Victoria. Queen Victoria was one of the most vital, effective Nephilim rulers in English history, while her husband, Albert, was actually partially Golobian, although this was a family secret that has been very well hidden. The hemophilia was passed through the Nephil line. Thus, it would follow that this disorder was one of the traits the medicine of Noah would cure."

"Surely it would have killed him," Azov said, echoing Vera's thoughts.

"Perhaps it would have," Valko acknowledged. "But Rasputin had little to lose in the gamble. He had promised not only to ease Alexei's bleeding episodes but to cure him completely. If Noah's medicine turned the tsarevitch human, the vow would be fulfilled; if it killed the boy, the hemophilia could always be blamed."

"Rasputin would have been sentenced to exile—even execution—if Alexei had died on his watch," Vera said.

"You should remember Rasputin's power over Alexei's mother," Valko said. "He was thought to have cast a spell over Alexandra. He was charged with every kind of evil practice imaginable—of holding black masses at the palace, of invoking demons to harm Alexandra's enemies, of the sexual practices associated with the Khlysty sect. Maybe there was a kernel of truth to the rumors. But if he hadn't come up with a cure, he would have lost all power over the imperial family." Valko looked out the doorway, as if the morning star were pulling him toward some distant memory. "I was a boy of nine years when the tsarevitch was executed with his family. Despite his Nephil lineage, despite all that I knew to be wrong with imperial Russia, I remember feeling a profound horror at the thought of his murder, horror at the pain he must have suffered as he and his family were led into the cold and shot. Horror, in the end, at the cruelty of humankind. I cannot say why, but I felt a strange kinship—something like brotherhood—for this murdered child. When his body disappeared and rumors abounded that he lived, I wondered if he was perhaps hiding somewhere, waiting to return."

Azov exchanged a look with Vera and said, "Just last month, genetic tests identified the remains of Alexei Romanov. They were found in a communal grave in Ekaterinburg."

"And so Rasputin's success or failure meant nothing," Valko said. "Revolution would have snuffed out any progress Rasputin had made with Alexei."

"What I don't understand," Azov said, "is why Angela became involved in all of this. What did she hope to gain from the formula?"

"Remember, it was Rasputin, not Angela, who actually attempted to produce the medicine of Noah," Valko said. "My daughter's efforts may have had the appearance of such an endeavor, but the true nature of her work was something else entirely."

"Such as?" Vera asked.

"Performing a wedding," Valko said and, seeing Vera's surprise, he added, "A chemical wedding. The concept is invoked as a symbol for chemical union: a female element and a male element being brought together in an unbreakable, eternal bond. This marriage of disparate elements brings forth a new element, often called the Alchemical Child." Valko turned to Vera and placed a hand on Rasputin's journal, brushing her arm. "May I?" he asked.

Vera felt an instant reaction to Raphael Valko's touch. Something about him made her profoundly aware of herself—she glanced down at her sweaty, wrinkled clothes, the same clothes she'd worn to work when Verlaine and Bruno showed up at the Hermitage, and wondered how she appeared to a man like Valko.

Valko turned through Rasputin's journal, finally stopping at a page of hastily written sentences. "I read this page thirty-two years ago with Angela. She understood the value of Noah's medicine, and she was intent upon re-creating it." Valko gave Azov a nod. "That is how you came into our acquaintance, Hristo. But it wasn't only Rasputin's recipe that caught her attention." He ran a finger along the page until it rested upon a drawing of an egg painted in a wash of gold and scarlet.

Vera recognized another egg, this one different from the others, the fourth of the missing eggs she had seen in two days.

"This aquarelle, made by one of the grand duchesses, probably the talented Tatiana, was of great interest to Angela. She believed it to have been copied under the guidance of Rasputin's predecessor, Monsieur Philippe—the spiritual adviser who undertook to give the tsar and tsarina an heir. You see, it is the Nécessaire Egg, one of the most practical of the eggs, holding all the important toiletry utensils an empress might need. Contrary to what historians believe about the egg, it was wildly expensive to make, with rubies and colored diamonds studding the egg itself and the toilet articles fashioned of gold."

"It looks," Vera said, leaning close, "as if there is a snake biting its tail drawn below the egg."

"Well spotted," Valko said. "It is something that Angela found intriguing about the egg."

"This symbol is very well-known," Sveti offered. "The ouroboros, the alpha and omega, is a sign of death and rebirth, regeneration and new life. The passage below it contains the words of Jesus, *'I am the Alpha and Omega, the first and the last, the beginning and the end.'* Revelation 22:13."

"Yes, of course," Valko said. "In this respect, the Nécessaire Egg is an echo of the Blue Serpent Clock Egg given to Grace Kelly on her wedding day, and one of the most elaborate and lovely of Fabergé's eggs, a masterpiece made with the *quatre couleur* technique of gold, diamonds, and royal blue and opalescent white enamel. Most interesting is the diamond-encrusted serpent coiled around the base, its head and tail pointing to the hour on the face of the clock—the ouroboros, the symbol of eternal renewal and immortality."

"But what does that have to do with a chemical wedding?" Vera asked. "Especially considering the fact that Monsieur Philippe's sole legacy was Alexandra's phantom pregnancy."

Valko smiled and said, "Bear with me. The quest of the alchemist, once upon a time, was to find the Philosopher's Stone, which supposedly had the power to turn base metals into gold. This has been discredited many times over as an impossible dream of the avaricious and mad. But the Philosopher's Stone also signified another human desire, a longing so universal, so persistent in culture and mythology as to be considered integral to the human psyche: The Philosopher's Stone was believed to be a panacea with properties that could grant eternal life."

"The Elixir of Life," Azov said.

Valko continued. "It has gone by many names throughout history: Aab-Haiwan, Maha Ras, Chasma-i-Kausar, Amrita, Mansorovar, Soma Ras. The earliest written records of such a phenomenon emerge in China and denote a substance that is made of liquid gold. In Europe the substance often took on the properties of water, and many well-known drinks that soothed the body were called Water of Life, in French *eau de vie*, in Gaelic *whiskey*. There is a biblical precedent to this as well in John 4:14: *'But whoever drinks the water I give him will never thirst. Indeed, the water I give him will become in him a spring of water welling up to eternal life.'*"

"Is that what you're growing up here in your garden, Raphael?" Azov asked. "While the rest of us work to fight the Nephilim, you're concerned about self-preservation?"

"It is not surprising that I would exploit the resources at my disposal to stay alive," Valko said, his voice soothing. "But I'm afraid that you're missing the point, my friend, when you say that this is not engaging in our fight. From the moment Vera removed Rasputin's book from her satchel, I knew what you had come here to do."

Valko pressed open the book and Vera saw his long fingers frame the heart symbol that had inspired them to travel to Smolyan in the first place."

"I can imagine the sequence perfectly," Valko said. "You correctly deciphered Rasputin's silphium symbol here. And then you turned a few pages and determined that Valkine was all you needed to re-create the medicine of Noah. Voilà, here you are in my home, waiting for it all to come together. But I would like you to take a step back and consider the language of this volume on the whole—including Tatiana's illustration of the egg and ouroboros. OUR FRIEND, both Monsieur Philippe and Grigory Rasputin, were heavily immersed in the sexual and mystical properties of the alchemist tradition. Their Book of Flowers is much more than a recipe book for the medicine of Noah. In language, symbol, and aesthetic, it is a paean to the chemical wedding—the apotheosis of alchemy, the height of human spiritual aspiration. To understand Angela's interest in the Russian artifact, you must consider its symbols and Enochian jargon on a metaphoric plane, a moral plane—even an anagogical plane."

Something clicked in Vera's mind. Just twenty-four hours earlier she herself had lectured Verlaine and Bruno on Angela's Jungian approach to the society's most revered texts. "This Book of Flowers was her Jacob's Ladder," Vera said, reaching for the journal.

"I could not have chosen a more apt analogy myself," Valko said, releasing the book into her hands and walking to an oak armoire from which he removed a thick collection of folders. "This extraordinary collection of firsthand accounts of Rasputin's life was smuggled out of the USSR. It was my daughter who first found the files more than twenty years before I bought it, during her search for documentation about Rasputin. She read through it and then buried it in a Soviet paper graveyard when she was done. Angela had hoped to find some mention of the flower book. There was nothing at all, but she did find allusions to Rasputin's friendship with an herbalist. This man practiced medicine, Tibetan medicine in particular. Badmaieff, as he was called, had the honor of making tinctures for the tsar, mostly teas mixed with cannabis to restore his calm—the tsar was a mess psychologically during the First World War. Angela found this rather commonplace—herbal medicines were popular among Russian peasants, who believed that they were 'God's cures.' Rasputin was, above all else, a peasant from Pokrovskoye, and there could be no importance whatsoever placed on giving the tsar tea. Badmaieff may have been just another quack."

"Or," Vera said, feeling a sense of satisfaction at the direction Valko was taking them, "he may have held information Angela needed."

"Precisely," Valko said. "It was at this point that my daughter came to me for help. Communicating through her friend and colleague Vladimir's contacts, I learned that Badmaieff's daughter, Katya, was alive and living in Leningrad. This was over thirty years ago, when there were still people alive who remembered Rasputin. Katya agreed to speak with me and invited me to her apartment near the Anichkov Palace."

"Risky business, that would have been," Vera said under her breath.

"As it turned out, Katya was relieved that I had found her. She had long wanted to tell her father's story to someone, but she hadn't known whom to trust. The burden of such a history had taken a great toll on her. She was haggard and twisted, her bones weak from osteoporosis. I listened to her story—which even I, who believed I'd heard everything under the sun, found utterly incredible—and then

I made her write everything down and sign it, so that I could deliver her account directly to Angela in Paris."

"I bet that was one amazing testament," Sveti said, giving a low whistle.

"Quite," Valko said, pulling a thin folio bound in red leather from the stack of papers. Vera recognized the society colophon on the spine and knew it must be an angelologist's field notes.

Vera reached for the folio. "This was written by Angela?"

"Her mother," Valko said, his voice grim. "Collected in this folio are things that my daughter was never meant to read. Officially, they are the reports of her mother, Gabriella Lévi-Franche, about her resistance work in Paris during the Nazi occupation. But between the lines lies the truth of Angela's true paternity."

"Forgive me for saying so, Raphael," Azov said, a hint of apology in his manner. "But Angela's connection to Percival Grigori is common knowledge."

"Common knowledge now, perhaps," Valko said, "but very closely guarded information during Angela's lifetime. After her murder, Gabriella and I both were devastated to find this red book among Angela's belongings. Not only did she die knowing I was not her biological father, she died knowing that her mother and I deliberately deceived her. It must have hurt her deeply to realize that she was descended from our enemy."

Valko sighed deeply, and Vera felt a stab of guilt that they were forcing him to recall such painful memories.

"Finding Katya's deposition inside the red book was like being slapped in the face," Valko continued. "Clearly Angela wanted to send her mother and me a message. She wanted us to know that she had learned the truth."

Vera looked from the red book to the file, knowing that the hundreds of hours she'd spent among Angela's effects at the Hermitage had been merely the first step in a greater discovery. The obsession with eggs, the cryptic trail of clues the woman seemed to leave behind her wherever she went—Vera had once believed these to be meaningless. In a matter of hours Valko had changed all of that. Feeling an almost irrepressible urge to grab Katya's testimony, Vera said, "I imagine there must be quite a few surprises in these pages."

Valko removed a sheaf of loose pages from the red book and gave them to Vera. "Yes, indeed," he said quietly. "I suggest that you see for yourself."

Verlaine stepped into a narrow bathroom, turned on a neon light, and looked at himself in the mirror. A black bruise had formed around the stitches across his forehead and was slowly eating its way under his left eye. After taking a piss, he turned on the tap and splashed cold water over his face, wincing as it hit the wound. He was in bad shape. The burn on his chest still ached, his head was still ringing, he was so tired he could hardly move. He only knew that he had to find the strength to get to Evangeline, wherever she was.

As he dragged himself back through the train to his compartment, he took in the sound of Russian. It was strangely sibilant, without the rough edges of English, and he found its rhythms soothing. He picked up a copy of the Moscow daily and tried to make out the Cyrillic, but the alphabet meant nothing to him. That he could puzzle over the angular symbols all morning and they would signify nothing at all was strangely pleasing to him.

A man brushed by him and he turned, feeling the hair stand up at the back of his neck. He recognized the static in the air, the sense of abeyance as everything froze and then broke apart. Looking more closely, he saw that the man's skin oozed a slick of plasma, that the structure of the shoulders and back corresponded to Nephil wings, that the distinctive scent of the Nephilim followed him. He recognized the velvet suit and the elegance of his comportment: One of the twins from St. Petersburg was on the train.

Verlaine began following the creature, retracing his steps back toward the bathroom, through the second-class sleeping berths with their tatty lace curtains, a smoking car, the dining car smelling of black tea. They were nearing the back of the train. The creature stopped at a door with a gold plate that read PRIVATE LOUNGE. He pressed a button on an intercom system and a voice responded in Russian. The words were incomprehensible and, suddenly, the pleasurable dislocation Verlaine had felt only moments before became irritating. It was imperative that he understand everything happening around him.

Soon a muscular hulk of a man opened the door, mumbled a few words to the creature—Verlaine recognized the voice from the intercom—and motioned him inside. Verlaine followed the creature. He made sure the bouncer was human, and then slipped him a wad of euros, which the bouncer shoved into his jeans as he let Verlaine pass. The thump of music echoed through a narrow, dilapidated compartment. The scent of alcohol and cigarette smoke suffused the air. There were neon lights, cocktail waitresses in trashy lace corsets and stiletto heels, and leather couches where Nephilim lounged with drinks. The Nephil creature nodded at the bartender, who picked up a phone, and, after speaking with someone, waved him toward the back of the room.

Verlaine remembered what the doctor had said—that he should stay away from danger of any kind—and wondered if it was wise to have put himself in such a situation. Everyone had heard stories of agents brutally slaughtered during failed stints undercover. It was a fairly common occurrence, especially in the provincial outposts. The Nephilim could kill him and nobody in Paris would know what had happened. Yana might send the news back to France, although who could say if she could be considered trustworthy. Instinctively, he and Bruno had accepted her identity at face value, taking her skill as a hunter as proof of her authenticity. As he moved deeper into the lounge, Verlaine began to feel a prickling sensation of fear. If he needed to escape, there was no way out of there.

Although Verlaine had never seen Sneja Grigori before, he knew at once that this was the matriarch of the Grigori family. She lay on a leather couch, her body stretched from one end to the other. Two Anakim angels hovered over her, one feeding her pieces of baklava and the other holding a tray with a flute of champagne. Sneja was so enormous that Verlaine wondered how she had walked onto the train, and how she would, when the train reached its destination, descend. She wore what looked like a silk curtain wrapped around her body, and her hair had been tucked up into a turban. As he came closer to the bed, Sneja lifted her great, toadlike eyes. "Welcome to Siberia," she said, assessing him with a sharp gaze. Her voice was gravelly, abrasive, smoky. "My nephews predicted that you would be coming, although they did not have the slightest notion that you would be making the trip as my personal guest."

"Your nephews?" Verlaine said. Glancing behind Sneja, he saw that the first twin had been joined by his brother. They stood side by side, beautiful as cherubs, their blond hair curling around their shoulders, their large eyes fixed upon Verlaine.

"You met them in St. Petersburg," Sneja said, taking a piece of baklava and placing it delicately on her tongue. "With our favorite mercenary angel, Eno, who I believe will be—with the assistance of my nephews—breaking free any moment."

Sneja nodded to the twins, who turned and walked toward the exit.

"Now," Sneja said, clasping her flute of champagne and taking a long sip. "Tell me what you know about my granddaughter."

Verlaine narrowed his eyes, trying to read Sneja's expression through the thick smoke. It seemed to him that she was a sea creature emerging from the murk of a dark ocean. "I don't know who you mean," he said at last.

"With the thousands of possible ways that I could kill you—the slow and painful death, the quick and bloody death, the playful death—you had better try to understand quickly. Evangeline is the single descendant of a noble and illustrious family, the sole child of my son, Percival."

"You don't have her already?"

Sneja growled something in German and threw Verlaine a look of contempt. "Don't play games with me."

Verlaine tried to understand what Sneja was talking about. Eno had taken Evangeline in Paris. If she hadn't given her over to the Grigoris, what had she done with her?

"You can't be right about her patrimony," Verlaine said, deciding to feign ignorance. "Evangeline doesn't even look like Percival."

Suddenly, Sneja's mood shifted. "You knew my son?"

"I worked for your son," Verlaine said. "I saw him dead in New York. He was broken and pathetic, like a bird with clipped wings."

She placed her champagne glass on the silver platter and, pointing her finger at Verlaine, said, "Remove him."

Moving with the easy grace of a trained agent, Verlaine pulled his gun from his jacket and trained it on Sneja. Before he could bring his finger to the trigger, angelic creatures appeared from all sides, stepping before Sneja, surrounding him. A wing slithered around him, knocking his gun from his hand.

"Tie him up outside," Sneja said. "I'd like to kill him here and now, but I cannot tolerate the mess."

One of the creatures yanked Verlaine's arms and bound them together, pushing him toward the end of the lounge. It kicked open a door and dragged Verlaine out onto a narrow viewing ledge and roped him to the metal banister. His head was pressed flat against the icy railing so that he saw the flash of the tracks flicking by, strips of brown against the white snow. Verlaine struggled against the rope, his warm breath rising into the frigid air. The freezing wind whipped against him, stinging his skin. Looking up, he saw an immense tableau of faint stars holding their light against the morning sky.

Looking beyond, he saw the endless crystalline white of the Siberian plain. The train moved onward, slowly, relentlessly toward the east, where the sun was emerging on the horizon. Verlaine felt ice forming in the crevices of his eyelids and knew, within the hour, he would freeze to death.

Deposition of Katya Badmaiova, St. Petersburg, 1976

I was a girl of ten years old when my father brought Rasputin to our home. I knew who he was—even I had heard the stories about him—but I was startled to find that he wasn't as handsome as I had imagined. I couldn't understand how the tsarina would fall under the spell of a man with such an ugly, gnarled, black beard, ruddy skin, and strange eyes. My first impression of him was as an ugly brute in peasants' clothes. But my impression soon changed. Over the next months, when he visited us frequently, I came to have another opinion of Rasputin. He did not have elegant manners, or even a tendency to flatter, but there was something about his way of being that worked upon me until I was open to his allure. By the third or fourth visit his manner had changed my view of him. I was transformed from judging him the most vile of men to thinking him very subtle, almost charming. I believe this to be the secret of Rasputin's seductive powers: He was an ugly man who had the ability to make people believe him to be beautiful. I, like so many others, was entranced.

Each time Rasputin visited our home—a small apartment near the Anichkov Palace in St. Petersburg—he and my father went to my father's study, and I continued with my piano lesson, my French lesson, my lessons in embroidery, or whatever activity I had before me that day. We were not rich, but we had a number of tutors to keep me occupied while my father worked. Most of the time, I had no more direct exposure to Rasputin than seeing him walk from the entrance of the house to my father's study. After a year or so, he gradually stopped visiting my father, and I began to think of him less and less often. After Rasputin's murder, and the revolution, there was no reason to think of him ever again.

Or so I believed. My father became ill with cancer in the 1950s. During the final days of his life, when the illness had made him insensible to the world, he told a tale that astonished me. He was delirious when he said these things, and I could not know for certain if they were the incoherent words of a dying man or if there was some truth in his bizarre tale, but my mother was at my side, and she confirmed that I had heard the contents of the story correctly. I write it all down as faithfully as I remember it, reserving judgment for those who read it.

My father confessed that Grigory Rasputin came to him in November 1916, asking for his assistance. My father had won favor with the tsar by making him a tea—a simple mixture of cannabis and wolfsbane—which had the desired effect of relaxing Nikolai. And then one day Rasputin told my father that the tsars—as he sometimes called Nikolai and Alexandra—had another request. They wanted my father to mix a medicine. Rasputin claimed that the mixture would help the tsarevitch, Alexei Nikolaevich Romanov, recover from a terrible disorder. My father knew of the child's illness—the boy had nearly died at Christmastime 1911, and he had heard at that time that the child was a hemophiliac. My father responded that a cure for hemophilia was unknown. Rasputin refused to accept this answer. The medicine, Rasputin claimed, required one thousand petals from one thousand different varieties of flowers. Many of the flowers, my father said, did not grow in Russia and would be impossible to find, especially during the war. It was 1916 and freezing cold; there was only snow and ice and suffering.

Rasputin countered this objection, showing him a book filled with flowers. The empress had been collecting the flowers herself over many years—she and the grand duchesses had gone on hunts together in numerous countries in Europe and had preserved the flowers in a diary they shared. My father would only have to confirm that the flowers were correctly labeled and mix them together in the elixir. Rasputin said that the empress herself promised a large sum of money and an elevated position in the tsar's university in Moscow to anyone who could make the drug. Rasputin gave my father the album filled with flowers and left.

One month later Rasputin returned to see if my father had finished. My father had gone through the flowers in the album and confirmed that the one thousand flowers in the formula were the one thousand flowers in the book—everything matched up perfectly. My father had been having doubts about the authenticity of Rasputin's promises, however. He didn't know if he could trust the peasant to give him the sum promised. And so he gave Rasputin the elixir but kept the diary with the flowers as a guarantee.

When Rasputin returned with the money, he was drunk. I remember the evening well, because I was in the sitting room during the visit. I listened as Rasputin bragged to my father about the empress's devotion to him, calling her "Mama," a name he was encouraged to use by the empress herself. Rasputin claimed that he knew all of Mama's secrets, that she kept nothing from him. As proof of her confidence in him, he told my father to visit Pokrovskoye, his native village. There he would find, in the care of Rasputin's wife, a treasure unlike anything the world had seen before, one worth more than anyone in Moscow or St. Petersburg could imagine. Rasputin told my father that he would send a telegraph to his wife, who still lived in Pokrovskoye, telling her to allow my father to examine the treasure himself. The story was so ridiculous, and Rasputin so drunk, that my father took his payment, gave him the flower album, and kicked Rasputin out. Some days later Grigory Rasputin was murdered by Feliks Yusupov and Dmitri Pavlovich at the Moika Palace and his body thrown in the Neva.

My father never went to Pokrovskoye to see the treasure. I believe he forgot all about it—our lives were filled with real concerns during those years. After Rasputin's death, however, a servant from Tsarskoye Selo arrived with a purse of money for my father, a gift of thanks from the tsarina herself, and a warning that he must never speak of what had transpired between them.

After my father's death, in the summer of 1951, my mother and I began to wonder of these strange events. After much consideration, we took a train to Rasputin's native village to see if Rasputin's widow was still alive. It was a long journey from Petrograd to Tyumenskaya Oblast, and it was somewhat silly to make the trip, but we were exceptionally poor and extremely curious, and so decided that we must confirm Rasputin's story, to put our minds at ease.

We found the widow without too much trouble. She lived in the same place she had shared with Rasputin decades before. She was a kind woman, and she invited us into their two-story house, sat us down, and served tea. My mother introduced herself and mentioned my father's name. Mrs. Rasputin ruminated over the name a moment, and then went to a wooden box and removed a telegram: It was Rasputin's communication from thirty-five years before, instructing her to show my father the tsarina's treasure. Rasputin's widow returned with a metal trunk, the Romanov eagle emblazoned on its surface. No doubt the poor woman had no idea what was inside or why she should keep it, only that a man—the doctor named in the telegram—would be coming for it. She seemed eager to be rid of it, telling us that it was just sitting around collecting dust.

We hoped for jewels or gold, something of value we might sell. And from the look of the trunk, with its elaborate buckles and fine leatherwork, it seemed that we would soon be rewarded for our efforts. Instead, we found, after we opened the trunk, another sort of thing altogether. Nestled in a bed of red velvet lay an enormous egg—a gold egg with flecks of scarlet on its shell. I picked it up and felt it in my hands. I must clarify that this was not an object like the famous enameled eggs that one could buy in Fabergé's shop in the days before the Revolution. This was a living egg, large as an ostrich egg, heavy and warm when I took it in my hands. I had never seen anything like it and instantly wanted to give it back, but Mrs. Rasputin insisted that we take it with us. And so we packed the living egg back into the trunk marked with the Romanov insignia and took it home to Petrograd.

Vera turned the paper over, looking for more. "That's it?"

"The account ends there," Valko said, taking the pages and sliding them back into the red book. "After Katya told me about this giant egg, I began to do some searching into the imperial family's past, looking for something that could explain how this egg could have come into existence." A look of frustration crossed his features, as if he were remembering the difficulties of the search. "But the last Russian monarch born of an egg was Peter the Great. His was also a gold egg dappled with scarlet, like the colors of the Romanov crest, but how such a birth had come to pass was never documented. The Romanovs longed for another golden era in their reign, a monarch with superior powers to unite the people behind the dynasty, and what better way to do it than this? But the golden era never came. And so they waited. Nearly three hundred years later, an egg finally arrived. And Katya had it in her possession."

"But you must know what happened after Katya left Siberia," Vera said.

"Katya refused to write down the events that occurred after her encounter with Mrs. Rasputin. It was too dangerous, and she couldn't risk someone reading what she'd written. But she did tell me that she took the Romanov trunk with her to Leningrad, where she kept it hidden in her apartment. If the Soviets had gotten wind of the trunk, they would surely have sent someone around to investigate."

Vera tried to imagine the existence of such a strange and wonderful object, something that Katya had risked everything to hide. "And it was never discovered?"

"No," Valko said. "Katya was careful. But in the spring of 1959, fifty-seven years after it was laid, the egg cracked apart. A child lay in the catastrophe of shells, a golden-skinned boy with eyes that burned red and wings that wrapped around his shoulders. Katya was entranced by the creature, and she kept it, raising it as her own son. She named the angel Lucien."

Vera felt her jaw drop. She stared at Valko, waiting for him to tell her more. Finally she managed to say, "It lived?"

"Oh yes, it lived. Not only did it survive, the creature thrived. He grew over time, moving through the normal stages of development, like any child. Katya tried to treat him as if he were human. Of course, he was never enrolled in a school and had no human contacts other than Katya, but he was taught to read, to write, to speak, to eat, and to dress like a human being. By the time I arrived in Leningrad he had grown to adulthood. I had never seen such a magnificent creature."

"It was a Nephil with antediluvian qualities?" Azov asked.

"Even a quick look at Lucien told me that he was no Nephil. He seemed to me to embody the ancient descriptions of the heavenly host, the passages that one finds in biblical literature, with skin like pounded gold, hair of silk, eyes of fire. I telegraphed Angela, and, after much difficulty, she came to join us in Russia. This was in the 1970s, when Westerners were not exactly welcome behind the Iron Curtain."

"Nor archangels, I imagine," Sveti said.

"True enough," Valko responded. "Which is perhaps the reason Lucien had been permitted to leave the apartment only a few times in his life. I was there with Angela the day she met Lucien. He looked from Angela to me, his eyes wide with curiosity. There was such purity in his gaze, such peace, that I felt that I was in the presence of divinity. I understood in a single moment the metaphor of the chemical wedding: that synergy, that renewal of existence that grows out of a perfect meeting."

"Angela felt this as well?" Vera asked, finding it hard to imagine the savvy Angela Valko falling prey to any mystical mumbo jumbo.

"I believe so," Valko said. "In any case, she convinced Katya to let her take Lucien outside. The creature was delighted by the air, the coldness of the snow, the blue sky, the open spaces. He had never seen the Neva, never touched ice, never heard music played at the theater. Angela showed him the human world, and, in turn, he began to teach her what it meant to be ethereal. I cannot say if Angela had planned to seduce him from the beginning, but from the moment she saw him, there seemed to be no other course for my daughter. They fell in love before my eyes. Soon they were having an affair. And in 1978, after Angela returned to Paris, she gave birth to Lucien's child."

Vera felt almost too stunned to speak. "Luca Cacciatore was Evangeline's father."

"Biologically, Luca had nothing to do with Evangeline's existence. The girl's biological father was, in fact, Lucien."

"Did Luca know this?" Azov asked.

Valko sighed. "It would be impossible for me to say. My daughter closed herself to me after Evangeline's birth."

"Are there records anywhere about this angel?" Vera forced herself to ask. The existence of such a creature mirrored her work so closely—and would prove her theories with such finality—that she was almost afraid to press ahead. "Photographs? Video? Anything that proves his existence?"

"There is no need for photos or videos," Valko said, crossing his arms and meeting Vera's eye. "Lucien is with us."

B runo's thoughts were so filled with Angela Valko's report, the details of her discovery in Godwin's lab, and the repercussions of what she had found that he didn't hear the metal door slide open. By the time he realized what was happening it was too late: The Grigori twins were already inside the carriage, surrounded by an army of Gibborim angels. As Yana pulled her gun, and the explosion of bullets rattled the car, he snapped into action, falling to the floor, groping for his gun, and backing Yana up. She was hitting her targets, but, as they both knew, ordinary ammunition did little to affect or harm the Gibborim. They felt the bullets the way Bruno felt the sting of an insect.

From a purely theoretical point of view, the twins were incredible to watch. Immensely tall, thin, pale as milk, their large eyes staring vacantly into the beyond—these Nephilim were the ideal specimens for study. That they were in duplicate, and that they were of such a rarified pedigree, only made them more desirable. He tried to see them through the masses of Gibborim, but they were so well protected that he wasn't even sure they were in the carriage any longer. A wave of anger washed through him: They should have captured these bastards in St. Petersburg.

Bruno stood and pushed through a line of Gibborim, calling for Yana to watch his back. The Gibborim surrounded him, their claws ripping into his clothes. He felt his arms and back burn, as if he were running naked through a twist of barbed wire. Fighting them put him in a space of pure movement, a place where he lost all thought and simply felt the rush of his fists, the power of his legs, the breath moving in and out of his lungs. A gush of cold air filled the space: The door to Eno's storage cell must have been opened. By the time he'd pushed through the Gibborim, the twins had Eno out of her cell and were making their way through the train, Eno between them.

Yana screamed something in the distance—he couldn't make out her words—and he felt a blow to his head. He hit the ground, closed his eyes, and willed himself to stay conscious. When he opened his eyes, the Gibborim were scattered throughout the room, their bodies black as electrocuted flies. Yana stood over him, her beautiful face filled with concern. "Bruno," she whispered. "Are you okay?"

Bruno took her hand and sat up. Looking more closely, he saw that Yana had decimated the entire population of Gibborim in one fell swoop. Bruno raised an eyebrow, sure that he looked like a smitten schoolboy. "How'd you do that?"

"Gibborish charm," Yana said, smiling as she helped Bruno to stand up. "One of the many tricks up my sleeve."

"Can't wait to see your next one," Bruno said, looking through the door at the empty carriages. The Grigori were long gone. "They've released all of your prisoners."

"Come on," Yana said. "We have to recapture them."

Bruno followed close behind Yana as they ran through the train. The carriages were uniformly quiet, the passengers unaware that anything out of the ordinary was happening. It was remarkable— with the noise and the movement, he would have thought someone would be asking questions, or at least complaining. But the human desire for normalcy outweighed all else.

After searching the length of the train they came to a door marked PRIVATE LOUNGE. Yana typed an access code into an electronic keypad. The door didn't open.

"It's strange," she said, trying a second time. "I don't recognize this car. It must have been attached in Moscow."

Bruno understood Yana's thinking—if the creatures were any-where on the train, it was there. "If we can't get in this way," he said, gesturing to the door. "We'll have to go out."

Yana considered this a moment, and then, turning on her heel, led Bruno back to the sleeping berths. She slid open one of the doors, startling the passengers, a man and a woman sleeping in opposite beds. The man jumped out of bed and began screaming in Russian, gesturing for them to get out and—if Bruno could read the man's intentions—threatening to call the conductor. Yana put her hand on his shoulder and, speaking in a gentle voice, tried to calm him down. Soon the man's wife climbed out of her bed and began speak-ing with great animation. After some time they opened the window to the berth. Yana gestured for Bruno to follow her as she hoisted herself up and climbed out the window. He saw her black leather boots gain footing on the sill. With a push, they were up on the roof of the train.

Bruno nodded to the Russian couple and climbed out into the biting wind. The cold was brutal, unlike anything he'd felt before. He blinked away tears, feeling them stick against his eyelids as they froze and melted. Yana stood at the edge of the train, balancing as if she were on a high wire, the glare of the rising sun setting her hair ablaze.

"What did you tell them?" Bruno asked, as he joined her on the roof. With the metallic grinding of the train and the howling wind, he had to shout to be heard.

"That my uncle got drunk and climbed out of the train," Yana said. "I told them we had no choice but to find him and bring him back inside."

"And they believed you?"

"This is Russia," Yana said, giving him a withering look. "Every-body's got an uncle who gets drunk and climbs out a train window at least once. Usually the police find these guys frozen in a snowdrift somewhere, bottle of vodka in hand."

"Charming," Bruno said.

"There's a reason why the average life expectancy for Russian men is sixty-three," she said, her voice rising over the noise. "Now we want to go there, to that car ahead. We have to be careful—too much noise and we'll have problems with the conductor. Think you can make it?"

Bruno felt his temper flare. Just because he'd had trouble with the Gibborim didn't mean he couldn't keep up with Yana. "Of course," he said. "I'll meet you there."

Pushing through the wind, Bruno made his way over the metal rooftop. A layer of snow capped the car, covering his shoes. His feet were burning hot, and then, after a few minutes, numb. He jumped the gap between the cars easily, but at the end of the third car, he landed hard on a patch of ice, lost his balance, and fell. He saw the landscape tip away from him, slowly, as if he were falling off the edge of a high cliff into a bottomless cloud.

He landed hard on the rooftop, his body pressing into the powdery snow. It was in the thrall of this sensation—a dry chill that froze through his brain—that he heard a meek voice from below. Pushing himself to the edge of the roof, he found Verlaine, tied to the metal bars of a railing, his body laid out on a narrow ledge. Bruno waved Yana over, and together they climbed over the edge of the roof and made their way down to the ledge, where Verlaine lay frightfully still.

Despite his efforts to speak, Verliane looked half dead. His skin was gray, his lips blue, his wire-rimmed glasses ringed with ice. Bruno untied the ropes with Yana's help and, after helping Verlaine stand, slid open a door and pulled him into a train car, where Yana proceeded to rub his hands and arms, trying to bring blood back to his extremities. Bruno ran to the restaurant car, ordered black tea, and carried the pot and cup back to Verlaine. By the time he returned Yana had helped Verlaine to sit against the wall. His shoes were off, and she had his feet between her hands, rubbing the skin. Bruno poured the tea and was relieved to see him drink the entire cup. He filled it a second time and noticed, with a shudder, that Verlaine's hair was encrusted with chunks of ice.

"You were supposed to stay out of trouble," Bruno said.

Sipping the hot tea more slowly, Verlaine said, "I can take you to the Grigori twins."

"Bad idea," Yana said. "They've nearly killed you twice. I wouldn't tempt fate."

Bruno looked at Yana. "If the Grigoris are there, Eno is too."

"Sneja is inside," Verlaine said, looking to Bruno for support. "She's running everything."

"That much was obvious from the way she tried to kill you," Yana said.

"How's that?" Bruno asked, restraining himself from arguing with Yana. She'd just saved his life; he owed it to her to give her the benefit of the doubt. Still, they'd been trying to corner Sneja Grigori for decades. And she was there, on the train, waiting for them to take her.

"Sneja likes her victims frozen to the brink of death before she executes them," Yana said. "The actual slaughter is less messy that way."

"Nice," Verlaine said, his face going paler.

"So now that you've been scorched and frozen by the Grigoris," Yana said, "that leaves only drowning and being buried alive, if you'd like to cover all the elements. Believe me, you've pushed your luck—and mine—enough. Sometimes these transports go awry, and when that happens, it's best to cut our losses. Besides, Bruno has his sights set much higher than a bunch of Nephilim."

Verlaine gave Bruno a questioning look.

"We're going to find Godwin," Bruno said. And although Bruno understood the massive risk he was taking; he knew that he would get this one chance to get inside the panopticon. He leaned against the wall, his gaze falling over the frozen landscape. It would be many hours before they passed the Ural Mountains into Asia, descending toward Chelyabinsk and its famous prison of angels.

Vera watched Azov closely, measuring his every gesture. She knew him well enough to see that he was struggling to contain his emotions. He was mad, and that wasn't something Vera saw often.

"You've known about this," Azov said, his voice little more than a whisper. "And you've said nothing all of these years."

"Ah, but that is because nothing has worked as we expected it would," Valko said.

"What went wrong?" Sveti asked.

"Evangeline was human," Valko said. "Or so her mother believed her to be. Year after year, Angela's hope that her daughter's angelic inheritance would reveal itself diminished. With every extraction of her blood, her mother's disappointment grew."

Vera thought of the film she'd watched in the storage rooms of the Hermitage the previous morning—the vials of blood labeled with various names. She understood now why Alexei's and Lucien's blood had been stored away. "Angela extracted her own daughter's blood?"

"She oversaw its extraction and testing, yes," Valko said.

"She wasn't afraid of putting Evangeline in danger?" Vera asked.

"It sounds as if there wasn't anything about Evangeline's blood to cause alarm," Sveti said.

"Alas, you're right about that," Valko said. "At that time, Evangeline's blood tested human. And Angela, accepting that her child was ordinary, occupied herself with other projects. One in particular became a kind of obsession for my daughter."

"You mean the virus," Vera said.

"Yes," Valko said.

"It was an incredible accomplishment," Vera said.

"I'm not sure that she was pleased by the virus in itself," Valko said. "There was more to her plans than simply the creation of an epidemic. A virus can be cured. Creatures can protect themselves from contamination. Angela understood that the virus she'd engineered wasn't enough. She wanted to utterly destroy the Nephilim race. To do so she needed a stronger, more certain weapon."

"This is why the Nephilim killed her," Azov noted, his voice uncertain, as if it were still a surprise to him that Angela was dead.

"Not exactly," Valko said. "Recall, if you will, Tatiana's egg in the Book of Flowers. I asked you to interpret this aquarelle as a gateway to a higher purpose, something more elevated than a mere recipe book for the medicine of Noah."

"Yes, of course," Sveti said. "Angela's Jacob's Ladder. Although I still don't understand how this interpretation actually led to anything. It doesn't seem to have any obvious significance to me."

Valko said, "Angela acted on a hunch that the drawing was more than just an effort from the grand duchesses' painting classes. She enlisted my help, and, after poking around, I found that Angela was right: The drawing had a much more pointed meaning than anyone could have guessed."

"But what?" Sveti said.

"I think I understand it," Vera said, taking the Book of Flowers from Sveti and turning the pages back to the beginning, where OTMA's dedication of the book to Our Friend was inscribed on the copper plate. "When Nadia gave me this book yesterday she explained that the first Our Friend, a Monsieur Philippe, had prophesied an heir for the tsar in 1902, after which the tsarina experienced her infamous phantom pregnancy."

"I looked into this pregnancy during my search for an explanation for Lucien's birth," Valko said. "I couldn't find a thing about the birth except, of course, that it had been an enormous embarrassment for the tsar and tsarina. They fired their entire staff of doctors, nurses, and midwives afterward. Monsieur Philippe was sent back to France. Depressing, to say the least."

"But what if Alexandra's pregnancy wasn't phantom at all?" Vera asked.

"You mean, what if Alexandra brought a baby to term?" Azov asked.

"No," Vera said, twisting her hair and tying it up in a quick messy ponytail. "What if Alexandra actually gave birth, but there was no child to show for it. What if she delivered the longed-for Romanov egg and then, to keep the truth hidden, dispensed with all possible witnesses?"

Valko considered this a moment and began to smile. "It's entirely possible, I suppose," he said. "But it doesn't explain how or why the egg birth came to happen. Why, after hundreds of years of waiting, did it happen then?"

Vera paused, considering how to best present the theory she had wagered her career on. "I am proposing," she said, with as much authority as she could muster, "that Monsieur Philippe prophesied that Alexandra would become pregnant with a son because he, like John Dee before him, and Rasputin after him, had learned how to communicate with angels."

The others stared at her, unsure of what to make of such a theory.

"That would explain," Sveti said tentatively, "the Enochian language written on every page of the journal. But what does that have to do with Alexandra's phantom pregnancy—egg or no egg, I don't see how there's a connection."

"If Monsieur Philippe was able to summon the Archangel Gabriel, it has everything to do with it," Vera said. "Consider this: The Watchers were not the only angels who consorted with human women. I believe that the Annunciation of Gabriel should more accurately be called the Consummation of Gabriel, that Mary's famous union with Gabriel was neither the first not the last instance of human intercourse with a member of the Heavenly Host."

"You can't be serious," Sveti said.

"She's serious," Azov whispered. "Hear her out."

"For the past years, I have been documenting historical representations of angelology and the virgin birth—and Luke's narration of the annunciation in particular—to discover if there is any truth to theories that Jesus could have been the result of a sexual encounter between the virgin and the Archangel Gabriel. Mind you, this isn't an entirely new idea. The controversy surrounding the annunciation was once a debate that occupied theoretical angelologists for centuries. One camp believed the birth of Jesus to be accurately depicted by Luke: Jesus was the product of the Holy Spirit descending upon Mary, God's son, a scenario that placed Gabriel in the position of messenger, the traditional role of the angels in Scripture. The other camp believed that Mary had been seduced by Gabriel, who had also seduced her cousin Elizabeth before her, and that the children both women conceived—John the Baptist and Jesus—were the first in a lineage of what would have become a race of superior creatures: moral, divine angels whose presence would have been a tonic to the evil of the Nephilim. Of course, neither John the Baptist nor Jesus had children. Their lines died with them."

"So you're suggesting that John the Baptist and Jesus Christ and Lucien Romanov share the same father?" Azov asked.

"I'm suggesting that exactly," Vera said.

"There are people in these parts who would burn us at the stake for making such claims," Sveti said.

"Then I shudder to imagine what they would do upon hearing the next conclusion we must draw," Vera said. "With his archangelic father, Gabriel, and his Nephilistic mother, Alexandra, Lucien is descended from the exalted and the damned."

"A true Manichaean," Sveti said.

"Throw Percival Grigori—Evangeline's other grandfather—into the mix, and you have a truly unholy cocktail," Vera said.

"Enough," Valko said, his voice steely. "You're speaking about my daughter's work, all that she lived and died for. I won't let you trifle with her legacy."

"Evangeline was her work?" Vera asked, incredulous to hear Valko speak of Evangeline so coldly, as if she were little more than a thought experiment.

"The conception of Evangeline was the most brilliant and dangerous risk of Angela's career," Valko said. "Angela knew what she was doing and did it with purpose." He folded his arms over his chest and looked at them, his features hardening. "The child was not some foolhardy whim. My daughter put her own body on the line, as well as her safety, to produce Evangeline."

"But you said before that Angela and Lucien were in love," Azov said.

"That was an unexpected consequence."

"What did she expect to happen?" Vera asked, realizing with horror that Angela was more calculating than she could have ever imagined. "Do you mean to say that she was fully aware of what she was doing? What did she expect Evangeline to become?"

"The ultimate weapon," Valko said. "A weapon that derived from the natural hierarchy of angelic beings. There are the spheres of heavenly creatures—the archangels, seraphim, cherubim—and then there are the spheres of devils, fallen angels, the creatures disowned by heaven, demons. Angela knew these distinctions intimately. She knew the power of an angel must be measured against the power of another angel. She knew that false creation—the genetic modeling of automatons, golems, clones, or any such engineered animate being—would not work, as it went against the divine hierarchy of beings. Angela also knew that in order to defeat a creature of human and angelic origin—a monster of the heavenly order—she must create another, more powerful creature. And so she attempted to engineer a new species of angel, one that was stronger than the Nephilim."

Azov's voice strained as he said, "You make it sound like Angela was some kind of Frankenstein constructing a monster."

"My daughter did something even more bold," Valko said, and Vera could not tell if he was proud of or ashamed by his daughter's work.

"Are you really saying," Azov said, "that Angela created a child to be used a weapon?"

"'Weapon' is perhaps not the ideal way to classify the girl," Valko said. "Examine her name. It contains the seeds of her destiny. She was called Evangeline. Eve Angel. The child was to be the new Eve, an original creature born to reconstruct a new world."

"Semantics aside, it is difficult to believe that Angela used her own child as a kind of genetic experiment," Azov said, his voice filled with doubt.

"In the end, it didn't matter," Valko said. "The experiment failed."

"Because Evangeline turned out to be human?" Vera asked.

"A female human with ruddy, opaque skin, crimson blood, a propensity toward illness, a navel, and a startling resemblance to her human grandmother, Gabriella." Valko looked away and his voice grew quiet as he said, "And so Angela tried again."

"What?" Vera said and, realizing that she was nearly screaming, changed her tone. "I don't understand. A lot of time passed before Angela could know that Evangeline wasn't the creature she wanted to create. How on earth did she try again?"

"Angela went back to St. Petersburg in 1983 and renewed her relationship with the angel who had fathered Evangeline. She never told Lucien of Evangeline's existence, nor did she reveal her reasons for renewing the affair. I don't think Angela had any notion that she was being heartless or even irresponsible. She did it all with the belief that her second child would be a boy and that he would be the warrior angel she had been waiting for. With the birth of her son, her work against the Nephilim would be finished."

"And did she succeed?" Vera asked.

Valko said quietly, "My daughter was pregnant when she was killed. During the autopsy it was discovered that an egg had formed in Angela's womb. The child was a boy. I saw his corpse. His skin was golden and he had the white wings of an archangel. Angela's second child would have been a warrior. He would have brought peace and tranquility to our world. But this savior child died with her."

"What became of the angel?" Vera asked.

"After Angela's death, I knew that I needed to find Lucien," Valko said. "And after searching for many months, I found him imprisoned in Siberia."

"They must have taken him to the panopticon," Vera said. Rumors about the existence of a great Siberian prison were forever circulating among Russian angelologists. It was just the kind of detention center to be found in the wilderness—old-fashioned, aesthetically complex, flawlessly designed, and impenetrable. But no one had ever verified if the panopticon actually existed.

"The very one," Valko said. "The same day Angela was murdered, Lucien was taken into captivity by the Russian hunters and transported by train to Siberia."

"They wanted to study him?" Vera asked.

"Clearly," Valko said. "With such a magnificent creature there would be much to examine and explore. The biological breakdown of an archangel's son could occupy researchers for years."

"But the society was founded to fight the Nephilim," Sveti said. "How could someone get away with the imprisonment of a creature proven to derive from an altogether different, truly divine angelic form?"

"I'm not sure the guards would have known the difference," Valko said. "And besides, that prison conducts its business outside of the confines of our conventions."

As if by a sudden impulse, Valko gestured for them to follow him back outside into the garden, where a table had been set with a breakfast of Valko's antediluvian fruit—orange strawberries and blue apples and green oranges. Vera shivered, feeling the crisp mountain air on her arms as she made her way to the table.

"Sit a moment," Valko said, pulling a chair out for Vera. "We'll have something to eat while we finish our conversation."

Vera sat alongside the others, watching as they chose fruit from a platter. Vera took a strawberry, picked up her knife and fork, and cut it in half. A thick orange juice seeped from the center. Valko opened a thermos and poured coffee into their mugs.

Valko continued where he had left off. "The panopticon prison is funded beyond anything you and I could dream of. As a result, it is extremely well equipped and secure. The scientists there are using captive angelic creatures as experimental subjects. They are taking blood and DNA samples; they are taking biopsies, bone samples, MRI scans; they are even operating on the creatures. They are very powerful and, as they say about absolute power, well . . ." Valko paused to cut a fruit that seemed a cross between a kiwi and a pear, "the aphorism is a perfect expression of the chief technician there— a British scientist named Merlin Godwin."

Vera nearly choked on her coffee. Hearing the name Merlin Godwin now, uttered in this Edenic garden, was so jarring that she could hardly swallow. She glanced at her watch. Almost twenty-four hours had passed since she had seen Angela's interrogation projected on a cellar wall of the Winter Palace. Finally, she found her voice. "Merlin Godwin is a traitor."

"Godwin has been in the Grigoris' pocket since the beginning," Valko conceded.

"Why has he been permitted to continue his work, then?" Azov asked. "Sveti and I are struggling to keep our projects going, and this criminal is set up with unlimited funding and equipment."

"The academy believes that the work he's doing is of benefit to them," Valko said. "Keeping him in Siberia is a form of containment: He is a permanent resident of the panopticon. He has absolutely no contact with the world outside."

"He's a prisoner himself," Vera said.

"As director and chief scientist of the facility, I would hardly call him that," Valko said. "He has ultimate control of the facility. But his power lies only within the walls of the prison. His work with the Grigoris is something he has managed to maintain, apparently, although I have no idea how."

"Or why," Sveti added. "How could they allow him to continue his work? I can't imagine the Grigoris using their own kind as experimental subjects."

"I have my own theories about that," Valko said, winking at Vera. "I suspect that they are attempting to develop a new genetic pool as a way to renew themselves. What they may not realize is that their efforts are hopeless without a creature who can give them the biological blueprint they need."

"Hence Lucien," Azov added.

"I took care of Lucien," Valko said, and Vera could hear the pride of a man who had spent a lifetime outsmarting the creatures. "I got him out of Siberia before they did any real harm to him."

"He's here?" Vera asked.

"All in due time, my dear," Valko said. "You came to me for answers and I will try to provide some." Valko leaned back in his chair, his coffee steaming in his hand. "As you know, the field of angelic genetics was founded by my daughter. What you may not know is that her work was closely monitored by her enemies. They hoped to use genetic engineering to create angels."

"But I thought you said Angela didn't believe cloning could work?" Azov said.

"She didn't think it would be viable," Valko said. "And her reasoning came from the most basic aspects of genetic inheritance— the nature of mitochondrial DNA and nuclear DNA."

"Ah, the pillars of ancestry societies everywhere," Azov said. "We've had a number of religious scholars at St. Ivan asking to exhume the remains of John the Baptist, hoping to run such DNA testing."

"And of course you tell them why that would not be prudent," Valko said.

"I tell them that it's the mitochondrial DNA of the female members of a family that acts as a time capsule: A girl's mitochondrial DNA is a replica of her mother's, grandmother's, great-grandmother's, and so on. So John the Baptist, being a man—a man who may have descended from the Archangel Gabriel, I would now add—wouldn't deliver the goods."

"Angela discovered that the same is true for female Nephilim," Valko said. "There is an exact replica of the maternal line in every female born, creating an enormous possibility to examine ancient DNA structures of female creatures."

"But the Nephilim are descended from angels and women," Vera said. "The mitochondrial DNA would, thus, lead back to humanity, not to angels."

"Correct," Valko said. "That was why Godwin ultimately found Lucien unusable. He was descended from an angel, sure enough, and was very, very pure. But with an angelic father and a very pure Nephilistic mother, Lucien's genes were impossible for Godwin to sequence with the technology available in the 1980s. His mitochondrial DNA was a direct match to Alexandra Romanov's. His nuclear DNA was a hodgepodge of his parents' combined genes—human, Nephil, and an unidentifiable strain that Godwin couldn't pinpoint and therefore deemed worthless to him and his project."

"And Lucien?" Vera asked again. She couldn't help but think of how alluring it would be to be able to see the creature, to touch it, to feel the heat of its skin.

"When I finally found Lucien in 1986, Godwin had him in their prison in Siberia. The terrible conditions didn't seem to affect him—he is a transcendental being, quite literally, and the realities of the material world cannot touch him. Even so, I knew that I needed to get him out of there, and so I convinced Godwin that I had the one thing on earth more precious than Lucien—an ingredient in the elusive medicine of Noah."

"Silphium," Azov said.

"There were two seeds in the cache you gave me in 1985," Valko said. "I gave one of them to Godwin in exchange for Lucien."

"But why?" Azov said, his voice rising. "How could you do something so irresponsible?"

"First of all, if Lucien had remained in Siberia, he would have eventually been used by Godwin—and by extension the Grigoris—in some fashion or another. This is most certain. Second, and more important, I knew that they didn't have a clue about the formula. It was recorded in one place and one place only."

"Rasputin's Book of Flowers," Vera said. "Buried in an old lady's antique shop, right under the Grigoris' noses."

"Until now, evidently," Valko replied, glancing at Vera's satchel, as if verifying that she was bringing it along. "But really, even if Godwin were lucky enough to get the silphium seed to grow, he couldn't use it."

"And so you took Lucien from Russia," Azov said.

"I came here, to these mountains, with Lucien. I hoped to study him, to listen to him, to understand his nature. It is no small thing, having a seraph's descendant at one's disposal—our discipline is the classification of angelic systems. Lucien is derived from the highest order."

"Is he here, in these mountains?" Vera asked, fixing Valko in her gaze, noting the determination with which he spoke about Lucien, the ambition that burned in his eyes. It had been only days since she had revisited the photographs Seraphina Valko had taken of the Watcher. That she might actually see such a creature in the flesh, might touch it and speak to it, was hard to believe.

Valko nodded, an air of pride in his manner. "I gave him a room here, in my cabin, but he was never able to stay there. He would leave to wander through the Rhodopes, spending days and then weeks in the canyons. I would find him at the summit of a mountain, luminescent as a ray of sunshine, singing praises to the heavens, and then I would find him in the caves, in a trance of introspection. And so I took him down into the Devil's Throat, where he has stayed for many years. Perhaps it is the proximity of his fellow angels, but he finds comfort there, close to the Watchers. There is something in his soul that finds peace in this circle of hell."

VIOLENCE

Valko stepped into his hiking boots, bent over, and tied the laces. Spring in the mountains was cold, and they would need heavy jackets and gloves to keep warm. He went into the greenhouse and found a number of Gore-Tex parkas. He went to a metal cabinet, unlocked the doors, and began pulling out tiny lacquered boxes, spoons fashioned of different metals, a mortar and pestle, and a number of glass jars and put them carefully in his backpack. He wrapped a portable gas burner in a cloth and added it to his supplies. Everything necessary had to be brought into the cavern.

As he zipped his jacket, he turned to the others, sizing them up. He distributed the parkas, and gave everyone a cap and a pair of gloves. Both Sveti and Vera were potentially worrisome. Although trim and tanned from her work on the Black Sea, Sveti was a linguist, whose greatest physical exertion was the moving of books from one shelf to another, and—if he was a good judge of character—Vera wasn't much different. Neither of them had the training or the strength for a real expedition.

He tried to remember that he'd been a novice himself once too, and that he needed to be patient with his younger colleagues. His first expeditions were in the Pyrenees Mountains, where he and his first wife, Seraphina, had fallen in love. They continued to find remains of the Nephilim in mountain sites in the years following their marriage. Her work in the Rhodopes had changed everything for them both. The discovery of Valkine, contact with the Watchers, the series of photographs Seraphina had taken of a dead angel, and—their greatest achievement—the recovery of the lyre: Such advances had never been made before, and although nearly seventy

years had passed, he'd never reached such heights again. He had remarried twice, but he'd never forgotten his brilliant Seraphina.
Maybe it was nostalgia for their time together, but he felt closer to
her in the mountains than anywhere else.

They set off toward the peaks above Smolyan, walking within the
thick forest. They would avoid the village roads near Trigrad and
descend to the Devil's Throat from behind. He'd done it many times
over the past years, filling his backpack with a video camera so that
he could record his observations about the site. Only now he didn't
pack his notebooks or his camera. He knew that this was his last
trip into the cave.

The snow had melted in March, and they climbed over a bed of
pine needles and rock, safe under the cover of enormous evergreens.
A patch of sunlight appeared overhead, sliding between the barren
branches of a linden tree and casting a golden gleam over the forest
floor. He glanced over his shoulder as they ascended, noting the
smoke rising from the chimney of his stone house—the smoke grew
fainter and fainter, until it dissolved away completely.

The sun had climbed into the sky by the time they reached the
Devil's Throat. The rocky surface of the mountain seemed silver in
the brightness. Valko led the way up the steep rise of the mountain
and through a dense patch of forest. Beyond the overgrown bramble
stood the large, dark cave. Once, many years before, this had been a
much revered entrance to the Devil's Throat. Thracians had created
shrines here; myths and legends grew around the site. The local people believed that Orpheus descended to the underworld from the
cave and that devils lived in the labryinthian structures deep below
it. Anyone who entered would be cursed, lost to life aboveground,
forever mired in darkness.

Approaching the entrance, Valko remembered the first time he
had seen it. It had seemed to him to be just a hole gaping in the side

of the mountain like so many other caves he'd seen in his travels, but of course it had been so much more. He would never forget the smile of triumph on Seraphina's face when she returned to Paris after the Second Angelic Expedition. She had found the opening to the underworld, and she had brought back its most precious treasure. Of course, everything had changed since her death. He'd stayed in Paris, remarried, raised a daughter, divorced, buried a daughter. Only then, after Angela's death, when the last of his connections to Paris was gone, had he made the trek to the Devil's Throat Cavern himself. For twenty-five years Valko had climbed the sheer rock face, the sound of the waterfall crashing in his ears, and spied on the Watchers, waiting for the day when he would return. For years his life had been in that secluded valley. He'd disguised himself so well that nobody knew who he was or what he was doing. He'd married a Bulgarian woman, spoke Bulgarian like a native, mixed with local men in the village bars, and done everything he could to fit in. If the Nephilim had discovered his identity, he would be dead. But they hadn't.

Leaning against the entrance of the cavern, he looked past his young comrades and through the tangle of birch trees beyond, letting his mind drift to the hours ahead. He threw a rope ladder over the ledge. Vera stepped to it, grabbed the first rung, and lowered herself down. The descent would be painstaking and dangerous. The familiar sound of water bounced through the gorge, echoing, filling the space with a deafening noise, and he wondered why Vera and Azov hadn't asked for more specific information about the layout of the Devil's Throat, why they had trusted him about Lucien, why they didn't verify his story. It used to be that agents trusted no one.

Valko knew the mythology behind the cavern, but he also knew the cave as a geological formation. He knew the depth and the general perimeters as precisely as the contour lines on a topographical map; he recognized the sound of water that came from the river and the water that came from the waterfall. Quickly he went, letting gravity take him downward. He counted each step, positioning his feet carefully, delicately on the ladder rungs, adding them up. He looked over his shoulder, straining to see in the swirling, infinite darkness. He knew that the noise would grow louder and louder as he descended. As the shaft deepened, the darkness would become thick. He could see no farther than the whites of his knuckles wrapped upon the ladder's rungs, and yet he knew that soon he would reach the bottom.

A s Vera followed Valko through the darkness, she saw a skeletal figure stretched out on the rock, its pale arms crossed upon its chest. Seraphina Valko's photographs of the dead Watcher had taken Vera's breath away when she'd first seen them a year earlier in Paris, and now here was the actual angel, in the flesh, its skin giving the illusion of life, its golden hair curling in tendrils to its shoulders. As they stood over its body, taking in its unearthly beauty, Vera felt a sense that she was following a path created long before her birth.

"It looks alive," Vera said, lifting the white metallic gown and rubbing the fabric between her fingers.

"I wouldn't touch it," Valko said. "The bodies of angels weren't meant to be touched. The level of radioactivity may still be very high."

Azov bent over the body. "But I thought that they couldn't die."

"Immortality is a gift that can be taken as easily as it is bequeathed," Valko said. "Clematis believed that the Lord struck the angel down as vengeance. It may be that angels live the way humans do—in the shadow of their Creator, wholly dependent upon the whims of divinity."

Valko, who had clearly seen the dead Watcher many times before, headed off into the cavern. Vera followed the trembling glow of his flashlight into the cold, wet space. He stopped before a declivity in the wall that, upon closer inspection, was a chiseled corridor that opened into a large room. In the depths of the space, removed from the roar of water, there was light and movement, the soft scraping of a pen on paper. A figure stood and walked toward them, his thin body barely discernible.

"Lucien?" Valko said, in little more than a whisper.

"What is it?" a soft voice said.

"Lucien, there are some people I'd like you to meet," Valko said. "Do you mind if we come in?"

The angel hesitated, and then, as if realizing that he couldn't refuse, stepped aside and let them pass into his chamber.

A candle burned on a table in the corner, throwing a flickering weak light over loose pages and an inkwell. The cave had little in it—a bookshelf packed with books, a tattered carpet, a small table and a matching wooden chair—and Vera had the feeling that she was walking into the spare, severe, cloistered space of a hermit. Vera knew that angels could exist without the comforts of the material world, their bodies made of fire and air. Lucien had an aura of tranquility, of a being that existed outside of time. Vera felt fear and awe and reverence at once. She wanted to fall on her knees and behold the angel's beauty.

Slowly Lucien opened his wings and, in what seemed to be a gesture of protection, as if he were too fragile to be seen by human eyes, folded them over his body. Vera tried to see the creature clearly, but his skin had the fluid consistency of candlelight. Even as her eyes moved over him, he seemed to melt away, his arms dissipating into his wings, his wings disappearing in the darkness. Vera was sure that if she placed her hand on his shoulder, her fingers would simply pass through.

She stole a glance at Azov and Sveti. It was clear that neither of them had ever seen such a magnificent creature before, either. For all their research and all their training, they were out of their element.

Lucien said, "Have you brought me more ink?"

"Of course," Valko said, pulling a jar from his pocket and placing it on the wooden table. "You have enough paper?"

"For the moment, yes," Lucien said.

Valko turned to Azov. "He is part seraph, and so it is his nature to sing praises to the Lord. He learned musical notation with Katya and has been writing his psalms down ever since."

"You haven't come here to hear my songs," Lucien said, fixing Vera, Sveti, and Azov with his gaze.

"Not today," Valko said. "I've come because I need the alembic." Vera could see a complicity between them, as if they were embarking upon a plan they had conceived long ago.

Lucien went to his bed and pulled a beat-up suitcase from underneath. Opening the buckles, he lifted the top and removed a wooden case. A Fabergé egg was inside, a golden egg set with diamonds and rubies, and with a large cabochon diamond on top. Lucien presented it to Valko, who, looking it over, nodded in approval. Vera watched as he inserted a fingernail under the cabochon and pressed the egg open. A mechanism popped and the top sprung, revealing a number of gold toiletry utensils. He removed these items and lifted the interior lining from its casement. The vessel was smooth and transparent rock crystal.

"It's the Nécessaire Egg," Vera said, almost to herself. "The real one, the one that Tatiana must have copied in her aquarelle."

"Well done," Valko said, taking two of the toiletry utensils and holding them up for her to see. They were long, thin pipes dusted with brilliants. He fitted them into tiny holes in the egg and the crystal vessel, screwing them in place.

"It appears to be little more than a worthless bauble. But, in fact, the egg acts as an alembic, the vessel in which an alchemical formula must be mixed. The quartz lining of the egg is the perfect material for the creation of the elixir. The golden pipes move the liquid from the first vessel to the second, like a still. And the golden egg seals the potion inside, protecting it. My daughter gave the alembic to Lucien. He has kept it with him. He hid it before he was imprisoned and, after I had him released, we retrieved it."

Vera looked at the alembic, her eyes drawn to its absurd brilliance. She could only imagine the foresight, the meticulous planning, that Angela Valko had undergone in leaving the egg with Lucien. She must have had everything planned—from finding the ingredients to assembling it to ensuring that Lucien remained close by. It struck Vera that this very egg had been touched by the empress herself. It had been the center of all M. Philippe's—and Rasputin's after him—schemes.

Vera touched the crystal vessel, running her finger over its smooth surface. "It is hard to believe that this led to so much searching."

"You have no idea," Valko said under his breath. "The progression from Noah to this cave is almost too incredible to contemplate. You have the original formula, passed down in secret through generations of magicians, alchemists, scientists, and mystics, all of whose efforts were thwarted because they lacked essential ingredients."

"Silphium," Azov said.

"And Valkine," Sveti added.

"Yes, of course," Valko said. "But, most important of all, an angelic creature like Lucien, one born of an egg, one descended from an archangel. The presence of such a creature is absolutely essential. With Lucien here, everything will come together."

"You believe it's really possible?" Azov said, and Vera could see the curiosity in his manner, the pure desire of a scientist at work.

"That we will soon know for sure," Valko said. "First we need fire." He withdrew his small portable gas stove from his backpack and, taking matches from the pocket of his parka, lit it. The hissing blue fire rose and fell to a soft steady flame.

"And now I need the formula," he said. Vera took Rasputin's book from her satchel and gave it to Valko. He removed the flowers from behind the protective layer of wax paper and dropped them into the vessel. The process took only a matter of minutes. Soon the flowers had been blended together into a resinous white liquid.

Valko picked up the tube and swirled it gently, until it began to bubble and melt, forming a sticky soup at the bottom. Soon a brown mixture, thick as caramel, clung to the rock crystal, solidifying and melting against the curvature of the vessel. Inserting a long copper rod, and turning it through the concoction, he said, "It is nearly time to melt the Valkine and the silphium."

Valko removed a glass tube from his pocket. Vera saw what looked like the stamens of flowers, each no bigger than the leg of a fly, collected at the bottom.

"This tiny amount of silphium is all I have been able to harvest, even after years of growing it," Valko said. "I can only hope that it will be enough." After uncorking the tube, he scattered the silphium stamens into the mixture. "I must add them slowly," Valko said, without looking up. "A few bits of resin at a time."

With the first drops, the thick brown concoction hissed and began to thin. With the next addition, the color transformed into the golden amber of the resin itself, a rich yellow that matched the Fabergé eggs in brilliance. Valko dropped in the remaining stems of resin, watching them disappear into the brew. Vera wondered—as she stepped away from the table—at those who had spent their lives in endless experimentation, hunting for ingredients that did not exist, working out fruitless recipes, following circular metaphors, and, in the end, wasting their lives in pursuit of an unattainable dream. She couldn't help but wonder if they were just following the same hopeless path.

"Vera, my dear," Valko said. "I will need your help." His eyes seemed to catch fire. "The pendant."

Vera went behind Valko and unfastened the necklace. The metal retained the warmth of his skin.

"It will dissolve?" Sveti asked.

"Valkine is extremely soft and should melt with ease," Valko said, stirring the mixture. Vera slid the pendant off the necklace and dropped it into the alembic.

"Now the blood," Valko said.

"Blood?" Vera said, surprised by this addition. She glanced from Azov to Valko, trying to understand. "You never said anything about blood."

"Why do you think we need Lucien?" Valko said. "Angelic blood—a certain kind of angelic blood—is necessary to complete the mixture. Blood from an egg-born angel is quite different from the blood of humans, or even of Nephilim."

"Which explains why Godwin wants Evangeline," Vera said.

"Not exactly," Valko said thoughtfully. "They are interested in Evangeline's blood, that is for certain, although she is simply a rare mixture, not an egg-born child, nor the product of angelophany. In any case, they cannot possibly create what we are about to create here." Looking to Lucien, Valko gestured for him to come to the table. The creature stepped closer, casting a column of light over the alembic. Valko took nail scissors from the Nécessaire kit and sliced Lucien's finger. The drops of blood fell into the mixture.

"Assist me," Valko said, giving Vera a plastic vial he'd taken from his backpack. She held it between her fingers, her hands steady as he transferred drops of the thick potion into the vial. Vera secured the top with a cork and held it up to the light. The alembic, which only moments before had been coated in a sticky resin, was perfectly clear, its crystalline curves as transparent as glass.

Azov looked closely at the vial. "There isn't very much."

"It is extremely concentrated," Valko said, taking it from Vera's fingers. He wrapped it in a cloth, placed it inside the egg, and snapped it closed. "A few drops released into the water supply of any major city would be enough to affect the entire Nephilistic population."

"If you do that," Vera said, "what will happen to Lucien?"

Valko sighed. It was evident that he had considered the question many times, and that facing the scrutiny of his fellow angelologists made him uneasy and defensive. "I believe that it will affect only the most base qualities of angelic creatures," he said at last. "But I can't be certain. It is a sacrifice Lucien must be willing to make. There is, indeed, much suffering ahead. We must strike hard against angelic creatures, with all the weapons at our disposal. Noah's medicine is one part of our attack. The Watchers—who are at the root of the entire history of evil—must be dealt with now as well."

"You can't be serious," Azov said, his anger rising as he stepped close to Valko, looking him directly in the eye. "You know the potential consequences of releasing the Watchers. They could fight the Nephilim, yes, but they could also turn on humanity. You will put all of us in danger."

Valko folded his hands on the table and closed his eyes. For a moment Vera believed he was saying a prayer, as if he were asking for divine guidance in what he was about to do. Finally he opened his eyes and said, "This was the case with our forefathers, the noble men who came here for the First Angelic Expedition, and it is our work still. Danger is something we accept in our work, Hristo. Death is something we accept. We cannot go back now." Valko slid the vessel into his pocket. "The time has come for us to move, Lucien. Let's go."

The black water of the twisting river rushed by, sweeping into the darkness beyond as they climbed into a wobbling rowboat. Sitting in the prow next to Sveti, Vera saw a waterfall at the head of the river, the thick mist rising before the endless hollow of cave. She understood why legend designated the river as Styx, the river of the dead: As they glided across the water she felt a heaviness descend, a dark emptiness so complete it was as though her life had been stolen away. The living could not enter the land of the dead.

With Valko and Azov's help, she and Sveti rowed toward the opposite shore, the boat rising and falling with the current. Lucien stood on the other side, waiting. He had gone ahead to open the door to the Watchers' prison. In the absolute darkness of the cavern, his body seemed even brighter than it had in his room. His white wings sparkled with a strange brilliance, as if each feather had been inlaid with crystals. Vera watched him carefully, realizing that she'd never measured herself—her body, her mind, her strength, her speed—against any angelic creature before. All of her limitations, all of her human weaknesses, became clear by comparison.

The opposite bank of the river seemed empty at first, but upon closer inspection, Vera made out a cadre of glowing beings arriving upon the shore, arraying themselves in a great fan behind Lucien, their skin throwing off a tempered, diaphanous light. There were between fifty and one hundred angels, each one as lovely as the next. Their wings seemed to be made of gold leaf, and rings of light floated over their masses of blond curls. But even in their pure angelic splendor, the Watchers were no match for Lucien.

Stunned by the spectacle, Vera was torn between horror that she'd gotten herself into this situation and a desperate desire to examine the angels. It became apparent that a small number of the Watchers acted as leaders to the others. They walked among their brothers, directing them to stand in rows, organizing their legions as if preparing for battle. After they had been arrayed in perfect regiments, fanning along the riverside in bands of light, the leaders stood at Lucien's side like royal guards.

With a clattering of wings, the angels rose to attention, their bodies blazing in brilliant bands of fire against the darkness. They were coming to the water, closing in on the boat, moving forward at a steady pace. Vera's awe and terror swelled as the creatures approached. As the angels moved closer, the fire burnished the surface of the river, gilding the black with gold.

In a flurry of wind and wings that seemed to come out of nowhere, Lucien rose into the air, landing between the angelologists and the Watchers. He was their superior in every way. The Watchers stopped before the archangel's son and, in a sweeping movement, knelt before him.

"Brothers," Lucien said, "in heaven, I am of a superior caste. But here, in the wilderness of exile, we are equals."

The Watchers stood, light undulating over the craggy walls of the gorge. Vera detected curiosity and fear and hesitation in the angels' silence.

Lucien continued. "Your story is famous in heaven and on earth. God imprisoned you. You have waited for him to grant you reprieve, to bring you back to him. And now you are free. Come with me to the surface. We will celebrate together. We will sing praises to heaven together. We will fight and kill the enemy together."

An angel stepped forward from the band of Watchers. He wore a silver robe, and his wings—majestic white wings that matched Lucien's—were wrapped about his shoulders. "Brother, we are preparing for battle."

"There is no fight between us," Lucien said.

"Not with you, but with them," the Watcher said, gesturing to Vera and Sveti. "They are the cause of our fall from favor."

"No," Lucien said. "The war is between the Nephilim and human beings. We, pure creatures, made of light at the beginning of time, do not notice the childish battles between them."

Another Watcher stepped forward. "But the Nephilim are our children."

"They are the result of your great sin against heaven," Lucien said. "Accepting them is denying your guilt."

"He's correct," another Watcher said. "We must throw them back, deny the Nephilim, redeem ourselves."

"Come, now," Lucien said, stepping toward the band of fallen angels. "We are made of the same airy material, there is no stain of human reason in you. Join me. Together we will rehabilitate you. Soon you will shine in the image of the highest angels. The creatures of the sun will meet the creatures of the shadows. Beings of the ether will fight side by side with beings of the pit. Angels, prepare! The war is soon upon us."

Suddenly, a blinding light filled the cavern. Vera felt a wave of heat fall over her, glutinous and sticky, as if she'd fallen into boiled tar. She heard Azov cry out in pain, and then the sickening, beating movement of wings. Valko was out of the boat and wading toward the shore when a second blast of searing heat seized her, this one more intensely painful than the first, as if her skin had been peeled away in one clean sweep. Crouching to the ground, she tried to escape the pain ripping through her body. Once she'd felt tremendous fear about dying. She had tried to imagine how she would fight if she came up against one of the creatures. She had believed that she would find courage, that she would lose herself in the battle, but she felt nothing of the sort now. There was only the simple truth of her life and her death, the base reality of translating herself from one state of being into another.

The moment Vera woke it seemed to her that she had died and emerged on the other side of existence, as if Charon had in fact taken her across the deathly river Styx to the banks of hell. Emerging more fully from sleep, a seizure of pain overwhelmed her. Her body felt stiff and hot, as if she had been dipped in wax. A glowing flashlight hovered above her. She felt someone's touch against her arm, a soft yet insistent pressure on her body, and she knew two things: first, she was not dead yet, and second, the angels had escaped.

Vera tried to sit up. The boat rocked in the still water. A wave of nausea overtook her, and she threw up over the gunwale.

"Wait a sec," Azov said, putting an arm about her. "Take it slow."

She knew that something terrible had happened. She glanced past Azov and saw Dr. Raphael Valko, curled upon the rock floor, burned beyond recognition. Azov walked to the body and gingerly—as if afraid to disturb a sleeping child—took the vessel filled with Noah's medicine from Valko's hands and slid it into his pocket.

"Dead," Azov said, his voice little more than a whisper. "He got the full force of the light."

"Where is Sveti?" Vera asked, glancing through the boat and beyond, into the frightfully still cavern.

For the first time in her life, she saw Azov at a loss for words. He simply gestured out over the water, his hand signifying the dark, silent recesses of the Devil's Throat. His eyes brimmed with tears. Vera wanted to say something but couldn't find her voice. She hoped her silence would be understood as a kind of vigil.

Azov cleared his throat. "Right now we have to concentrate on getting out of here. You're hurt. You need medical attention."

Azov touched her arm, and she flinched. Her body was filled with a sharp, searing pain. Slowly, and with great care, Azov helped her stand. As she leaned against him, she knew that her face was burned.

"You're in bad shape, Vera," Azov said. "I don't know how I'm going to get you over the river without causing you more pain."

A band of white light fell over the rocks. Vera's terror at the sight of it overtook her, and she vomited again as Lucien landed. Lucien looked her over and, lifting her slowly, held her in his arms and flew over the river. She held on to his neck, nestling into the downy warmth of his wings as they made their way back to the rope ladder. The ladder twisted up into the darkness, disappearing into a fold in the rock.

"Hold on to me tightly," Lucien said, positioning Vera's hands around his shoulders and wrapping her arm about his waist. "I'll bring you up."

"No," Vera said. "Bring Azov here first."

Lucien considered this a moment before setting Vera down and flying back for Azov.

Vera collapsed against the wall of the cavern, her ears ringing with the sharp, rapid-fire noise of the waterfall. Without the light from Lucien's body, the cave fell into a fathomless darkness. She strained to discern the space. She tried to stand, but her legs gave out from under her. She fell to the ground, feeling as if she might lose consciousness. She closed her eyes for what seemed less than a moment. When she opened them, a faint glow emanated from the distance. Lucien was coming back; she needed to prepare herself for the searing pain of movement. Easing herself up, she watched the light come closer. She saw a glow of white wings, the shimmer of a silver robe, and she knew that it wasn't Lucien at all but one of the Watchers. It stood before her, looking her over with curiosity.

"You are human?" the angel asked at last.

Vera nodded, all the while staring at the angel. There was something soft in his features, something divine, and for the first time she truly understood how unfair it had been that such beautiful beings had been punished so severely. Vera wanted to understand how an act of love—because the Watchers had, after all, disobeyed God out of love—had brought so much treachery to the world. The angel had spent thousands of years in this underworld of stone and water. He had lost paradise and now he had lost his companions.

The angel introduced himself as Semyaza and placed his hand on Vera's shoulder. A gentle burst of warmth moved through her muscles, easing the pain, as if she'd been given a shot of morphine. The relief was so profound that Vera felt as if she had the strength to stand.

"The others are up there," Vera said, pointing up the rope ladder to the ledge high above. "Don't you want to join your brothers?"

"I've decided to remain here," Semyaza said.

"But why?" Vera didn't understand. They were offering the angel its freedom, and it had chosen to stay in the cave in solitude and darkness.

"In the presence of other beings like yourself, one can endure great suffering. For thousands of years I've been a creature of hell. I don't know if I can adjust to the light." Semyaza smiled. "Besides, the earth belongs to humanity. There is no place for me there. I am a prisoner not of this cave but to eternal life as a fallen angel. I would like, for just one minute, to understand what it is like to be human. My memories of falling in love are so vibrant. There is nothing in my experience like it. To feel warm blood in my veins, to hold another body close, to eat, to fear death. For that, I would return to earth."

The Eighth Circle

FRAUD

I

D r. Merlin Godwin pressed his thumb against the screen, and the thick, iron doors opened. He made his way into a dark concrete tube, neon bulbs lighting his path. Each morning he entered the tunnel via the south entrance, walking the thirteen hundred feet leading from the exterior to the interior chamber, his briefcase in one hand and a cup of coffee in the other. It was a dark and solitary commute. And while it lasted less than ten minutes, walking through the corridor gave him a few moments of total peace and isolation, allowing him to leave the normal world, where people lived without the slightest knowledge of the truth, and enter a place that seemed to him, even after twenty-five years, a place of nightmares.

In truth, he was only traveling one hundred thirty feet below the ground to a space carved into the soft rock below the Siberian permafrost. It was something of a miracle that the facility even existed. Although the society had a long and well-documented history of observing and studying live specimens—their first contact with an angel had been in the twelfth century, when the Venerable Clematis had breached the Watchers' prison—the angel storage facility in western Siberia was the largest angelic incarceration project in the history of angelology. It contained holding cells, examination rooms, laboratories, a complete medical center, and solitary confinement chambers for angelic life-forms and, when necessary, human beings who obstructed their work. There were facilities for intake procedures and facilities for disposing of dead creatures. There was a crematorium. As the scientist in charge of this massive operation, every possible technological advantage for the containment of the enemy was at his disposal.

The prison had been in various stages of planning since the 1950s, when the Russian Angelological Society had begun searching for a site that could accommodate the masses of creatures they had taken into custody. After two decades of fruitless attempts the society made a deal with the Kremlin to occupy the space directly below Russia's largest nuclear facility in Chelyabinsk. The agreement was controversial among the angelologists—especially Western angelologists, who objected to any alignment with the Russian government, which had blocked their efforts in Eastern Europe—but, after negotiations, a deal was struck: Below the frozen fields, molded out of the concrete foundation of the plutonium nuclear reactor, there would exist an immense secret observatory and prison facility.

While similar observatories existed elsewhere—Godwin had personally visited a structure in the American state of Indiana and another in China—there was nothing that could compare with the magnitude of the Siberian panopticon. The storage capacity of the facility was enormous, with thousands of cells below the earth. The prison could hold up to twenty thousand angelic beings, from the lower angelic life-forms to the highest. At present, it was filled to capacity.

Access to the panopticon could be gained only with security clearance, and only via specialized tunnels. Godwin always traversed the south tunnel, but passageways opened through each quadrant, each one equidistant from the central cavity, where the glass-and-steel holding cells stretched in a seemingly endless curve, each one lit by a neon light, and each—when the prison was full—containing an angelic being. The prison had three levels. The ground floor held the lowest angelic life-forms. The next ring of cells contained the more dangerous breeds—Raiphim, Gibborim, Emim. Level I held the Nephilim, and it required the highest level of security. The three levels formed an elegant and intricate ovoid structure that, when one first encountered it, seemed like a glass honeycomb, each cell crawling with an angry wasp.

In the very center of the rings of cells, separated from the creatures by a vast expanse of blue-lit space, stood an observatory tower, a large glass capsule that rose from a concrete floor like a spaceship. The observatory tower was constructed entirely of tinted panels, and it remained darkened, so that the glowing holding cells seemed like rings of fire around a dark center. Inside the capsule, scientists worked night and day, monitoring the creatures.

It was an ingenious structure, modeled on a classic panopticon prison of the variety developed by Jeremy Bentham in the nineteenth century. A team of engineers had adapted this original concept, re-inventing it to suit the particular purposes of angelology. The original intention of a panopticon had been to enforce a psychological control over the prisoners. A central tower was equipped with blinds so that the prisoners could not be sure when they were being observed by prison guards. When the blinds were closed, the prisoners behaved as if they were being watched. Angelologists hoped to employ the same principle. An observer standing inside the tower had the power to watch each and every cell. When they changed the opacity of the Plexiglas, the angels could no longer see the scientists standing behind it. The creatures did not know when they were being watched and when they were not. The effect was the illusion of continual surveillance. The angels were severely punished for any infraction of the rules and in time became obedient and docile.

The angels had nowhere to hide. The cells were ten feet by ten feet, cold, and gray, as if the harsh Siberian climate had been translated into the interior realms of the compound. There were no blankets, beds, or toilets, nothing more than what was absolutely necessary to sustain the creatures. Some of the imprisoned angels had been held in these conditions for decades, and would continue to live out their lives under the observation of angelologists. These creatures were listless and resigned. Recently captured creatures, the hope of release still burning in their eyes, stood whenever Godwin came into view. The gesture was so pointless, so pathetic, that Godwin had to stifle an urge to laugh.

As he walked toward the tower he passed through a wash of grainy blue that fell over the concrete floor, over the metallic steps leading up to the rings of cells, over the thick glass of the cells themselves, giving the space the texture of an aquarium filled with exotic fish. Whenever the creatures stood at the glass, pressing their incandescent hands against it, it seemed to Godwin as if thousands of white starfish floated in a murky sea. At so many feet below the earth, there was no natural sunlight, and so the creatures were suspended in a perpetual bath of neon. The absence of the rhythms of night and day proved useful—the captured angels existed in a zone of timelessness, floating in a state of suspension, where—Dr. Godwin imagined—a creature must mark the passing time by the slow, shallow beating of its inhuman heart.

For the most part, his prisoners were unusable creatures, undesirables picked out and captured by the Russian angelologists. Many were Nephilim affected by the virus that Angela Valko had introduced into the angel population decades earlier; others had strong human characteristics, physical and behavioral, that set them apart from the Nephilim ideal; others had betrayed their clans by marrying a human being.

The irony of his position wasn't lost on him. Godwin was working for the enemy, plain and simple. There were Russian agents who had sold out to the Nephilim—he wasn't unique by any stretch of the imagination—but the extent of his betrayal was unprecedented. He blamed the baser elements of human nature, of course. He was greedy, vain, and power hungry. He had helped to create an angelic containment program far superior to anything the angelologists could have made alone, and he offered its use to the enemy. When he was feeling self-analytical, he wondered if he weren't rebelling against his parents, dedicated British angelologists who had insisted that he follow their calling. Once he had tried to please them. He had been an earnest young angelologist whose work was used as a weapon against the Nephilim. He had assisted Angela Valko in exploring the genetic codes of the creatures so that angelologists could destroy them. And now, years later, he'd built upon this research to assist the Grigori family, performing the experiments that Angela had only fantasized about. If he succeeded in creating the population density they required, he would be the most powerful human being in the new world.

Even after all these years, he marveled at the irony of his apprenticeship to Angela Valko. She had been the society's most devoted soldier when it came to overcoming the Nephilim. And she had nearly succeeded in doing so. Developing an avian flu designed to attack their wings was the act of a thoughtful scientist; releasing it into the angelic population through the Grigori family was the act of a genius. Percival Grigori spread the virus to all the major Nephilim families, ensuring that many of the elite died. For decades Godwin admired and cursed Angela for it. The virus eluded every cure he had attempted to develop. Even now he'd only found a way to halt its progress, to alleviate the symptoms, and to contain it.

After his recruitment, when the Russians brought Godwin to Siberia to survey the site, he'd stood at the edge of a vast field, an eternity of ice stretching before him, and he understood the incredible potential of the prison that existed below his feet. But the true, secret goal of his work was far more exacting, and momentous, than to re-create the strength of the original Nephilim—to elevate their race, as Arthur Grigori had liked to say, with the qualities of the angels that they had lost over the millennia. For several years he had been riding on the promise of his first and only triumph: The twins were an impressive feat of breeding, genetic manipulation, and luck. The successful cloning—twice over—of the late Percival Grigori—using frozen cells harvested from Percival during his lifetime—had bought him carte blanche with the Grigori money. Godwin had been left in peace, working without interference.

Godwin looked up, taking in the full height of the observation tower, an edifice bound by impenetrable panes of glass. Inside, along the spiraling floors, were angelologists on duty, some busy at computers, others at observation posts, watching, making notes, updating inmate files. The night shift would go home and the day shift would arrive, a routine that ensured the perpetual motion machine of the panopticon.

Godwin always felt an odd, phantasmagoric sensation when he traversed the moat of concrete surrounding the observation tower. Thousands of eyes trailed his movements, and he couldn't help but feel the unnerving power of their gaze. Sometimes it seemed to him that their positions were reversed, and that he had become a prisoner, a spectacle paraded out for the pleasure of the Nephilim. Each day he had to remind himself that he was the master, and they, these beautiful beasts whose bodies were stronger than his own, were his prisoners.

II

Under normal circumstances, Yana wouldn't go to the entrance to the panopticon for any amount of money. It had been more than two decades since she had last set foot at the nuclear waste facility known as Chelyabinsk-40, and yet the structure still had the power to fill her with dread. While her family had always been angelologists, tracing their first efforts to the time of Catherine the Great, she had an uncle who had been imprisoned in the panopticon as a spy in the 1950s. Stripped of his rights, he was thrown into an isolated holding cell. He worked both in the reactor and at cleaning up the nuclear waste that leaked from the facility. The lakes and forests were saturated with radioactivity, although the citizens of nearby villages were never informed. Yana's uncle had wasted away with cancer and been buried at the site. Now most of the trees around the facility were dead, leaving a wasteland of ashy soil behind. The Russian government had only recently admitted to the nuclear contamination—for decades it had denied that the reactor existed at all—and newly posted signs warned of radioactivity. Yana wasn't prone to doomsday scenarios, but she had the feeling that if the world were going to end, then the disaster would emerge from that desolate, godforsaken place in Chelyabinsk.

She halted abruptly before a fence ringed with barbed wire. Making her way into a corrugated steel outbuilding—a rusted-out shack that served as an entrance to the east tunnel—she pulled out her wallet and fingered her Russian Angelological Society identity card. At least she could identify herself, which was more than she could say for the others, whose French identity cards would mean nothing to these security goons. Getting them in would be difficult. For that she was going to need to call in a favor or two.

A pair of burly, stupid-looking guards—Russian military flunkies hired by the society in Moscow—greeted them.

"I have an appointment with Dmitri Melachev," Yana said, imperiously, daring them to turn her away.

A guard with bloodshot eyes and the smell of vodka on his breath looked her over, sneered, and said, "You're a bit old for Dmitri, honey."

Another guard said, "His girls always come in the West entrance."

"Tell him Yana Demidova is here."

Yana crossed her arms and waited for the guard to place a call to Dmitri's office. He relayed her name to another functionary at the other end of the line and then waved them toward some plastic chairs near an elevator. "Wait there. He's sending someone up for you."

Yana closed her eyes and took a deep breath, praying that Dmitri would give her a break. Before she'd been assigned to angel hunting in Siberia, she and Dmitri had been childhood sweethearts in Moscow. They had been deeply in love in the way that only teenagers can be—madly, blindly—and had been engaged until Yana broke things off. Yana had helped Dmitri get his first job as a bodyguard to one of the high-level angelologists. His career took off from there. Now he was the chief of security in the panopticon, a man with clout over everyone and everything barring their path, and if she had to put herself on the line a little to get them inside, then so be it. Besides, Dmitri owed her.

After fifteen minutes of waiting, the elevator doors parted and Dmitri himself emerged. Yana hadn't seen him for twenty years, but he hadn't changed much. He was short and muscular, with sharp blue eyes and streaks of gray in his hair. She could see that she had surprised him.

"Bring us to your office, Dmitri, and I'll explain everything,"

Yana said, meeting his eye, hoping that he was still her friend after so many years.

Dmitri nodded and the security guards went to work. They searched the angelologists' bags and clothes, examined their weapons, and then allowed them to go into the lift. Dmitri pushed 31, and the elevator began to descend, moving slowly deeper and deeper into the earth. Yana couldn't say if it were her imagination, but she felt as if the pressure of the earth were pushing into her, as if she had to struggle to breathe.

Finally the doors parted, and they stepped into the east tunnel. Cool air blew through the shaft, sending a shiver of freezing air over her. She'd forgotten about the descriptions she had heard of the prison—it was cold, bereft of light, as if one would wither in its sterile darkness. They would walk for a few minutes through a narrow tunnel, the neon lights playing above, and emerge at the other end. It was a short walk, and yet Yana felt as though they were making a journey to another universe. She had always found it eerie that people aboveground knew nothing about the space. It could cave in, killing thousands of living beings, and nobody would know the difference.

When they reached the core of the panopticon, the immensity of the space pulled her eye up, and then, just as her vision adjusted to the scale and grandiosity of the structure, closed in on the rows and rows of creatures locked in their glass-and-metal cells, each angel back-lit by harsh neon.

Yana glanced at Bruno and then Verlaine, wondering what they would think of the state of their underground prison. Unlike other facilities she'd visited, where the ambiance was sleek and clean, orderly and antiseptic as a hospital, the panopticon was a dungeon of the classic medieval variety. The floors were concrete and stained with blood. Dim lights shone overhead, creating pools of murky light. There was, somewhere in the mass of cells, a lab where countless men and women labored over biological samples of angelic creatures.

Every living being could be opened, studied, and classified. There was a pretension toward research and scientific progress, of course, but in the end they were there to exploit the prisoners for their own benefit. Every creature, Yana knew from her own experience, belonged to its captor.

"The security offices are this way," Dmitri said, walking toward an alcove off the panopticon.

Yana slowed her pace to match Verlaine's and, speaking quietly, so that the others wouldn't hear her, said, "If your Evangeline is here, she's in one of these cells."

Verlaine gave her a grateful look. She squeezed his arm and gestured for him to come closer before she pulled a wad of material from under her sweater and pushed it into his hands. He looked at it, puzzled, and then smiled: It was the drunk security guard's jacket. She'd lifted it off his chair as they passed through the elevator doors with Dmitri.

III

This is one of the only spots in the facility without security cameras," Dmitri said, bringing them into an office and locking the door. "It's safe to talk here."

Verlaine paced the room. "There isn't much to talk about," he said. "We just need to know where Godwin is holding Evangeline."

Bruno didn't know if he should admire Verlaine's obsessive pursuit or if he should tell him to back off and let Dmitri guide them. It was Verlaine's nature to push harder the closer he came to his target: He always wanted to go in shooting, no matter what risk was involved. It was an admirable quality when they were on familiar terrain, with plenty of backup and weapons at their disposal. Being a million miles underneath a Siberian nuclear wasteland, in a security office loaded with plasma screens displaying hundreds of Russian angelologists and thousands of creatures in their cell pods—that was another story. Yana had assured them that Dmitri would be safe, but he couldn't help but be wary of a man who had spent most of his career in the frozen tundra.

Bruno searched the video monitors for Godwin, but all he could make out were various office spaces filled with people in lab coats. "You ever get Godwin on one of these things?"

"I have been monitoring Merlin Godwin for fifteen years," Dmitri said, waving a hand dismissively at the plasma screens. "Believe me, it would be a pleasure to nail him. But I can tell you that Godwin and his crew would never be stupid enough to let me see anything too important." Dmitri leaned against his desk and crossed his arms across his chest. "My surveillance only goes so far."

Bruno tried to imagine Dmitri spying on Godwin—eavesdropping on phone calls, monitoring his electronic correspondence. He was beginning to understand how frustrating it might be. "Let's hear what you've got on Godwin first."

"I should start by making one thing clear," Dmitri said. "I'm not easily impressed by criminal behavior. Russia is full of thieves. But most of them want money and power and prestige. Not Godwin. He's after another thing entirely."

"Such as?" Verlaine asked.

Dmitri said, "Godwin has been working with the Grigori family to remove weak Nephilim from the general population, testing them for certain genetic qualities, and then disposing of or incarcerating them if they fail to yield the desired results."

"Sounds like the bastard has been doing us a favor," Yana said.

"He might have been helpful if he'd just continued on his genocidal path," Dmitri said. "Unfortunately, his ultimate goal seems to be to repopulate the world with creatures superior to the Grigori—a master race of angels, if you will. For this he needs a superior angelic specimen."

"We have reason to believe he acquired a creature he has been pursuing for a very long time," Bruno said.

Dmitri glanced at Verlaine. "This is the Evangeline you mentioned?"

"The very one," he replied, his manner measured. He turned back to the bank of plasma screens. "Could she be here?"

"On paper there isn't anyone in the panopticon that I don't know about," Dmitri said. "All prisoners are checked by security before intake."

"And in reality?" Yana asked.

"In reality, Godwin can do what he wants," Dmitri admitted. "He has ways of getting around the regulations. He could have Evangeline here and I wouldn't have a clue."

"The question, then," Verlaine said, scrutinizing the screens, "is where."

"What about the nuclear plant?" Yana asked.

"Security at the plant is extreme," Dmitri said.

"Godwin could get around it," Yana said. "He could access the panopticon via the nuclear reactor itself."

"That would be a suicide mission in the extreme, even for a psychopath like Godwin, but not beyond the realm of possibility." Dmitri stepped to a screen and, releasing a catch, pushed the screen up, revealing a vast interior garage stacked with long white bricks of plastic explosives, blue and red wires twisting around them. "This belonged to Godwin."

"PVV5A," Yana said, astonished.

"I intercepted a shipment in January," Dmitri said.

"You've got enough of this stuff to bring down the whole prison," Bruno said.

"Considering the fact that we're below a nuclear reactor, that's what we don't want to happen," Dmitri said, taking one of the white bricks and placing it on his desk. "Godwin, on the other hand, has planted this stuff in every nook and cranny of the prison. After I intercepted the PVV5A, I knew he was up to something, and so I used dogs to find the rest of the explosives. What you see here is a collection of what was found in the panopticon itself. I can't guarantee he hasn't rigged his private research center or the nuclear reactor, and I can't promise he hasn't planted other kinds of devices."

Bruno was surprised to see sweat dripping down Dmitri's face. His voice cracked as he spoke. "So he likes to play with fireworks," he said. "But to what end?"

"Godwin knows that explosions in the cells would trigger the panopticon's security system," Dmitri said. "A series of mechanisms are in place that, once activated, cause a large-scale self-detonation.

The structure will continue to destroy itself over the course of several hours, tunnel by tunnel, level by level, until the entire prison is incinerated."

"Melt down to what extent?" Yana asked.

"To the extent that everyone and everything—including the caged angels, the laboratories, and all the data collected in the past four decades—will be destroyed. It's a protective mechanism," Dmitri said, "like torching fields and villages to deprive the enemy of food. The tower will go first. Then the labs. When the various pieces of the facility have been destroyed, a gas will be released into the panopticon, and every living thing—human being or monster—left inside will be poisoned. The system was meant to cover all traces of our presence here. The panopticon was built underground for this very reason: If they need to destroy it, the ruins will be hidden below the earth, a tomb containing thousands of dead angels."

"Makes sense to have a safety measure in place," Bruno said. "But why would Godwin want to trigger it?"

"That I don't know," Dmitri said, quietly. "I can only guess that he has no intention of leaving his work unfinished. If he's under threat, he'll bring the whole thing down."

"Then we have to get to Evangeline before Godwin has a chance to self-destruct," Verlaine said.

"There are hundreds, if not thousands, of guards patrolling this compound," Dmitri said, reaching into the recesses of the crawl-space and pulling out three canisters of gas, face masks, two semi-automatic weapons with ammo, two stun guns, and three bulletproof vests. "Godwin's movements are like clockwork. He got here this morning, entered through the south tunnel, and went to his lab. He'll leave for an hour at lunch. I estimate that you'll have half an hour to get in, look around, get the angel, if you find her, and get back out. All of this depends, of course, on your ability to get to his lab without being detected. I can take care of the security cameras in the panopticon itself, but that's as far as I go. You can leave Russia when this is over. I have to continue my career here."

As Bruno slid into a bulletproof vest, he couldn't help but wonder if what they were doing was worth the risk. Gabriella would have wanted him to go after Evangeline at any cost—he knew this in his heart, but he also knew that more was at stake than recovering a half-human half-angel traitor who may or may not turn against them. Yet Evangeline had touched him. He could almost see her as a little girl running through the courtyard outside the academy, a wild and happy child. It was impossible for him to imagine then that, one day, he might not be able to save her.

IV

Verlaine had waited long enough; he couldn't listen to any more talking. Bruno had his method—he would gather information, divide the hunt, and move out with a deliberate plan of attack—but Verlaine couldn't follow him now. Evangeline was here, somewhere, and there was nothing on earth that would keep him from finding her. Tagging along behind Bruno wasn't going to happen. His time for simply taking orders was over. He was going after Evangeline alone.

He slipped on the security guard's jacket, left Dmitri's office, and began walking the pathway alongside the cells, searching for Evangeline. The lower levels were filled to capacity with ragged, emaciated creatures. Never had he been so close to so many varieties of angelic beings. It was as though he had stepped into a museum packed with specimens.

Verlaine stopped and gripped the metal railing as he looked over the vast prison, the observation tower rising at the center. Suddenly the screens shifted and slats of light sliced across the walls of the panopticon. Verlaine saw the enormous sweep of the space, the chambers stretching away in a path of diminishing visibility. He turned once more to the honeycomb of cells, each one filled with an angel, many with unfurled wings. The cells were deep but narrow, leaving no room for full expansion of the wings, and, as a result, the creatures had pressed their wings against the glass until they curled with pressure, so that the details of feathers were imprinted upon the panes. Angelologists sat behind the glass of the observatory tower studying the creatures' movements, their manner clinical. Suddenly the panels turned opaque, obscuring the observers behind a shield of smoky glass. It gave Verlaine the creeps to think that they were there, be-hind the glass, watching him. He didn't want to be part of their ex-periment.

Heading up a set of metal steps, he climbed to the top level. If they had Evangeline in custody, she would probably be there, among the Nephilim. The lights were dim, enhancing the effect of the neon bulbs in the creatures' cells. As he walked along the cells, he glanced inside. The prisoners were large, powerful Nephilim who scowled and hissed as he went by, thrashing their wings, spitting, and cursing at him. One of the creatures scratched at the glass, leaving streaks of blue blood behind. The conditions were horrendous and must have ensured that a steady number of the creatures died each year, perhaps making way for new ones. Over the years he'd lost all ability to feel empathy for the Nephilim, and yet, when he looked at the tortured state of the prisoners, he wondered if the Russian angelologists weren't being too harsh in their methods.

The sound of footsteps broke his thoughts. Looking into the re-flective glass of the window, he saw that a security guard was walking in his direction. He glanced over his shoulder and saw another guard, on the opposite side of the panopticon, staring at him. He turned up the collar of his jacket and walked away, realizing that the curve of the complex offered no escape. It was clear that if they caught him, he wasn't going to be able to fool anyone with his disguise. He didn't speak Russian, his face didn't match the security badge pinned to his pocket, and he was wearing street shoes and jeans. He was an angel-ologist, and could prove his identity, but they would still take him into custody for questioning until someone in Paris came to the res-cue. If these guards stopped him, it was all over.

The guard behind Verlaine called something to him in Russian. Verlaine walked faster, scanning the cells, as if the glass doors might magically open and reveal an escape route. The guard began to run— Verlaine heard the heavy clomping of shoes on the cement—and the second guard, taking his cue, came at Verlaine from the other direction. Looking ahead and behind, he saw that there was nowhere to go but over the railing. In a burst of movement, he leaped over the bar, holding tight as he swung onto the second level. He landed hard next to a cell packed with Mara angels.

He ran, pushing himself faster, his heart racing as he passed the cells, each one filled with a creature in various states of unrest. Verlaine increased his pace, the soles of his shoes hitting the concrete in a hard rhythm. Finally he came to a metal door at the far end of Level 2. Hearing the sound of more and more guards shouting behind him, he tried the knob.

The door was locked. Swearing under his breath, he rattled the lock, pushing against it, as if his weight might force the mechanism to spring open. The voices of guards ricocheted through the panopticon. Bruno and the others would be wondering what in the hell had happened.

Verlaine grabbed his gun and shot the lock. The report made a tremendous amount of noise, and the guards would now be able to follow the sound to his location, but there was a chance that he could escape through the door, and that was all he needed. He kicked it in and looked inside, unsure of what to expect. It looked like an empty closet, just big enough to hide in. Whatever it was, he didn't have any choice but to take cover. He stepped into the space, slammed the door closed behind him, and flicked on a light.

The closet opened into a number of metal airshafts, huge aluminum tubes that distributed air to distant parts of the prison. Hearing the guards in the distance, Verlaine pulled away the grating of the nearest one and crawled inside. Distributing his weight, he inched forward. If he moved too fast, the thin metal would begin to buckle under him. After thirty feet or so, a metal grating opened up below, and he could see that he was traversing the very top of the structure, crawling high above the concrete floor. His stomach lurched. He felt as if he'd found himself on a wire high above the world, looking down into a fathomless canyon. As he glanced down into the depths, he couldn't help but imagine falling to the concrete below. In his mind, he plummeted into the space, gravity taking hold as he fell past the caged angels.

He swallowed and crawled ahead, listening to the guards shouting below. Metal gratings appeared at regular intervals, and he was able to glimpse what was happening in the panopticon. He saw the gray concrete of the pillars, the metal walls, the central tower, each part of the structure coming to him in fractured pieces that he reassembled in his mind. He saw the chaos of security guards running past the cells; he saw the caged creatures behind the glass. For ten minutes he moved onward, following the curve of the air pipe until the shaft abruptly tipped, and he found himself pulled downward. Catching himself as best he could, he struggled against gravity until, unable to resist, he let go.

Verlaine landed heavily at the bottom of the shaft, breaking through a metal grating and tumbling onto the hard concrete floor. For a moment he lay stunned, struggling to breathe, trying to discern if he'd broken any bones. In the past forty-eight hours he'd been beaten and burned and frozen. His muscles hurt, and he was bruised and broken. It was a miracle that he was still alive and, in reaction to the absurdity of his situation, he began to laugh. He drummed the opening beats to the Rolling Stones' "Sympathy for the Devil" with his fingers on the concrete. He wiggled his toes, feeling his muscles flex, and had the strangest feeling of joy as his body reacted to his will. One of these days his luck would run out. But for now, he'd made it.

He pulled himself up and began examining his new surroundings. It was clear that he'd fallen into an entirely different quadrant from the rest of the prison. At first glance it seemed that he'd landed in some kind of exterior hallway, perhaps an access route around the facility. There were doors on either side of the hallway. He tried one, found it locked, and continued walking until he heard voices coming through a wall. Checking over his shoulder to be certain he was alone, Verlaine pressed his ear close, straining to understand the muffled words.

"I've done my part," a female voice said. "You can't expect me to wait."

Verlaine recognized the voice as belonging to the Emim angel he'd chased through St. Petersburg. Verlaine felt his entire being concentrate to a single point of attention. If Eno was there, Evangeline must be close by.

"And you cannot expect that I can work on her in her present condition," a man replied. Verlaine assumed it to be Godwin. "The blood is still filled with sedatives." Godwin's voice softened. "Look, we've waited a long time for this. We can wait a few more hours."

Verlaine heard footsteps as Godwin walked closer to the wall.

"In the meantime, I'll tell you how the procedure will work. It's a bit of a departure."

Verlaine heard Eno grunt her approval, and Godwin's voice grew still louder. He had walked closer to the wall.

"This machine," Godwin said, "will extract the angel's blood and filter it. We are interested in the blue cells, as you know, and this machine over here will separate the blue from the red and white blood cells. Evangeline is interesting to us, just as her father was interesting to the Romanovs one hundred years ago, because of the rare quality of her blood. Hers is red blood, not blue blood, but it contains an abundance of blue blood cells, which, if one were to get technical, contain stem cells of an extremely adaptable and creative variety, far superior in their generative power to human stem cells. The precision of this equipment gives us great advantage over blood used in the past. Rasputin, for example, used blood that had been withdrawn from an angel, but he could not filter it. It was an inseparable conglomeration of white, red, and blue cells. He must have fed it to the tsarevitch whole, which would have made the child desperately sick before he began to improve. Not us. We will use just the cells we need. And with these cells, we will continue the project I began with your masters. Soon we will see the results of our labors."

"This should be ten times more fun than what you did for my masters," Eno said. "If you can pull it off."

"No creator since God has been as successful in fashioning a living being as I have been," Godwin said.

"That may be true," Eno said. "But can you do it again or are you going to disappoint my masters?"

"The panopticon cannot possibly disappoint," Godwin said.

"Don't be so sure," Eno said. "The Grigori capacity for disappointment is very high. They have me here to make sure you don't fuck this up."

Suddenly the door flew open, and he stood face-to-face with a man with a deathly white face topped by a shock of carrot-orange hair. Verlaine stepped back in surprise and grabbed for his gun, but Godwin took hold of his jacket and pulled him violently into the room. Eno glared at him, her eyes narrowed, her whole manner that of a predator. Verlaine couldn't believe he'd been so stupid. Godwin had sensed that he was behind the door, waited until the optimal moment, and jumped him. Before he could fight back, Godwin pushed him into a restraining cage and slammed the door closed.

In his ten years as an angel hunter, Verlaine had been exposed to almost everything he could imagine. He had seen every variety of creature, he understood the physical conditions in which the angels lived, and he accepted the level of violence necessary to bring the Nephilim in. But in all his time in the service of angelology, he had never witnessed anything quite like the scene before him. It took him a few seconds to fully process what he was seeing.

At the center of the room, strapped to two examining tables near Godwin and Eno, were the Grigori twins. Verlaine couldn't tell if they were alive or dead: They'd been stripped and laid out like corpses. Their golden wings were wrapped around their bodies, covering them from chest to ankle in scintillating plumage. Their skin was bluish gray, the color of ash. *Surely they must be dead*, Verlaine thought, but then he saw one of them blink his eyes, and he knew that they were somehow part of Eno and Godwin's experiment.

Verlaine heard a voice behind him.

"I knew you'd come," Evangeline said.

Verlaine turned and found her sitting cross-legged in the far corner of the cage, her wings folded over her and her body subsumed by shadow.

"I felt you standing outside the door. I wanted to warn you, but Godwin got to you first."

"I can't believe it's you," Verlaine said at last, lacking the words to describe his relief and joy at finding her.

"Hard to believe, I know," she said, smiling slightly.

As Evangeline spoke to him, Verlaine felt as if the order of the universe were changing shape. Somehow when he was near her, he understood everything perfectly. He knew why he had thought of her so often; he understood why he'd followed her halfway around the world. Verlaine's heart was beating too hard, sweat falling from his forehead and dripping down his neck. This woman had changed everything. He couldn't go forward without her.

"We have to get out of here," he whispered, sliding his hand over her hand and squeezing it. He looked from one end of the laboratory to the other, trying to find a way out. Their prospects didn't look good. He pushed against the wall. The Plexiglas was impenetrable.

"We're going to have to perform some serious Houdini to get out of this."

It was only a matter of minutes before Verlaine heard a commotion at the door—Bruno and Yana had broken into the lab. Verlaine strained to see what was happening, but his view was blocked as Godwin unfurled a white sheet and threw it over the Grigori twins, as if to protect them. Bruno went after Godwin as Yana snatched a set of keys and ran to the cage. As she unlocked it, Verlaine grabbed Evangeline and pulled her free, leaving the others to fight.

They were in the hallway when a great explosion shook the air. Within seconds, smoke and ash billowed from the lab. An alarm began to sound; it rang through the panopticon, echoing and distorting. The toxic smell of burning plastic, mixed with the syrupy sweet scent of scorched flesh, created a noxious and sickening aroma. Verlaine tried to navigate his way through the smoke, desperate to find a way out. As a second series of explosions went off in the distance—the blasts stronger, more pronounced than the first—Verlaine knew that they were in danger.

Suddenly, he made out Godwin ahead, running into the fire. He tried to follow, but felt Evangeline resist.

"We're going in the wrong direction," she said, pulling him back.

"How do you know?"

"I can't feel the presence of angelic creatures any longer," she said. "I don't know why, but it's as if I'm wired to sense them. There are definitely no Nephilim this way. The panopticon must be in the other direction."

They turned around and ran in the opposite direction. Soon the floor began to shake, as if something nearby were being detonated. As the sound of explosions grew louder, he realized that they were approaching the very center of the destruction. The hallway opened into the panopticon and, as they sped past the wide arc of the Level I cells, Verlaine found nothing but deserted chambers, many of them encrusted in dried plasma, its golden hue charred to gray. Verlaine could see creatures across the panopticon, running toward the tunnels, trying to escape. The prisoners were disoriented and stunned, assessing their surroundings with wariness, as if they suspected that they had fallen prey to a cruel test. At the tower, a group of Raiphim formed a mob. They screamed and struck at the tower with whatever was at hand—metal folding chairs and rods broken from the cots in their cells. A pair of Gibborim leaped from the railing and swooped down over the scattering humans below, snatching them up, lifting them into the air, and dropping them to the ground. Men and women lay bloody on the concrete floor of the moat, some screaming in agony, others unconscious or dead.

Pushing through the smoke, he and Evangeline found a metal staircase that brought them down past the second- and third-level cells. The smoke grew thicker as they descended; the chaos Verlaine had witnessed from above grew harder to navigate as he moved into it. Evangeline's hand was small and cold in his. He held it tight, as if she might disappear into the smoke.

Together they hurried toward the tunnel exit, stepping over creatures that had collapsed, their bodies trampled and broken. Verlaine could feel Evangeline hesitate. Men in uniforms lay in pools of blood on the concrete floor, some with their guns still in hand. The guards had been slaughtered while fighting to keep the creatures from escaping. The great iron security door began to roll closed.

"They are trying to contain the angels," Evangeline said.

Verlaine held his hand over his mouth and nose, but it was impossible to breathe without taking in the thick chemical fumes. Another explosion sent shards of glass through the air. Within an instant, the panopticon plunged into darkness.

"There go the lights," Verlaine said. Although he had no way of knowing for sure, he had a terrible feeling that the nuclear reactors were connected to the panopticon's power source.

Evangeline's hand slipped from his grasp. He stumbled forward, trying to reach her. "Evangeline," he called, but the noise had become deafening as thousands of creatures stampeded past.

"I'm here, above you," she said, and he saw, floating in the darkness, a concentration of brilliant light.

Verlaine blinked, coaxing his eyes to look at her hovering like a hummingbird overhead. The dome of the panopticon filled with a strange, warm light. It seemed to him as if the sun had been captured and concentrated into a single point. Evangeline could not possibly be a Nephil, nor a descendant of a lower order of angel, nor any of the common creatures serving the Nephilim. She was not one of the Anakim, Mara, Golobians, or Gibborim. It was such a simple truth that he was astonished he hadn't understood it before: No angelologist could possibly gauge how far the Nephilim had fallen from grace until beholding the beauty of a pure angel.

"We need to find an exit tunnel that hasn't been blocked," Verlaine called up to her. "If the nuclear reactor is affected, this is going to be a death trap. If we don't find an open tunnel, we'll die here."

"Maybe there's another way out," Evangeline said.

Verlaine looked up, trying to imagine her perspective. She was at the top of the structure. "Can you see something from up there?" he shouted.

Evangeline swooped close and Verlaine grabbed hold of her without giving it a moment's thought. She flew fast and reckless through the panopticon, rising up and falling back, as if she were afloat on a stormy sea. Verlaine clung to her, overwhelmed by the pure adrenaline of losing contact with the ground. The thrill of their ascent made him giddy. He wanted to hold Evangeline closer, to move as her body moved, to fly higher and higher with her. He was sure that all of the thoughts and all of the desires that he'd ever felt had collected in his heart at that moment. It didn't matter what happened, as long as he was with Evangeline.

Another explosion ruptured through the panopticon, sending a cascade of fire in their path. Evangeline dipped and rose, and Verlaine felt breathless as he lost hold of Evangeline's body. He fell, reaching for something solid to grasp, his hands flailing in the air. Before he had a chance to call her name, Evangeline appeared, her green eyes sharp, her body as bright as the sun as she swooped underneath and caught him. He never wanted to let her go.

He looked at her in wonder. There was a profound serenity in her features and—despite the fact that she was much stronger than him and had just saved his life—a gentleness he admired.

"Thank you," he whispered into her ear. "I owe you one."

"I wouldn't let you fall," she said. "Ever."

They flew to the ground and he stepped away from her, examining her among the ruins of the panopticon. In the smoke, with her wings retracted, she looked almost human.

"Can you see?" he asked, gesturing toward a tunnel. "Can we get out that way?"

Evangeline nodded. "It's open," she said. "It's probably the only one, though."

Verlaine grasped her ice-cold hand and pulled her toward the tunnel. Thick, toxic smoke obscured his vision. "We have to go now, before it closes."

Ahead, at the end of a passage, grew a golden light. As he approached, the light grew stronger until, in a burst of brilliance, it consumed the darkness entirely. Verlaine stood in a blaze of illumination. The walls of the panopticon—polished titanium with bolts the size of his head—gave off a wavering reflection. The light seemed to twist through the air, creating a cone so distinctly overpowering he could not make out what was before him. He removed his eyeglasses and the source came into sharp focus. Verlaine found a creature of such marvelous beauty he was certain it had come directly from heaven. He fell to the ground, covering his eyes with his arm, blinking against the light, falling into a painful blindness.

By the time Verlaine recovered his sight, the angel stood with Evangeline. Despite his huge white wings, there was something simple, something almost childlike about him.

He could see Evangeline staring at the archangel, her eyes narrowed, her body tense. "What are you?" she asked at last.

"You know very well what I am," the angel said, opening his enormous white wings. "And I can sense what you are, too. Nevertheless, I'll stand on convention and tell you my name. I am Lucien. And although it is merely an exercise, and I know who and what you are, I will ask you to identify yourself."

Evangeline circled the angel, sidestepping to the left and right. Then, in an elegant flourish, she snapped open her wings, displaying them in the glow of Lucien's body. The purple and silver feathers seemed electric in comparison to Lucien's white wings. Verlaine felt his heart beating in his chest as he realized that Evangeline's beauty, her luminosity and grandeur, were on par with the creature before her. Together, they were the most pure and rare angels he had ever seen.

"You are lovely," Lucien said, smiling slightly. "And unusual, too." He stepped forward and bowed to Evangeline. "I have waited many years to see you again."

Evangeline stared at Lucien a beat too long, and Verlaine knew that something had passed between the two angels, something that he could never understand completely.

"We've met before?"

"Once, when you were just a baby, I held you in my arms. Your mother brought you to me."

"You knew my mother?" Evangeline asked.

"You were so fragile when I held you, so small, so human that I could only bear to keep you in my arms a moment. I was afraid I would hurt you. I could never have imagined what you would become."

"But why?" Evangeline asked. "Why did my mother bring me to you?"

"I've been waiting for this moment for many years," Lucien said.

Verlaine stepped forward. "Evangeline," he said, holding out his hand. "We have to get out of here."

"I am here to tell you everything," Lucien said. "But in your heart you know already that I am your father."

Evangeline stood in silence for many minutes. Then she looked from Lucien to Verlaine and, before Verlaine could prepare himself, she kissed him, pressing her body against his with passion and tenderness.

"Go," she said, pushing him gently away. "Get out of here. You have to get aboveground before it's too late."

The Ninth Circle

TREACHERY

s Verlaine opened his eyes, he understood that he was lying in a snowy field. He couldn't say how long he had slept. The snow around him was stained with blood; he realized that it was his own. His leg was injured; the wound to his head had opened yet again. As he examined the cut to his leg, he remembered crawling out of the panopticon, fire rising around him, the noise of explosions ringing in his ears. Looking back toward the prison, he saw that the only landmark remaining was a plume of smoke rising in the far distance. The whole compound had collapsed.

A sound grew in his ears, a buzzing as grating and persistent as an insect. It was a truck approaching through the snow. As it got closer, Verlaine could make out Dmitri at the wheel of a Lada Niva. Yana jumped out of the backseat, leaving Bruno—whom Verlaine could see was badly injured—hunched against the door. A man Verlaine didn't recognize followed behind Yana and Dmitri. He greeted Verlaine and offered his hand, introducing himself as Azov and explaining that he'd come at Vera's request.

"What happened in there?" Verlaine asked Dmitri, brushing the snow from his clothes.

"Exactly what Godwin hoped would happen," Dmitri said. His face was streaked black, his clothes singed.

"Is he inside?" Verlaine asked.

"There's no way to know for sure," Dmitri said.

Verlaine felt his heart sink. Godwin could be inside, or he could have escaped. He could be anywhere.

"What about the nuclear plant?" Verlaine asked.

"It's supposed to be able to resist this kind of rupture," Dmitri said, glancing over his shoulder at the rising smoke. "But I don't think we should stay and take our chances. We have to get as far from here as we can. Now."

"We can't leave," Verlaine said. "Not yet."

"If we stay," Dmitri said, pointing to the far side of the field, "we face that."

The escaped prisoners—every variety of angel—filled the landscape. Verlaine scanned the chaos of movement, searching for Evangeline, spotting her everywhere and nowhere at once until, in the center of it all, he found her. She walked hand in hand with Lucien at the edge of the panopticon. Verlaine saw, as they walked closer, the image of the father in his child. The delicate shape of her face, the large eyes, the luminosity that surrounded her—it was obvious that Evangeline and Lucien were made of the same ethereal substance.

"Evangeline has to come with us," Verlaine said, feeling more helpless by the second.

"I don't know if Lucien will allow that," Azov said, looking circumspect. "We traveled together for thousands of miles. I know his strength, but also, more important, I know that he is a gentle and kind creature, one whose motives are good. Evangeline, if I can believe what I've heard about her, would never fight against him, or allow you to harm him. If you want to bring Evangeline with you, there is only one certain way."

Azov removed a vessel from his pocket and showed it to Verlaine. He remembered Vera's confidence that Azov could help her understand Rasputin's journal. Somehow they had succeeded in making the formula.

Verlaine reached for the vessel, but Azov stopped him. Instead he started toward the angels himself, calling their names, his voice filled with a desperate hope that Verlaine understood: He felt the same violent need to call Evangeline back, to convince her to leave Lucien behind. To Verlaine's surprise, Azov caught Evangeline's attention—she walked across the snowy field, approaching them, Lucien at her side.

"Who are you?" she asked. "And what do you want with us?"

Lucien glanced at the vessel in Azov's hand. Whatever Azov was doing, Lucien understood it immediately. "Don't go closer," he said, opening his wings and wrapping them in a protective gesture around Evangeline's shoulders.

Azov took a plastic vessel from his pocket and held it out to her. "This is for you," he said. "It will bring you—and the other creatures like you—back."

"Back to what?" Evangeline asked.

"You have a choice," Azov replied.

"You don't have to be one of them anymore," Verlaine said, stepping closer to Evangeline.

"If I'm not one of them," she said, her gaze falling upon Verlaine, "what will I be?"

"Human," Verlaine said. "You'll be like us."

Without taking her eyes from Verlaine, she said, "I'm not sure I know how to be like you anymore."

"I can teach you," Verlaine said. "I'll help you return to what you were. If you let me."

Evangeline extricated herself from Lucien's wings and, her feet crunching in the snow, walked to Azov and took the medicine of Noah. Verlaine could almost see her thoughts as they crossed her mind—her expression changed from consternation to curiosity to determination. She brushed the cork of the vessel with her fingernail and tilted the vessel back and forth, sending the liquid from one end of the tube to the other. Then, with a quick, decisive gesture, Evangeline slid the potion into her pocket. Turning away, she ran to join Lucien.

Verlaine started after her, but Dmitri and Azov wrestled him back, pulling him across the field, toward the Neva.

"Come on," Yana yelled from the driver's seat. "We have to go now."

As he struggled, using all his strength to reach Evangeline, he could see that the dense black smoke rising from the reactor had grown thicker. A noise filled the air. It began as a vibration, a clattering as sharp as the hum of a cicada. The daylight faded to a thin light, pale and pink, as a series of flashes rocked the earth. Within seconds, the air filled with ash. Then the exodus began. From the depths of the smoke, a swarm of wings swirled up from the crater, rising, creating a mass of creatures so thick that the sky fell dark. In the shadow of the escaped angels, the reactor burned.

Bruno clung to the door. Yana drove fast and erratic, the tires sliding as she sped through the tundra. Each bump was torture. Glancing out the window, Bruno could see that the world had begun to change. The sky turned ashy, and then blood-red. They drove past villagers staring up at the heavens; they passed herds of goats struck dead, the bodies lying in the snow; they passed streams of water flowing with blood; they passed the decimated, charred trunks of burned trees. Increasing her speed, Yana careened along the road, sliding ever more dangerously close to the sheer icy edge. A flock of Watchers broke from the crust of the earth, lifting into the sky like crazed birds. Lightning coursed above, crackling through the ionized atmosphere, alighting upon the craggy mountain peak ahead of them. The earth appeared to tip upon its axis and a nexus of stars fell overhead, glowing with a strange, bright fervor. The moon grew large and purple. Rain fell, hissing upon them, staining the snow black. The fallen angels were rebelling. The battle had begun.

Yana pulled over. At the roadside Verlaine packed snow into his hands and returned to Bruno. The snow formed hard, wet packs. Bruno felt the delicious cold against his singed body as Verlaine held the melting ice to his skin, pressing it lightly against his cheek. The cold gave him some relief. Bruno realized that he was shivering, whether because of the cold or the pain or the terrible fear that was growing inside of him, he could not tell.

Somewhere in that sizzling hole in Chelyabinsk lay the man who had started all of this. Bruno closed his eyes, trying to forget what he'd seen. Of all the horrors of that day—the Nephilim breaking free of their cages, the Watchers bearing down upon them from above, the explosions thundering through the underground prison—nothing compared with the terrible end Merlin Godwin had met at the hands of Eno. Bruno had watched it all from a distance—the way Eno rose up like a cobra behind Godwin, curling her black wings around his body until Bruno saw nothing but a stream of blood falling over the floor. When she'd finished she left Godwin's mangled remains among the ruins of the laboratory. What disturbed Bruno most of all was the fact that the surveillance reports had been wrong—Eno didn't keep the trophies of her kills. When she'd finished with Godwin, she turned to Bruno, her lips red with blood, and he understood the true horror of what she did to her male victims. Bruno knew that Godwin's fate could have been his own.

As they drove onward, Bruno tried to make a division between the pain he felt burning through his body and the clear, direct movement of his thoughts. Despite the agony, he must remain sharp; he must keep his mind directed on the future. The real battle would be coming. If they made it out of Siberia alive—and, with Yana at the wheel, their chances were strong—the fight would be at its beginning. The greatest difficulties lay ahead. Soon there would be nowhere to hide.

"You're going to get us back to St. Petersburg in one piece?" Bruno said to Yana, his voice little more than a whisper.

Yana kept her eyes fixed on the road. "Even if I do," she said, "What are we going to do then?"

Bruno felt the ice melting against his cheek. The cool liquid fell along the curve of his hand and along his neck. Before Bruno could respond, Verlaine spoke. "We'll fight them," he said. "We'll fight them together, and we'll win."

Academy of Angelology, fourteenth arrondissement, Paris

Easter Sunday

Verlaine sat at the long oak table, listening to the church bells in the distance. The council would arrive any minute, and Verlaine wanted to be ready. For two days he had practiced the speech. He knew that, despite their tendency to make conservative decisions, it wouldn't be difficult to convince them. The damage alone was enough to warrant full and immediate deployment of all their agents. The meltdown had poisoned a third of the planet. The Watchers were free. Human beings were terrified and had begun forming armies. Angelologists had no choice but to fight.

A door opened and, with a great shuffling of feet, the council members entered the athenaeum. Verlaine, Yana, Dmitri, Azov, and Bruno stood, waiting as the council sat around the table. Bruno met his eyes and smiled, his expression weary. Even if they got everything they wanted, there would be nothing to celebrate. They all knew that they were bound to fight until the last creature had been killed.

A council member, a woman with gray hair and large eyeglasses, nodded to Verlaine and his companions. "My fellow angelologists, we have called you here to ask for your assistance."

The council member cleared her throat and met Verlaine's eyes. He felt a shiver of admiration. There was something in her manner that inspired a sense of fearlessness.

"Our council has spoken at great length about the current situation. We are fully aware of the danger of our position. We are also aware that we are fighting for the very existence of our world." She took a deep breath and continued. "And so, we have decided, after much consideration, to disband the council. It is clear that we are entering a new era, one of great destruction, one of terrible danger and sadness. At the same time, we are aware of the prophesies that have been made, the apocalypse that is at hand, and the possibility that this time of pain has arrived so that we might rise into a new and better world. To do this we need a leader, one who knows the enemy, one who has the strength to see this battle through. We expect this leader to be chosen from our elite angel hunters."

Verlaine felt the eyes of the council members burning into him as he realized, suddenly, that they expected him to volunteer. Bruno nudged him softly, as if pushing him forward. In that moment, with the council members gazing at him, with Bruno at his side and his body seething with fear and anger, Verlaine knew what he must do. He would stand and lead the battle. He would kill the Nephilim, destroy the Watchers, and bring human beings to victory. Above all, he would find Evangeline. And when he did, he would look into her pale green eyes and he would kill her.